Tecumseh's Curse

Tecumseh's Curse

W. C. Madden

To order additional copies of this book, contact:
Xlibris Corporation
1-888-795-4274
www.Xlibris.com
Orders@Xlibris.com
100504

Chapter 1

Present Day

A fter putzing around the house all afternoon, watching college football, eating popcorn until near explosion, and completing a crossword puzzle, Patrick decided he and his German shepherd, a former Seeing Eye dog, needed some exercise on the Saturday afternoon in early November, a day that would be his last. Little did he know this before he began their walk; otherwise, he would have stayed at home. Only a psychic, or God, would know that fact. He had died before, but it was a fake death, done for the amusement of others. He felt perfectly healthy, but it was not his health that would come into play.

As he prepared for the walk, Scamp stood by the door, tail wagging, panting in anticipation of the stroll. He loved walks. Patrick or Pat, like his friends called him, buttoned up his jacket, a tan coat made of deerskin like what Daniel Boone wore that was a little ragged due to wear and tear. Underneath, he had on a denim shirt and jeans, comfortable, cozy clothing to keep him warm. To keep his balding head warm, he wore a cowboy hat; to keep his feet dry and toasty, he wore long white tube socks inside his cowboy boots; and to keep his spirit high, he whistled the Purdue fight song in honor of them winning their football game over Wisconsin earlier in the afternoon. He stepped out of his front door, the bright sun nearly blinding him, the smell of burning leaves filling his nostrils, the cold air hitting him in the face like standing in front of an air conditioner, sending a chill down his spine as his sinewy body lacked the fat to keep him warm. It was near freezing out. The day was coming to an end, the sun sinking to the western horizon in the cloudless sky, a sky containing many shades of blue like a watercolor painting on the Hoosier community of

Battle Ground, a town named after a famous battle there two centuries before, a small sleepy community near the big city of Lafayette, considered a suburb by some of the bigger city.

As Daviess started to walk his furry friend, he saw his neighbor raking leaves to the street, her long gray hair blowing in the stiff breeze, the wind making the leaves fly all around her like a dust devil.

"Hi, Sharon," he greeted her as he walked toward her, Scamp pulling hard on his leash, wanting to greet her too.

"Oh, hi," Sharon said, stopping her raking for the time being to speak to him. She knew him well for she had been his neighbor for many years, for she spoke to him on many occasions, for she cared for his house when he was away. "Are you in tomorrow's ceremony?"

"No, I'm going out of town in the morning. Please keep an eye on the house for me." He was going to drive to Saint Louis for a historical conference on Indian heritage, a subject that he loved to research.

"How long are you going for?" she asked, leaning on the rake for further support, her middle-aged body needing it. She zipped up her chestnut brown vest, the wind giving her a chill.

"Until Wednesday," he said, letting Scamp sniff at her.

She reached down and petted the dog on his large head. "I'll get your newspaper and mail for you."

"That would be great."

"You have a good walk," she said, wanting to get back to finishing her raking so she could go in and fix dinner for herself as she was a widow and lived all alone.

"We will. Don't work too hard."

"I'm just about done. See ya later."

As usual, Patrick headed to the old battlefield for their walk, a walk that would last only a half hour as the sunset was quickly approaching. The pair strolled down the road, a blacktopped road leading from the small downtown area to the old battlefield. Across the street, a slow freight train lumbered along the railroad track, the train laden with coal going in the direction of Chicago.

While Patrick walked, he scratched the short graying beard that hung from his face as the beard had reached the point where it got itchy. When it got a little longer, it would no longer itch, and he could play Santa Claus for Christmas to earn a few extra bucks. The many wrinkles on his face—reminiscent of the Chinese Shar-Pei—showed he was getting old and had been a smoker and sunbather. In fact, a scar on his nose was the result of skin cancer from too much exposure to the sun. Now that he was retired, he walked his dog several times a day because he had the time to do so, and he wanted to because it was good for his health and the health of his dog. He also wanted to avoid another heart attack; he had previously had one resulting in seven stents being inserted into his heart to repair the damage. The next step would be a bypass operation if the stents didn't do the trick. He didn't want that.

Patrick passed the sign at the entrance to the Battle of Tippecanoe Park, the sign reading Park Closes at Dark, at dark because there was no supervision to watch over it and because the lighting was inadequate. The museum staff had closed an hour or so before, and the staff was gone by now as darkness was quickly approaching. The only vehicle in the parking lot was an official museum pickup truck, an old blue truck. Before entering the wooded battlefield, Patrick stopped at the box marked "All pets must be kept on leash, please clean up after your pet." The box had blue plastic bags for people to use to clean up after their dog, so he pulled one out of the box just in case Scamp did anything on the battlefield, which had been given the status as a national historic landmark in 1963. Ironically, his dog was retired after his own eyesight began failing. Patrick had rescued him from the Tippecanoe County Dog Shelter. His coat was dark on top and blond underneath, like most shepherds. The box was attached to the black iron fence that had been restored recently to its original look, a cleanup that had cost quite a bit and lasted for months as the four-foot fence went all the way around the large battlefield area, covering several acres.

"Come on, Scamp," Patrick urged his dog, who was more interested in smelling around the fence than following his master. He tugged hard on the black leather leash, and the dog responded by coming closer to him.

He entered the battlefield, a large shaded expanse with many oak, maple, and other indigenous trees to the area, and took his dog over by some trees to sniff them out and hike as the male dog did many times on the walk. First, he went over by the black marker that honored his great-great-greatuncle. The marker read,

STRICKEN DOWN IN THE PERFORMANCE OF DUTY
In tribute to Major Joseph Daviess, Grand Master of Masons in
Kentucky, who fell in the battle here, and to the many freemasons
of general harrison's command, whose valor is held in grateful
remembrance.

Then Patrick strolled around the nearby tall monument, a monument with the same shape as the Washington Monument in Washington DC but on a much smaller scale—about fifty feet in height—and it was made of limestone from Southern Indiana. On the monument was a statue of the battle's commanding general, William Henry Harrison, who was also the governor of the Indiana Territory at the time of the battle. Next to the monument was a wreath made of dried twisted twigs and decorated with dragonflies, Indian corn, an eagle feather, and red-white-and-blue ribbons, placed there to honor the two hundredth anniversary of the battle.

As they walked, golden brown leaves from the three-hundred-year-old oak trees nearby fell like little parachutes to the ground. Many of the old trees, who had been silent witnesses to the battle, had already lost their leaves. Patrick heard many birds chirping as if they were saying good night to one another, the black crows being the loudest of the flying creatures, although a flock of sandhill cranes was making quite a commotion of their own high up in the sky as they headed south to Florida for the winter. The smell of burning leaves filled his nostrils, the smell coming from homes near the battlefield, where the residents were burning their leaves rather than bagging them up and putting them in the trash. Since the town had no ordinance against burning, nearly everyone had a burn barrel in their backyard for burning leaves, trash, or whatever they decided. The town council had discussed passing a law against it, but residents opposed. And the thousands of visitors to the battlefield park liked to build campfires just as their ancestors did years before.

After making a complete circle around the monument, Patrick retraced his way back to the gate that led into the battlefield, because darkness was minutes away now and the woods were getting dark. He was paying more attention to his dog than watching where he was going. Suddenly, out of the corner of his eye, he saw a silhouette of a man near the entrance to the battlefield, a man wearing what looked like feathers coming from his head like an Indian might wear, a man aiming a musket in his direction.

Bam! The loud bang was followed by a puff of smoke from the musket. A split second later, he felt a tremendous pain in his chest. He brought his hand up to his chest and felt the blood rushing from it. He fell over like a tree being struck by lightning. Thoughts raced through his mind: his ex-wife waving good-bye . . . his time in Vietnam during the war . . . him as a child. He gasped his last breath of air.

Scamp wrenched the leash from the grasp of his unmoving master and charged in the direction of the fleeing figure, barking loudly as he ran. The dog followed the figure as it disappeared into the nearby woods, sniffing his trail until he came up to a creek, a small creek but a creek nonetheless and enough to stop the scent. Scamp's eyesight wasn't good enough to see the man disappear into the dark woods. The dog turned around and ran back to the side of his motionless master, nudging him, not understanding why his master wasn't responding. Patrick Daviess was dead.

Chapter 2

Northwest Territory, August 20, 1794

T he night rain pounded the tent like a hundred drummers drumming, keeping Lieutenant William Henry Harrison and his bunkmate, Lieutenant Kenton Pogue, awake for most of the night. So they talked instead of slept at a place the Indians called Fallen Timbers, not far from Lake Erie to the northeast, an area that got its name after a tornado ripped through the forest during the preceding spring and caused a tangled mess of uprooted trees, the downed oaks, maples, pines, poplar, and other kinds of trees in the forest providing a natural cover, much like a fort would to the natives. It stretched for a couple of miles.

"When do you think the general is going to attack?" Lieutenant Pogue asked as he slipped on his white pants over his long legs, legs that supported a six-foot muscular frame.

"Good question," replied the smaller Lieutenant Harrison, who put on his boots as they talked. "Your guess is as good as mine."

"But you're his aide. I would think he would have told you by now."

"I may be his aide, but I'm not a mind reader. He hasn't told me anything about when the attack will be, but I think it will be soon, maybe today."

"I sure hope so," said Pogue, who would rather fight than wait to fight. The American army of more than four thousand men had camped for three days, waiting out Chief Turkey Foot and his two thousand warriors, who had taken a position in Fallen Timbers, rendering General Anthony "Mad" Wayne's cavalry useless in an attack. The general had earned the nickname Mad when his light infantry surprised and captured the British garrison at Stony Point in

1779, but he wasn't crazy enough to attack the well-entrenched Indians. He had decided to wait them out and make them wonder when he would attack. He wanted them tired, worried, and hungry.

"I'm going to wake him up in a few minutes, so maybe I'll find out then what he's got in store for us today."

"Good, I'm tired of waiting."

Harrison put on a gray rain smock over his blue uniform to protect him from the pouring rain outside as he left the tent, sloshing through the mud the rain had turned the earth into. He could see the night sky was turning lighter with dawn approaching. He made his way to the largest white tent in the camp, the tent with a white flag flying high with the name Wayne on it. Harrison woke General Wayne up before reveille sounded. The twenty-one-year-old officer had been promoted the summer before because of his strict attention to discipline. Then he was promoted to his current grade when he became the general's aide. Harrison first became an ensign in the US Regiment of Infantry when he was eighteen. He was assigned to Cincinnati in the Northwest Territory. The army was at war with the Indians there for control of the territory. The United States had organized the territory in 1787 after the British ceded the area at the end of the Revolutionary War, but they still maintained a presence there as did the Native American Indians. Born before the Revolutionary War, Harrison was the son of Benjamin Harrison V and Elizabeth Bassett. His father was the governor of Virginia at that time. The elder Harrison would later be one of the signers of the Declaration of Independence. William's oldest brother also got into politics as representative of Virginia in the United States House of Representatives. After his father's death, William was persuaded to go into the military.

As the general put on his uniform, a white shirt covered by a dark blue overcoat with gold features and gold pants, Harrison told him, "The Indians are getting restless, sir. A number of them have left the forest and are hunting. Our scouts have seen traders at McKee's Trading Post handing out food to them."

"They're getting hungry after three days of sitting behind those trees. Make sure the men are ready to attack in an hour if this rain ever lets up," the curly blond-haired general said as he pulled up his black knee-high boots.

"Yes, sir. The men are ready. They have been for three days," said Harrison, who had brown hair in comparison. He also had a dark blue overcoat with red features and a white shirt, vest, and pants with black leggings.

"Good. Have my breakfast brought. I want something to eat before we attack."

"Yes, sir." Harrison ordered a private to bring the general some breakfast while he went to the other officers to tell them to get ready for the attack.

"Thank you," the general replied. General Wayne, a veteran soldier of the Revolutionary War, had been recalled from civilian life by President George Washington to lead an army against the Indians in the Northwest Territory. Washington had tried to come to peace with the Indians of the Six Nations but with no success. Washington's only option now was to attack them and force them into peace. Wayne had built an army in Western Pennsylvania at a settlement named Legionville, so he called his army of dragoons and soldiers the Legion. After peace negotiations with the Indians failed, his army was injected with a shot of courage when a large body of Kentucky volunteers showed up, fighters who were fearless and obsessed with a hatred of the Indians, who had inflicted death among them with raiding parties on their settlements many times.

In July, Wayne made his move, leading his army up the Auglaize River and building Fort Defiance at the mouth of the Maumee River. When he received word from the Indians that they weren't interested in talking peace, the general launched his attack from there. His advance patrols encountered some resistance in the Maumee River Valley that led him to Fallen Timbers, where Turkey Foot had taken up a defensive position. The Indians were protected on one flank by the Maumee River. And to their rear was Fort Miamis, a British outpost, where the chief planned to retreat to if necessary.

Meanwhile, Turkey Foot, whose Indian name was Me-sa-sa, was awakened by the sound of thunder. His tent in the forest was enough to keep the rain out, but it didn't help with the clapping going on in the heavens above. The chief of the Ottawa Indian Tribe had also become the leader of this group of Indians made up of warriors from the Chippewa, Delaware, Miami, Mingo, Ottawa, Potawatomi, Shawnee, and Wyandot tribes. While Turkey Foot was keeping dry and well fed, many of his Indians had little protection from the rain in the forest and were wet, cold, and famished. Hunger gnawed at their bellies after days of not eating. Their war paint was now streaked and smeared from the rain, making them look even more menacing. Turkey Foot applied some fresh war paint to his face and then put on large earrings, a necklace of bear claws, and large eagle feathers on his head. The chief had a strong angular face with large lips. The Indians were cold because their blankets and deerskin leggings were soaked. Only the trees provided protection from the elements.

As the chief painted his face for battle, a young scout entered his tent, his clothing and body soaked thoroughly from the rain.

"Chief Turkey Foot, the bluecoats are not moving," he reported. "They remain in their tents."

"Then we will eat. Tell the other chiefs to send one out of every four men to the rear to eat," the chief said. The chief could not let his men go without food. They were getting weak.

The runner left Turkey Foot and went first to tell Chief Tecumseh, the war leader of the Shawnee. The young Tecumseh, who was now twenty-six years old, had followed in the footsteps of his father, Puchsinwah, who had fought in the French and Indian War and died at the Battle of Point Pleasant when Tecumseh was just six years old. When Tecumseh turned fifteen, he became a warrior and began fighting with his older brother Cheeseekua. In one fight with thirteen white men, he outshone the other warriors of his war party by killing four with a war club. He had remarkable agility for his age and moved with grace and speed in slaying the white men, who were hunting; however, when his warrior brothers burned a white man to his death, Tecumseh objected to them doing so as he had principles even at his young age, earning the respect of other warriors. The young warrior had turned into a man almost six feet in height with a broad chest and shoulders, his hazel eyes blending well with his light brown complexion. Tecumseh meant "crouching tiger" in the Indian tongue. He lived up to that name and became an extraordinary warrior and a war chief of his tribe at an early age. Along with him at Fallen Timbers were his nineteen-year-old triplet brothers: Sauwaseekaw, Kumskaka, and Lowawluwaysica.

On the way to see Tecumseh, the scout ran into his brother, Sauwaseekaw, as he came into the area where the Shawnee were protecting their position. He told him about getting some food to eat.

Sauwaseekaw approached his brother cautiously as he knew Tecumseh was against eating anything before a battle. "My brother, Turkey Foot is allowing us to get some food."

Tecumseh's copper face turned red as he immediately got angry. "No. We should stay here. Keep our position."

"But I am hungry, brother."

"We will not eat until after the battle," Tecumseh insisted.

"Yes, my brother. I will do as you ask."

Tecumseh was just as hungry as Sauwaseekaw, but he did not trust the Americans to stay in their tents all day. He thought they might attack after the rain subsided. He wanted to be ready. Tecumseh was concerned about when the Americans would attack because his warriors were getting hungry after days of not eating, extremely hungry for that matter as they hadn't eaten anything in three days. The Indians traditionally fasted before a battle for spiritual and cultural reasons, fearing that if they were injured with food in their stomach or bowels, they would have a better chance of infection. The lack of food was making them anxious and irritated to the point they were becoming increasingly angry at the situation.

The rain eased up just after 6:00 a.m., and General Wayne gave Lieutenant Harrison the order to move forward to attack the Indians. An hour later, the army moved out of its encampment at Roche de Boeuf and followed the Maumee River downstream toward Fallen Timbers area. When they arrived, General Wayne gave an order to Lieutenant Harrison, "Have an advance guard of Kentucky cavalry charge toward the woods. After the Indians fire, have the troops retreat back to draw the savages out of the woods. Then we will counterattack before they have a chance to reload."

"That sounds like a good plan, sir."

"I just hope they take the bait."

"I'll inform the Kentucky commander to attack immediately."

Harrison rode his black stallion to where the Kentucky force was waiting for the battle to begin.

"General Wayne wants you to send an advance guard to the edge of the forest to see if the Indians will attack your force," Lieutenant Harrison said as he saluted the Kentucky commander.

"I will do as the general commands," replied Colonel Grant Morrison, returning the salute. "I suppose he wants to attack once they are in the open."

"You are correct, Colonel."

"We will be ready with a counterattack if this brings them out. If they do not come after us, what then shall we do?"

"Nothing, until ordered to do so."

"Very well, Lieutenant."

Colonel Morrison did as the general had ordered and sent an advance guard of about fifty Kentucky cavalry to the edge of the forest to entice the Indians. The Kentuckians, dressed in hunting clothes and black hats, rode their horses at a quick pace toward the forest, sending mud flying in all directions from the horse's hoofs. As they got close to the forest, one Ottawa gave a war cry and the Indians opened fire at them, one shot and shout leading to hundreds of them. Five Kentuckians and their horses fell from the flying lead. The other Kentuckians returned one volley, turned their horses around, and retreated quickly. Just as General Wayne had thought, the naked Indians in their war paint came running after the Kentuckians, whooping and hollering at the top of their lungs.

When Tecumseh heard the shots, he climbed up a fallen oak tree like a squirrel and saw the sea of blue-coated soldiers approaching quickly in a four-abreast column with banners waving through his British spyglass. "Get back. It's a trap!" the chief yelled to the warriors. They didn't hear him. They were too busy running after the Kentuckians. When the savages saw what Tecumseh saw, they turned back around and quickly retreated, but it was too late as the bluecoat army was quickly advancing on their position.

Some of the Indians stood and tried to fight without the cover of any trees, and they were quickly killed by the Kentuckians or foot soldiers with bayonets, as they had no time to reload their muskets. So they had to fight with their tomahawks, war clubs, or knives, which were no match for muskets with bayonets fixed or pistols of the soldiers. Some Indians were able to retreat to the cover of the fallen timbers, but the American army was in hot pursuit, giving the savages no time to reload, and their comrades couldn't return fire in fear of hitting them as they retreated. The dilemma only played into the hands of the Americans. Meeting little resistance, the Kentuckians rode into the forest, their horses leaping over the fallen trees as if they were in some kind of a steeplechase. Legionnaire foot soldiers came right behind them. They fought the Indians from tree to tree in the tangled forest with the Indians quickly losing ground, so Blue Jacket ordered the savages to retreat, but some found that difficult as they were blocked by the same trees they thought would provide them protection.

"Charge!" ordered Lieutenant Harrison as he led his column of blue-coated soldiers into the tangled forest behind the Kentuckians. He fired his pistol at a group of Indians fleeing deeper into the woods. He ignored the knot in his stomach and the sweat streaming from his body. Oh, he was scared, but he couldn't show it to his soldiers, even though it was his first time in battle, and he didn't want to make it his last, so he ducked behind a downed oak to reload his revolver. Bullets whizzed by him. "Keep moving," he shouted to his soldiers. He looked cautiously around the oak, aimed his pistol, and fired at an Indian; his shot hit the warrior in the leg, and the savage fell to the ground. An arrow hit the tree next to Harrison's head. He got behind the tree to reload again. While he did so, an Indian charged at him, so he pulled out his saber and drove it into the savage as he was about to strike him with his tomahawk. The young Indian fell to the ground. The slain savage was Tecumseh's brother Sauwaseekaw. The awful reality of war hit Harrison after killing his first Indian, sickening his stomach, but he had to lead his men, so he shook off the feelings and pressed on through the forest.

Tecumseh, busy fighting the soldiers hand to hand, did not see his brother go down. He too was hit by several buckshot, and blood squirted from his wounds. As the Americans converged on him and his Shawnee brothers, he broke the cover of the timbers and attacked an artillery squad and their cannon. The squad retreated, so Tecumseh and his warriors freed the horses and rode away from the attack toward the British fort. They could do nothing else to stop the Americans' advance, but they could retreat and fight another day. The American army continued to push the other warriors through the forest out the other side.

Turkey Foot came upon a large rock at the base of Presque Isle Hill. He jumped up on it to rally his warriors. The chief became a clear target for a Kentucky rider and was shot, dying at its base. Blue Jacket took his place and ordered his followers to retreat to nearby Fort Miamis. When the Indians arrived at the fort three miles away, the British refused to open the gates. As the Indians clamored to get in, the Americans advanced on their position.

"Let us in! We fought for you, now help us!" Tecumseh yelled in English at the British commander, Major William Campbell. "Father, can you not remember your promise?" The Shawnee chief thought that the British were too afraid to help the warriors.

Campbell ignored the pleas as he had orders not to help the Indians, because the British and Americans were about to sign a treaty that would turn his garrison and others over to the Americans.

Tecumseh and the other warriors quickly gave up as the Americans were advancing on their position. The bloodied and bruised chief turned to the other warriors and said, "These are not our allies! They are cowards! Come with me downriver to bury our dead." Some warriors had carried their dead with them, and now they wanted to give them a fit burial.

The Americans advanced to within firing distance of the walls of the fort, but not a single shot was fired their way, nor did they fire on the fort as General Wayne had not given them permission to attack the fort, which he could have done if he so desired, but after fighting the Indians for more than an hour, he decided his troops had done enough fighting for one day. Plus, Wayne had lost thirty-eight men, and another hundred men were wounded and needed treatment. The Indians had lost a lot more, and more importantly, they were devastated and demoralized after losing to the Americans. So instead of attacking the fort, Harrison's troops burned the buildings around it, including a small trading post owned by Alexander McKee. They also burned the crops surrounding the fort, so the British watched their food supply for the winter go up in smoke.

Wayne's force returned to Fort Defiance to rest. After a week, the army marched out again. As they moved on, they burned Indian villages to the ground and destroyed their crops to put a finishing touch on the Indians. The battle put an end to the Northwest Indian War.

Lieutenant Harrison received a commendation from General Wayne for communicating his orders in every direction and leading the troops to press for victory. He deserved the award and was proud to receive it.

A year later in July, more than a thousand Indian warriors and their chiefs gathered at Fort Greenville in the Ohio Territory to negotiate a treaty with the Americans. General Wayne and his officers, including Harrison, were there representing the Americans. Harrison had been promoted to captain and was now in charge of Fort Washington near Cincinnati. He also had married a young woman named Anna, daughter of the territorial judge Benjamin Symmes.

The treaty opened up part of the Native American territory to white settlers. The Greenville Treaty Line ran south from Lake Erie to the middle of the Ohio Territory, then west to the Indiana Territory, then south to the Ohio River. The tribes would get $20,000 worth of goods for signing the treaty and $9,500 every year after that.

After several days of speeches, General Wayne read the treaty for the last time and asked, "Do you approve these articles?" The chiefs of the twelve tribes who attended agreed. Little Turtle, the chief of the Miami Indians, was the last to sign on August 2. The chief was not at the Battle of Fallen Timbers but was still considered one of the most powerful chiefs of his time. He had a large forehead and was known as Fivehead. Except for this occasion, he wore a headdress of eagle feathers to cover his balding scalp. He generally wore a necklace of bear claws as well and large earrings. After the signing, he buried a hatchet as a symbol of peace.

One of the chiefs who didn't attend the conference and refused to sign the Greenville Treaty was Tecumseh. He did not want to make peace with the whites and was against the treaty that gave almost all of Ohio to the Americans. However, he would honor the treaty and move his people after the harvest to satisfy the Americans because he didn't want to fight them at this time.

However, Harrison and Tecumseh were destined to meet again.

Chapter 3

Present Day

The plain-black Motorola cell phone played an island-type song and
vibrated on the dark walnut dresser next to the twin-sized bed. The
melody woke up Detective Sergeant Jackson O'Mahern in a matter of seconds.
The detective reached over and picked up the department-issued cell phone.
He fumbled with it in the early-morning light until he got it open. The phone
displayed 7:24 a.m., Sunday, November 7.

"Yeah," he answered sleepily as he sat up in the bed.

"Did I wake you?" Sheriff Joshua Andrews said from his own bedroom;
however, he was already dressed in a dark blue suit before he went off to
church at 8:00 a.m.

"Yep. What's up, Chief?" O'Mahern held the phone with his left hand
into his left ear as he rubbed the sleep from his greenish-blue eyes with his
right hand. Then he stroked his bushy brown-haired eyebrows, which needed
trimming from his favorite barber, a female hairdresser that he sometimes
dated.

"We have a murder in Battle Ground."

"Where?" O'Mahern was still groggy and could hardly believe his ears.

"I said Battle Ground. Now get your butt up and get down to the Tippecanoe
Battlefield Monument. Do you know where it is?"

"Yeah, I've been there before." He had once visited the famous battlefield
in the small town just north of Lafayette when he was a teenager. His class had
gone there on a field trip. "Do we know who it is?"

"Some local guy. I don't have any details. That's your job."

"Yes, sir. I know it is," O'Mahern said in a raspy voice, caused by his smoking cigarettes for so long.

"I'm giving you Julie Palmer to help investigate this case."

"Anyone but her," O'Mahern said disgustingly. Although he didn't particularly like her detective skills, he sure liked her looks and nice figure. He definitely wouldn't kick her out of his bed.

"I know she's a rookie detective, but that's why I'm assigning her to you and this case, so she can learn."

"I understand, Cap, but this is a murder case," he pleaded.

"She needs to investigate murders as well. That's part of her learning process. Plus, she's originally from Battle Ground, so she knows the territory better than you."

"That's true. Whatever you say, you're the boss," he relented.

"Now you're talkin'. And don't screw this one up or you'll be back in a uniform."

"Yes, sir."

That last comment by the sheriff got his attention and certainly woke him up. He hurriedly got out of bed and stretched his medium muscular frame.

Across town, another black department phone played "No Surprise" by Daughtry until Julie Palmer awakened from her deep sleep and reached over to get it. She knocked over a picture of her boyfriend, Fred Schultz, as she did. She had set the alarm for 8:00 a.m. because she had planned to go to church at 9:00 a.m. this Sunday morning since she had the day off.

"Palmer," she answered and swiveled around to take a sitting position on the side of the queen-sized bed. Her dark green silk pajamas contrasted with the white sheets and tan bedspread.

"Rise and shine."

She recognized the husky voice of the sheriff. "What's up, Sheriff?"

"There's been a murder in Battle Ground, so we need someone who knows the town on this case. That would be you. You'll be working with Jackson O'Mahern. He'll be the lead in this case."

"Oh, him," she said downheartedly. She had only worked with him once before, and it hadn't been a great experience. He seemed to be more interested in her body than her abilities.

"Yeah, him. I know you're not in love with the guy, but he's an experienced detective and you can learn a lot from him."

"Since you put it that way, then that's what I hope to do—learn a lot."

"The murder is at the battlefield. He'll probably get there before you do since he lives closer. Just meet him there."

"Who's the victim?"

"I don't know. They didn't have an ID on him when I spoke to the deputy at the scene. You'll have to find out who it is."

"Sure. I'll get down there ASAP."

"Great."

"Good-bye, sir."

"Bye."

Palmer jumped in the shower but didn't mess with shampooing her short dark brown hair that she had frosted with blond streaks. During her shower, she thought about the upcoming assignment as a breath of fresh air, as she had been assigned to drug investigations and hadn't had much luck with that, drugs not being a big problem in the county, except for the production of meth, a drug that was produced at some remote locations in the county, or the growing of marijuana hidden in the middle of cornfields, making it difficult to detect except from the air.

After her shower, she slipped into her white bra and panties before quickly brushing her hair, the bra not covering a dark brown mole at the top of her cleavage that drew even more attention to that part of her body than normal. She typically wore blouses that covered the mole when she was on duty, but off duty or when in a swimsuit, it was a different matter. She couldn't really cover it up. She had thought about having it removed, but she was against any doctor performing torture on her. This would be a light-makeup day since she needed to rush to the murder scene, yet she was the type of woman who didn't need that much makeup to look pretty.

Meanwhile, O'Mahern had decided not to shave to save some time, a look that was acceptable in today's world, and his light brown hair didn't make him look too shabby anyway. He jumped in the shower for a quick one, thinking about the last time he had worked with Palmer. It was a robbery with drugs involved because the man doing the stealing was doing it to get money to support his drug habit. The suspect was wanted by both detectives for two different crimes, so they were hooked up together by the sheriff to hunt the guy down and arrest him. When O'Mahern got out of the shower, he looked at his physique in the mirror as he put on deodorant, his frequent workouts at the police gym keeping his forty-year-old body slim and trim, although his face did show some wrinkles from the stress in his life and a few gray hairs peppered his thick scalp. Then he sprayed himself with some cologne as he wanted to smell good to his partner and the public he would be dealing with later.

The six-foot O'Mahern pulled on a pair of blue jeans and a long-sleeved blue shirt to go under his black leather jacket, since he knew it would be cool out on this November morning. He usually wore business-casual clothing to blend into the area, but it was cool out and he'd be outdoors, and jeans would blend in better in that small town. He was free to wear what he thought was appropriate for the occasion. The department only required a suit or sport coat when facing a jury or special occasions. It was now 8:00 a.m., and the sun had only been up for half an hour.

O'Mahern put on his holster and then checked the magazine of his Glock 40mm before putting it away under his jacket, the gun being the standard police issue he had for three years. He also checked his backup pistol, a personal North American .22-caliber Magnum derringer, a little gun with a powerful kick that he wore in a small holster strapped around his ankle. He left his apartment and breezed down the two flights of stairs to his red 2008 Ford Mustang. A clear blue sky had created a light frost over his car and windshield, so he pulled out a credit card from his wallet—he could have gotten an ice scraper out of his trunk, but he figured he could do it with the card—and started scraping after he started his car. A large pickup truck next to him was putting out diesel fumes, and he didn't much like the smell from it, so he quickly scraped and got back into his car. From his downtown apartment on Fifth Street in the Lahr Apartments, he drove across the bridge that crossed the Wabash River to West Lafayette, the home of Purdue University, and took Indiana 43 to go to Battle Ground.

He lit up a cigarette, one of those generic cheap types, and smoked his first butt of the day as he drove along the Wabash River, which was low this time of year as it hadn't rained much recently. His mind was running like the river. *What kind of murder was it . . . who did it . . . what was the motive . . . what was the means?*

Detective O'Mahern drove faster than the speed limit as he whizzed under Interstate 65. He stopped at a McDonald's to grab a quick breakfast to eat while on his way to the murder scene, which was now only minutes away. Instead of waiting in the drive-through, he rushed inside. It was a wise move. Nobody was waiting in line inside. He ordered a large coffee and a breakfast burrito. They hand it to him in a couple of minutes. When the manager saw his gold badge on his belt, he said, "It's on me, Officer."

"Thanks much," O'Mahern replied.

O'Mahern munched on his breakfast burrito as he finished the short drive to the crime scene. As he approached the battlefield, he could see the parking lot was filled with government vehicles. A crime scene team from the state police, an ambulance, and the Tippecanoe County coroner were already there. Also, there was a local television station truck parked there with a film crew. A TV reporter was interviewing a person from the small group of people who had gathered to get a glimpse of what was going on. He wouldn't be answering any of their questions as it was too early in the investigation, and he usually left that up to the public affairs officer.

He parked next to a two-tone brown Sheriff's car, lit up another cigarette, and walked the short distance to the entrance of the fenced-in battlefield. The black iron fence had recently been restored and repainted. Yellow tape wasn't needed to mark off the crime scene; the fence did an adequate job of that. The entrance read, Battle of Tippecanoe, November 7, 1811. O'Mahern noticed the date and remembered it was the same as today but the year a couple of centuries ago. In the distance, by the monument, he saw a number of officials standing around the body.

"Good morning, Detective O'Mahern," the young officer at the gate entrance greeted him. "You working this case by yourself?"

"No, my partner will be here shortly."

"Who's that?"

"The sheriff stuck me with the rookie Julie Palmer," he said and shrugged.

"I used to work with her myself. She's a smart cookie and cute."

"I agree with cute. It's the smart part I have a problem with. Well, I hope she can help me with this case."

"She will. You need to put out that cigarette before you enter. You know how they don't like those things around a crime scene."

"Oh yeah, I almost forgot." He tossed the butt down on the ground and stomped on it.

O'Mahern continued to the crime scene a short distance away from the entrance, located very close to the monument that towered above the battlefield like a giant stone spike, although not nearly as high as some of the oak trees that surrounded it. Some of those trees were there at the time of the battle and had seen it firsthand, but of course, they couldn't tell how it went. He saw a film crew by the monument and wondered why they were let in the crime scene.

"Hi, Jackson," said Sergeant Pete Duncan, who was the duty officer in the middle of the night. He had been called to the scene by a patrolman. Duncan was in uniform, a two-tone brown outfit like the police cars they drove. The pants were dark brown with a lighter stripe down the side. The shirt and jacket were both dark brown with patches on both shoulders. The hat, called a Smokey Bear campaign hat, was a lighter brown.

"What the hell is a film crew doing at the crime scene?" O'Mahern asked.

"I guess you didn't read the e-mail the other day explaining that Real TV was going to be in Lafayette starting yesterday to film us in action," Duncan said.

"No, I didn't see that memo. I think that's bullshit."

"The e-mail said it was to help raise money for our department."

"I guess they're looking at any way to raise money. Get me up to speed, Sergeant Duncan," O'Mahern said.

"The body was discovered just after dawn by ground maintenance here at the museum," the sergeant explained. "There were no 911 calls about it last night."

"We have an ID on him?"

"No, but one of the maintenance workers said he lives around here."

"Do we know what he was doing here?"

"They said he usually walked a large shepherd around here, but we haven't found the dog."

O'Mahern looked around. "We need to find that dog."

"We've got people looking for it."

"Have the crime scene techs found any evidence, like shell casings?"

"No."

"How about footprints?"

"This historic site has too many visitors for something like that."

O'Mahern raised up his left hand, put it on his chin, and scratched it while he thought at that. "Let's see. No evidence and no witnesses."

"That's about right."

"Nothing like landing a tough case on a Sunday morning, my day off." He took both arms and threw them out to the side as if he was giving up already. He was just starting.

Palmer pulled up in her car, a 2006 Chevrolet Caprice, midnight blue in color. O'Mahern saw her coming, so he stayed by the sergeant and continued chitchatting until she caught up with him. He noticed she was dressed in a purple pants suit for the occasion, an outfit that would keep her warm in the chilly temperatures, but the sunny sky was beginning to warm the air somewhat. O'Mahern thought she was overdressed for the occasion, but he figured as much coming from a woman. He thought they always overdressed.

"Good morning, Julie," O'Mahern greeted her.

"Morning to you too, Jackson."

He passed on the information from the sergeant to her as they moseyed over to the body. As they talked, they put on blue latex gloves before examining the body lying on a carpet of leaves not far from the monument, next to some bushes. The oak trees loomed over the monument as if they were looking down at the horrible site.

"And this film crew is here from Real TV to film us in action."

"Yeah, I know. I read the e-mail the other day."

"Well, I didn't. They just better stay out of our way."

A crime scene team was finishing up photographing the body and the scene as the coroner, Dr. John Jurgenson, waited patiently for them to finish before checking out the body lying facedown on the grass. A crime scene photographer motioned to Jurgenson that he was done with his photographs and it was his turn, so the tall, heavyset coroner kneeled down next to the man and turned him by grabbing his shoulder and waist and pulling the stiff body toward him with little effort. The forty-year-old coroner weighed more than 250 pounds and kept in shape; lifting and moving bodies were something he did all the time. Jurgenson showed a frown on his round face, a face with a high forehead showing signs of going bald. How the man died became obvious to the coroner and the detectives. His deerhide jacket had a red blood spot the size of a watermelon. He unbuttoned the victim's shirt to examine the wound.

"Get your film crew back a little, please," insisted O'Mahern as he motioned for them to step back.

"Yes, sir," the producer said without any argument. "Let's move back a little for the detectives, shall we."

"Oh my god," said Palmer. "I know this guy."

"What's his name?"

"Yeah, his name is Pat, but I don't recall his last name," Palmer said. "I don't know much about him other than he was a member of the Tippecanoe Historical Society."

"That guy reminds me of somebody out of the Wild West," O'Mahern said.

"Yeah, he always dressed like that. He could even pass as a settler of this area, which was in the mid-1800s."

"You know your history."

"Well, I did grow up here. What kind of gun do you think did that?" Palmer asked the coroner.

"I won't know for sure until I get 'em on the table."

"Can you give me a good guess on what it might be?"

"No. I couldn't even begin to give you an idea of what gun was used at this point." Jurgenson was a little perturbed by the question.

"When do you think he died?" Palmer continued, probing.

"I'd say at least twelve hours ago as the body is almost in full rigor. I'd guess around dusk last night. I'll narrow that down later for you as well once I get him back to the lab."

"You're probably right. Supposedly, he was walking his dog around yesterday afternoon," O'Mahern said.

"That makes sense," Jurgenson said. "That would be my best guess at this point."

Two ambulance workers stood by waiting like turkey vultures over a roadkill while Jurgenson and the detectives did their thing. As soon as the detectives were done, they would take the body away.

The coroner stood up, so O'Mahern kneeled down and started checking the victim's pockets. He found a set of keys in the left pocket of his jeans. He checked the other front pocket and found a cell phone, which he handed to Palmer. He then rolled the body over to check the back pockets—empty.

"Okay, we're done," Detective O'Mahern said to the ambulance workers as he rose to his feet. He turned to Palmer and commented, "I don't think we can rule out robbery as a motive since I didn't find any valuables on him."

"I doubt it was robbery."

"Maybe, but unless we find his wallet at home, I think it could be just that."

"Really?"

"Yeah. People have been killed for less."

"I guess."

The ambulance workers swooped down on the body to pick it up and put it on a gurney to take to the waiting ambulance.

O'Mahern looked over at the sidewalk leading to the gate they had entered, scratching his chin whiskers as he thought about where the bullet had come from. "I'd say he was probably standing on the sidewalk when he was hit. Then he fell over sideways and ended up the way he did—facedown."

She nodded. "Uh-huh."

"I think the shot came from over that way," O'Mahern said, pointing to the entrance of the battlefield.

"I agree," Palmer said. "For your information, there's also a ghost story involving an Indian here at the battlefield. Supposedly, at dusk, this Indian appears at the gate armed with a musket. Then he retreats like they did in 1811. People swear they've seen him."

"That's interesting, but ghosts don't shoot people."

"You're probably right about that."

"Okay, let's see. Patrick went to take his dog for a walk. Somebody follows him here and pops him just before dark when nobody's around." O'Mahern held his hands up as if he was shooting a rifle.

"And that somebody takes his dog as well."

"That's a possibility since we can't find the dog."

"Or the dog chased after the killer."

"Yeah, that's a possibility."

"Or the dog went back to his house."

"Do you know where this guy lives?"

"No, but we can ask the town marshal. He's right over there."

They walked ten yards to where the marshal was talking to a crime scene technician. After he was done talking, Julie said, "Hi, Marshal. I'm Detective Palmer, and this is Detective Sergeant O'Mahern."

"Glad to meet you. I'm Marshal Joshua Redbird."

They all shook hands.

"We've been assigned to investigate this case," O'Mahern said.

"I'm glad you're here."

"Do you know the vic's name?" Palmer asked.

"Yeah, it's Patrick Daviess," the marshal replied.

"I couldn't remember his last name," she said. "Do you know where he lives?"

"Yeah, he lives in that yellow house over on Prophet Street near College Avenue," said the marshal, who was dressed in his all-navy-blue uniform. His shirt was adorned with a patch that said Battle Ground Police. He had a dark olive skin like his Indian forefathers. "You know where that is?"

"Sure do. I grew up on Jewett Street, not far from there. That's awhile ago, before I went off to IU."

"You knew my predecessor then—Marshal Norberg." Jason Redbird was the new marshal in town. He had been hired to replace the previous marshal, who had retired after thirty years of service.

"Oh yeah. He showed me a few things about law enforcement."

"I'll bet he did. He showed me some things as well."

"When was the last time a murder occurred in Battle Ground?" O'Mahern said as he couldn't recall any murders there since being on the force.

"I heard that a woman was killed in Lafayette in 1970, and the body was dumped here," the marshal explained. "It wasn't found until four years later."

Battle Ground had only 1,400 people and was known most for its historic and tourist attractions, such as Wolf Park, which featured a pack of wolves, assorted coyotes, foxes, and other animals that created a sort of wild Indiana sanctuary. Some people who worked in Lafayette or West Lafayette lived there to get away from the bigger cities, so it was sort of a bedroom community.

"I heard about that," Palmer said. That murder occurred before she was born, but it was one of those stories that passed down from generation to generation.

"We're going over to the house to check it out," O'Mahern said.

"I'd give you a hand, but I need to get ready for the ceremony later today. We're celebrating the two hundredth anniversary of the Battle of Tippecanoe. Give me a call later if you need any help."

"That's okay, we can handle it. You've asked for our help in this case, and that's what we're here to do."

"Thanks. I've never handled a murder case before," Redbird said as his cell phone rang. "I gotta get that." He turned around and walked away to answer the call.

"Hi, I'm Jeff Shortridge, producer for Real TV. Could I have a moment of your time, Detective?" asked the producer of Real TV, a short man dressed in a black jacket with Real TV on the back. He put out his right hand to shake O'Mahern's, but the detective didn't respond as his hands were in his pockets, keeping warm.

"We're kind of busy right now," O'Mahern replied.

"Just a second," Palmer interrupted. She whispered in O'Mahern's ear, "The e-mail said that we should cooperate fully with them."

O'Mahern nodded. "Oh." He turned to the producer and said, "What can I do for you?"

"Just a couple of questions."

"Okay."

The film crew moved in for a close-up of O'Mahern. "What is your name?"

"Detective Sergeant Jackson O'Mahern."

"Do you have any idea about why this murder occurred here last night?"

"Not at this point. We have very little to go on. We should know a little more after the autopsy is performed."

"Do you know who the victim is?"

"Yes, we have identified him."

"What's your next move?"

"We are going to the victim's house to see if there are any clues there to what happened here."

"Thank you, Detective."

"Let's go over there now," O'Mahern said. "There's nothing else here for us."

"Okay."

As the detectives left the crime scene, O'Mahern said, "You drive since I don't know where the house is."

"As you wish. My car's parked next to yours."

"I know. I saw you pull in."

Ahead of them, the red ambulance was leaving the parking lot with the body to go to the coroner's office for autopsy.

Chapter 4

Indiana Territory, August 1810

"Brother, the Great White Indiana Chief has asked me to come to Vincennes to talk of peace," Tecumseh said to his brother Tenskwatawa. "I want you to be the chief of Tippecanoe until I return."

"Yes, brother. I will do that," Tenskwatawa said. "You better show him strength and go in numbers."

"Yes, brother. I will take several hundred warriors with me and paint our canoes in war colors. Pray for me."

"I will speak to the spirits."

Tecumseh left the medicine lodge of his brother and went to see the other chiefs who had come to Tippecanoe to live with him. He had recruited Indians from many different tribes, including the Potawatomis, Shawnee, Kickapoo, Delaware, Winnebago, Wea, Wyandotte, Ottawa, Chippewa, Menominee, Fox, Sauk, and Creek, who had come to live there in peace and start creating the nation. He envisioned a strong Indian confederacy that united all tribes under a revolutionary goal: the common ownership of all Indian lands. His goal was similar to the American goal back in 1776 when the thirteen colonies united to create the United States of America.

Tecumseh went to the chiefs of the other tribes in the village, told them to meet with him at dusk, and bring their best warriors to the Council House, the largest building in the village, called a msi-kah-mi-qui, a building that was 150 feet long and 35 feet wide, a log building that could hold up to five hundred Indians. Yet the village had grown to more than a thousand warriors, so the structure wasn't large enough to hold all of them at once. In fact, the whole village had grown tremendously in the two years since it began and now contained some sixty permanent log cabins and over one hundred each of wegiwas (huts) and tepees made of poles, bark, and skins. For smaller meetings, a council building was constructed. Another large building was built to act as a hotel for transient Indians and was called the House of Strangers. The dwellings were built in rows with lanes between them. The town's location was perfect for the red men as there was plenty of game available as well as fish—salmon, bass, redhorse, and pike—from the Wabash and Tippecanoe Rivers. The rich soil was ideal for growing corn and vegetables. As it was being built, some called it Prophet's Town, but the majority of Indians referred to it as Tippecanoe.

That evening, Tecumseh spoke to the hundreds of Indians that had gathered in the Council House. The Indians packed the place to hear the leader speak, creating a sauna-like atmosphere inside the place. Tecumseh told them of the letter that had been sent to him from Governor William Henry Harrison, asking for his presence. "The Great White Chief of Indiana wants to know why I refused a shipment of salt as part of the Treaty of Fort Wayne," he said at the top of his lungs to the gathering. "Brothers, why should I honor a treaty I did not sign? Come with me tomorrow morning to see this white man, see what he wants."

The Indians whooped it up to show their support.

The next morning, the hot summer sun shone down on the hundreds of Indians as they began their trip down the Wabash, which was as tame as a garden snake due to the lack of rain instead of the nasty rattlesnake it can be when it's flooded. The river conditions were ideal for a trip south down the river, from the Tippecanoe village in the northern part of the territory to Vincennes in the south, the capital of the Indiana Territory for the white man.

A few days later, when Tecumseh and his four hundred warriors in eighty canoes arrived in Vincennes, they struck fear in the residents there, who thought they might attack as their canoes were painted in bold red-and-white colors and their bodies were painted with streaks and swirls of red, blue, white, and yellow. Their party was stopped by the American forces at Fort Knox and allowed to camp along the Wabash riverbank two miles downstream and only a mile from the governor's mansion, Grouseland Estates.

It took a couple of days for the parties to settle on a schedule and agree on guidelines for the peace talks. They agreed to carry only sidearms with them, which meant knives and tomahawks for the Indians and pistols and swords for the Americans. Governor Harrison invited Tecumseh to his residence and set up benches and chairs on his portico, where they would be protected from the elements. Harrison was also protected by seventeen crack armed soldiers dressed in their finest dark-blue-and-gold uniforms. In close proximity, a couple of hundred civilians had gathered to witness the historic meeting on the muggy August day. The humidity was as thick as the tension between the two parties.

When Tecumseh, some other chiefs, and about forty warriors finally arrived at Grouseland, he stopped short of the mansion in a grove of tall oak trees. The Shawnee chief decided he didn't want to meet the governor on his territory. Harrison sent Joseph Barron to find out why he wouldn't come to the mansion.

"The governor wants to know why you are not coming to the mansion," asked Barron.

"No! I will not meet at the white man's house," Tecumseh insisted. He didn't want to sit in the white man's chair. "The earth is where I will recline. Tell your chief I prefer to council here."

Harrison, dressed in a white shirt and black frock and pants despite the warm weather, walked out to the chief. He placed one hand on the sword that hung from his belt on the right side and said, "I think having our meeting in the open will be pleasant." Then he turned to his soldiers and said, "Bring the seats and benches here for us to sit in."

Before the talks began in earnest, a sudden downpour sent Harrison and his men back to the estate to take cover. Seeing that the rain was going to last awhile, Tecumseh and his men headed back to their camp. The rain washed their red-and-black war paint away and canceled the talks for the time being.

A week went by before the weather got better and the parties were able to come together again. The parties again met in the grove near the mansion. On this day, the weather was much better as the clouds had been swept away by a sea of blue sky, yet it was still a hot summer day.

Besides having different opinions, Harrison and Tecumseh were completely different in appearance. Harrison was slim and of average height while Tecumseh was taller and much more muscular. Harrison had a long, thin, angular face with a fair complexion that was distinguished by a long sharp-bridged nose. As an Indian, Tecumseh's complexion was darker, although it wasn't as dark as some Indians, and his nose was shorter. Harrison's eyes were set close together and his lips were thin, but he had a strong jaw. The governor wore a double-breasted gray coat over a white shirt with matching gray pants. Tecumseh wore deerskin britches, beads around his neck, eagle feathers in his hair, and beaded moccasins. He carried a knife and tomahawk.

Although Tecumseh spoke English, he preferred to use his own Shawnee language to speak to the Americans. Governor Harrison chose Chief Winnemac of the Potawatomi to be one of his interpreters while Tecumseh chose his nephew Spemica Lawba. Tecumseh was not happy that Winnemac was interpreting for the Americans. Harrison allowed the Shawnee chief to speak his mind first. Tecumseh vividly remembered Harrison from the Battle of Fallen Timbers sixteen years before, when he was a young lieutenant still wet behind the ears. Now he was the most powerful white man in the West. Tecumseh was a young aspiring war chief back then. Now he was trying to form the largest alliance of tribes into an Indian nation in the northern part of the Indiana Territory.

Tecumseh began his demands by talking about the white man's crimes against the Indians dating from the Revolution. The chief spoke about broken treaties and promises. "I don't know if I can ever be friends with the Seventeen Fires (United States) in view of the cold-blooded murder," his interpreter translated in English. "You butchered the Moravian Indians at the Gandenhutten Massacre." His diatribe went on for about two hours. Of course, what he had to say took twice as long because all of it had to be translated into English. And his nephew did a good job of it.

At one point, Tecumseh retrieved a letter from Saugnash, a lieutenant of his. The letter from Harrison had made him an offer to go to Washington with three other chiefs. He looked at it for a few seconds and refolded it.

"Hear me!" Tecumseh shouted, jolting the Americans and Harrison. "We will have a great council at which all the tribes will be present, when we shall show to those who sold you land that they had no right to do so," he said, referring to the Fort Wayne Treaty. The treaty was signed by the Delaware, Potawatomi, Miami, Eel River, Kickapoo, and Wea tribes and deeded over 3,000 acres in the Indiana Territory to the Americans for $8,200 down and annuities of $2,350.

"I heard that you had threatened the lives of the chiefs who signed the Fort Wayne Treaty because they had no right to sell it," Harrison said. "Is that true?"

"Yes, and you will see what will be done to those chiefs that did sell the land to you." It was clear Tecumseh meant to kill them.

Then he turned to Chief Winnemac and threatened him in his own native Potawatomi tongue. Tecumseh's meaning was clear to Winnemac, and a fearful look crossed his face. Tecumseh's words to the chief weren't translated to the others, but all present knew they weren't comforting words. The tension in the air suddenly became thicker.

Then Tecumseh finally came to the point of the meeting. "The Treaty of Fort Wayne must be repealed," Tecumseh said through the interpreter. "I have already threatened to kill the chiefs who have signed the treaty. I have asked them to turn over their power to the war chiefs that I have assembled here. We will not speak to the Great White Chief until all the tribes are united."

"It is ridiculous that you think that all tribes are one nation," Governor Harrison said. "If the Great Spirit wanted you as one, he would have you speak the same language and have the same customs. You don't."

The interpreter started to convey the information, but the chief understood what Harrison had said. Tecumseh suddenly lost his temper. He leaped to his feet once more, his copper face turning red, his dark eyes flashing, his fist clenching. "You are a liar!" he shouted in Shawnee. "You are like many other white eyes. I cannot trust you."

General Gibson understood enough Shawnee to know that Tecumseh meant trouble. He turned to a young lieutenant and said, "These fellows intend mischief. You better bring up the guard." The lieutenant quietly did as the general ordered. At the same time, Reverend Winans, a Methodist minister, slipped into the governor's house and retrieved a musket. He too sensed trouble.

Then Tecumseh started waving his arms as he spoke. The more he spoke, the more agitated his warriors became. Some took their tomahawks out of their belts and readied to attack.

Harrison struggled to get out of the deep armchair to his feet. When he finally got up, he withdrew his small sword by his side to show them he could defend himself if necessary.

To the side, Chief Winnemac withdrew a pistol and cocked it, ready to shoot. Captain William Whitlock was nearby and aimed his pistol at Chief Tecumseh.

At that moment, the governor's guards came running up to defend the governor. Their arrival turned the advantage back to the Americans. The civilian crowd that had gathered for the meeting wanted nothing to do with what looked like a fight about to break out. They scattered, knocking down a rain fence in their haste to get away. An uneasy silence filled the air as the guards and Indians faced one another down.

Harrison broke the silence. "At ease, gentlemen. No need to get alarmed just yet," he said in an effort to prevent any conflict. He slipped his sword back into its sheath. Then he turned to the interpreter and said, "What has the chief been saying?"

Specima replied, "Tecumseh said that all of what you have spoken is false."

Harrison commented, "Tell him I say that he's a bad man and that I will have nothing more to do with him. I will allow his men to go in peace, but they must leave tomorrow."

Tecumseh raised his hand and signaled his warriors to follow him as he left the grove to go back to camp. On the way back, he realized he had left a bad taste in the mouths of the Americans, so he told Wasegoboah to go back under a white flag and ask for a meeting at the first light of day.

After Tecumseh was out of sight, Harrison turned to his officers and ordered, "Be ready for an attack in the middle of the night, just in case he decides to do so."

That evening, reinforcements consisting of three companies of Indiana militia and a company of Knox County Dragoons arrived at Vincennes, as well as a battalion from Newport Barracks, Kentucky. The Americans posted sentries during the night to guard against any surprise attack from Tecumseh and his men.

The next afternoon, Governor Harrison rode into Tecumseh's camp on a gray warhorse with four other men, two being soldiers. The governor had other soldiers and dragoons nearby if needed. The two leaders shook hands, and Tecumseh offered him a seat on a nearby log.

"Brother, I want to apologize for my bad temper and manners," the chief said.

"Apology accepted."

As the two sat on the log and talked without an interpreter, Tecumseh began to inch closer and closer to the governor, making Harrison a little uncomfortable and he moved over to the end of the log. When Tecumseh got to the point of being right next to Harrison, the governor said, "If you come any closer, I will have no place to sit."

Tecumseh flashed a brilliant smile of teeth and said, "Now you understand. If you force my people to move any more, they will have no place to live in the territory of Indiana as a free people."

They agreed to meet again the next day to talk some more.

The next morning, Harrison met with Tecumseh at the same place they had met the day before. However, this time, he had his soldiers ready with their muskets at the meeting site. Tecumseh didn't seem to mind. Also, he was more dignified and respectful than the previous day. He introduced chiefs from several tribes: Kickapoos, Potawatamies, Ottawas, Winnebagos, and Wyandots. They took turns in telling the governor that they had joined with Tecumseh.

"If you return our land, we will be faithful to you and not the redcoats," Tecumseh spoke up. Then he clapped his hands and shouted as if he was calling to a dog. He was demonstrating to Harrison how the British treated their Indian allies. The history of the British and the Indians extended back to revolutionary time when the British first enlisted Indians.

Harrison acknowledged what the chiefs had told him. "I will take your request to President Madison for consideration," Governor Harrison replied. Harrison would do that, but he doubted the president would consider it.

"Are your intentions really as you stated?" Harrison asked without a translator present.

"It would be with great reluctance that I would make war with the Seventeen Tribes," Tecumseh replied. "If your Great White Chief gives the land back and agrees to make a treaty with all tribes, then I will be a faithful ally and assist you against the British. If not, then I will join the British."

"I will tell the president of your propositions."

Tecumseh replied through Spemica Lawba that he hoped the Great White Chief would be directed by the Great Spirit in considering his request. "If your leader does not agree, you and I will raise weapons against each other. He may sit still in his town and drink his wine whilst you and I have to fight it out," he concluded.

"I understand. Thank you for your frankness. Have a safe journey home," Harrison said and rose to his feet.

Tecumseh nodded.

Chapter 5

Present Day

Detective Julie Palmer drove out of the Battle of Tippecanoe Museum parking lot, making a left-hand turn and then another left at the next block. She pulled over to the side of the road and parked in front of the murder victim's house. The old one-story cottage-style home was in need of work. The yellow paint was faded, blistered, and worn; the roof also needed new shingles as the asphalt shingles were curled and cracked.

Detective Sergeant Jackson O'Mahern led the way and knocked on the front door. Palmer drew her gun from her back where she carried it. About ten seconds went by before he tried the doorknob. It was locked. Then he dug out the set of keys from his left pocket.

"Don't we need a search warrant?" asked Palmer.

"No, Rook. We have probable cause, plus I have the keys. I know all about search warrants now after my last murder case." He always called her Rook when he thought she was asking a question she should already know.

"Why is that?"

"Before you became a detective, I investigated a murder in which I made an illegal search. The case got thrown out because of that," O'Mahern explained.

"They call that fruit from the poisonous tree or something like that," she said.

"Yeah. The sheriff suspended me for a day just to teach me a lesson. And he told me I better not screw this one up or I'll be back in uniform directing traffic or riding a desk."

"Ouch. Was that the Juan Mendez case?"

"Yeah. As it turns out, Mendez got his own justice in Indianapolis. He got whacked in a drug deal gone bad."

"Well, that's good—seems like he earned that bullet anyways."

O'Mahern had investigated only a couple of murders since becoming a detective a decade ago while his partner had none to her credit. Murder was a rare crime for the sheriff's department to investigate as most of those types of crimes were more prevalent in the cities of Lafayette or West Lafayette. In his first ever murder case, O'Mahern couldn't get any witnesses to come forward in the investigation; it was like getting an illegal immigrant to complete a census form. Because he couldn't get any witnesses, he never solved that first murder case involving a woman who was killed on the street in the small community of Shadeland, southwest of Lafayette, in broad daylight. He swore someone must have seen the poor woman get gunned down, but it involved drugs.

They went inside with their guns drawn as if someone was inside waiting for them, but that was how they were trained, training that taught them never to take chances, training that made them act more instinctively, training that would prevent them from being injured or killed. For all they knew, the murderer could have come to the victim's home. They were going to make sure they weren't caught off guard.

"Clear," said O'Mahern as he passed through the living room and went into the kitchen. O'Mahern could smell dog in the place, but it was nowhere around.

"Clear," Palmer said from one of the bedrooms that was on the right down the hallway. Palmer stayed in the master bedroom and began looking through things after she slipped on a pair of rubber latex gloves. She opened the closet first to make sure nobody was in it.

O'Mahern returned to the living room to check it out first. He also put on a pair of gloves before touching anything. Unlike the outside, the inside was neat and clean. The antique furniture was very primitive, including two rockers with a six-legged walnut occasional table in between them, a plain cocktail table sitting in front of the chairs, and on it, a stack of *National Geographic* magazines and a woven basket with miscellaneous items inside, such as a television controller, toenail clippers, and a dog grooming brush. Also in the room was a simple television stand made of pine, which contained an old analog television with a video recorder. What caught O'Mahern's attention was a gun cabinet, painted mushroom brown, over in the corner of the dark living room.

"Hey, Julie! Come look at this!" he yelled.

She came rushing in from the bedroom as if it was some kind of emergency.

He tried one of the keys on the keychain and it fit, so he opened the cabinet and pulled out an antique muzzle-loader with a shiny wood stock and black barrel from the collection of rifles, shotguns, and pistols in the oak cabinet.

"That's an original Kentucky muzzle-loader," Palmer explained. "It was first made in the mid-1700s and used until the mid-1800s."

"Wow, you even know gun history. It must be worth a lot."

"Oh yeah, thousands, but it depends on its age and condition though. I'd say this one would get a pretty penny on eBay or at an auction."

"Check out this one." O'Mahern handed her the rifle and picked up a box carrying two revolvers and all the accessories that went along with them.

"That's a set of dueling flintlock pistols, probably French."

"Is there anything you don't know about history?" he said kiddingly.

"Yeah, what's your mother's maiden name?"

"Inglestadt."

"I won't even ask how you spell it."

"I-t—"

"Very funny."

"So this guy was really into antiques and history."

"Yep. I think he was involved in portraying historical figures—a reenactor—based on what I saw in his closet."

"Looks as if he lives alone, like the maintenance man at the museum said."

"Yeah, he was married, but I think he got a divorce several years ago."

"Let's see what other things are of interest. Why don't you go back to the bedroom?"

"Well, that's where I was before you interrupted me."

She returned the rifle to the cabinet and walked back to the bedroom. The queen-sized bed was neatly made up, showing it hadn't been slept in, confirming that the victim was killed the evening before. She found his black leather wallet on the walnut dresser and began looking through it, the driver's license picture confirming he was the victim and showing his name as Patrick Daviess, a sixty-three-year-old. Birth date was October 1, so he was a Libra. She also found his Social Security card, Tippecanoe Historical Society membership card, and other information, none of which was probably of any help, so she stuffed that back into the wallet.

Meanwhile in the kitchen, O'Mahern continued to look through things that might point him in the direction of the murderer. He opened one drawer and found a large bowie knife. He wondered why it was in the kitchen and not in the living room in the gun cabinet. The knife reminded him of the illegal search he had made in the Mendez case. He'll never forget that search. It was an unusually warm evening in June when he jimmied the lock to get into Mendez's house. He started going through the criminal's things when he found a bowie knife in a dresser next to his bed. The knife contained some dried blood on the blade near the handle, so he took it with him. On his way out of the house, Mendez pulled up in his car, a Cadillac sports utility vehicle. He arrested the Hispanic drug dealer and took him downtown. The knife turned out to be the murder weapon, but because the evidence was obtained during an illegal search, it got tossed out by the judge, and the case had to be dropped for insufficient evidence.

Palmer found a personal laptop computer on a simple wooden desk made of pine. She picked it up to take back to the office for analysis by an expert in that sort of thing. She also found a personal telephone book in a nightstand next to the bedroom. It contained the names of relatives, which she could use to notify next of kin. She took it out to her partner.

"I found his phone book. You wanna notify the next of kin?"

"Not really. As lead detective, I'm assigning you that job."

"Thanks for nothing."

"You're welcome."

"Okay, I'll call them," she relented.

Palmer pulled out her cell phone from its holder on her belt. She had only done this a couple of times before, so she was a little nervous. She called the first Daviess in the book, hoping it was his mother. She lived in Denver, Colorado.

"Hello," a female answered.

"This is Detective Palmer from the Tippecanoe Sheriff's Department. Are you related to Patrick Daviess?"

"Yes, I'm his sister. What's the matter?"

"I'm sorry to break this news to you, but your brother was found dead last night."

"Oh god," she responded and started crying.

Julie waited patiently until Wanda Daviess got her composure back.

About a minute passed before she came back on the phone. "How can I help you, Detective?"

"Did your brother have any enemies?"

"Not that I know of. He did have an ex-wife though."

"What is her name?"

"Her first name is Barbara. I think she still goes by the family name. I don't recall her maiden name offhand."

"Do you know where she lives?"

"No, I'm not sure. They divorced a few years ago."

"Is there anyone in the area that you know of who could ID the body?"

"Yes, I'll call my son, he lives in Indianapolis."

"Just tell him to go to the Tippecanoe County Coroner's Office on Sixth Street in downtown Lafayette. We appreciate it."

"You're welcome. I'll be on a plane later today."

"Thank you for your help," Palmer said and gave her a telephone number to call if she could be of any assistance later. She turned to her partner and told him about the ex-wife.

"That's always a possibility," he commented. "Pretty much everyone's a suspect at this point."

They suddenly heard a scratching coming from the rear of the home. At the back door was none other than Scamp, the victim's dog. Palmer opened the door and let the dog in.

"That's a good dog," said Palmer. She was a dog person; O'Mahern was not.

The dog turned his attention to O'Mahern and smelled him.

"Sit!" commanded Palmer.

The shepherd obeyed her command. She went over and petted it under the mouth; he was fine with her action. The large dog was nearly waist high on her.

"You see, Jackson. You just have to know how to handle them."

"Yeah, you can have them," he said. O'Mahern had been bitten by two dogs when he was a child and didn't really trust them. He even killed a pit bull once when he was a patrol officer.

"You sure don't like them, do you?"

"No. What are we going to do with it?"

"It's not an it. It's a he by the name of Scamp," she said, looking at the dog tag on his collar.

"Whatever. I'll call dispatch and have Animal Control come here to pick him up."

O'Mahern made the call. Dispatch told him they would have the unit come to the house to pick Scamp up.

Meanwhile, Palmer gave the dog some water and a can of dog food she found in the pantry.

"Hey, that ex-wife of his is probably listed in his phone book. Where'd you put it?" O'Mahern said.

"It's over there on the kitchen table," she said, pointing to it.

"What did you say her name was?"

"Barbara, and it's probably listed under his last name, unless she changed it."

He turned to the Ds in the directory, and she was listed with a local number in West Lafayette. He called the number using his cell phone.

"Is this Barbara?"

"Yes, it is."

"This is Detective O'Mahern from the Tippecanoe Sheriff's Department. I wanted to speak to you about your ex-husband."

"Okay, what's the matter?"

"Well, that's what we're looking into. Could we come over to your house and talk to you sometime today?"

"Later. I'm on my way to church right now, then lunch. How about two o'clock?"

"That would be fine. We'll be over about two. Are you still living on Edgewood Drive in West Lafayette?"

"Yes, good-bye."

"Okay, then see you about two. Bye."

While Palmer messed with the dog, O'Mahern went about looking through things in the house, finding Daviess's checkbook, scanning through it, and seeing a recent payment of $500 to his ex-wife. Nothing else in the checkbook looked suspicious.

There was a knock on the front door, so Palmer went to answer it. It was Animal Control, so she turned Scamp over to them, making O'Mahern happy that he was gone.

"Find anything else of importance?" Palmer asked.

"Yeah, a $500 payment to his ex-wife. It's time to canvass the area now."

"Yeah, we should talk to some neighbors about him. The more we know the victim, the better chance we have figuring out who might have wanted him dead."

"You're right about that."

As they walked out the door, O'Mahern made sure to lock the front door behind him. He didn't want any unwanted visitors to the house. "Let's go this way," he said, pointing north.

"Okay."

The houses in the neighborhood ran the gamut in style and age, one- and two-story structures, ranch, trilevel, and even a double-wide trailer. Nobody answered the first couple of doors that they knocked at. O'Mahern figured they were either in church or overcoming a hangover from the night before. In either case, they weren't having much luck, and he started to get disgusted with the results. Finally, someone answered his knocking at an old two-story house. They introduced themselves, and O'Mahern asked, "Did you see Patrick Daviess last night?"

"As a matter of fact, I did. I was raking some leaves when he came by with his dog. He always takes his dog for a walk in the evening," Sharon Wishart commented. The middle-aged woman, clothed in a long black dress with short-heeled black shoes, was getting ready to go to church.

"What did you talk about?"

"Oh, he said he was leaving town today."

"Do you know where he was going?"

"No. I didn't ask him that, but he said he was going to be back on Wednesday."

"Was he with anyone else?"

"No, he was just with his dog. Is he okay?" She was not getting suspicious on why the police was there.

"No, he was found dead this morning."

"Oh my god," she said as a tear came to her eyes. "What happened?"

"We found him over by the battlefield monument. Did you hear or see anything unusual around dusk last night?"

"I heard a real loud bang around sunset just as I was finishing up outside. I thought it was a car backfiring."

"Could it have been a gunshot you heard?"

"Was he shot?" she said with her lips quivering.

"I'm not at liberty to say at this point. The case is under investigation."

Palmer jumped in. "Did he get along with everyone in the neighborhood?"

"Of course, he was a nice man. I need to get going, Detective. I don't want to be late for church. I'll say a prayer for him."

"Sure, thanks for your cooperation, ma'am," O'Mahern said.

As they walked away from the house, O'Mahern commented, "I think we have what we wanted. Let's go to the coroner's office and see if he's got anything for us yet. Drive me back to the crime scene so I can drive my car back to headquarters. After that, we can ride to the coroner in my car." Their office was on the way to the coroner's office.

"Whatever you say, boss," she replied. She didn't want him to think he was anything but her boss.

O'Mahern had to ask her some questions that had been bugging him about his new partner. "Why in the hell did you attend IU when you lived so close to Purdue?" he asked. Purdue and Indiana University are bitter state rivals in sports. They competed for the Old Oaken Bucket each year in football, and he played against them.

"Because I wanted to be a lawyer and they offered me a scholarship," she explained. "But along the way, I switched majors to criminal justice and became a police officer instead."

"I see. Why did you switch?"

"Police work seemed more interesting than the other side of the law. It was also a little easier to get into."

"That's for sure. I hate lawyers. They end up getting the criminals off way too often."

"Why did you become a cop?"

"Runs in the family. My grandfather was a Chicago beat cop during the Roaring Twenties. I have his 1902 .38 Smith & Wesson. It's a nice antique. He even killed a robber with it in 1915."

"How did he do that?"

"He was actually off duty at the time. He went into a liquor store that had just been robbed, and the thieves were fleeing down the alley when he told them to stop. They turned around and started shooting at him. He pulled out his gun and shot one dead. The other got away. He got an award for that. Then he became a bank guard."

"How long have you been with the sheriff's department?"

"About twenty years now. I started with them right after graduation."

"What about your dad?"

"He was in the army as an MP during Vietnam. When he retired, he started a security company right here in Lafayette. Now he's retired from that too. I might do that myself after I retire too."

"You've got a long way to go before that happens."

"True, but it's never too early to start thinking toward retirement."

"Unless you're young, like me."

"Yeah, I guess. I don't remember when I started thinking about retirement."

"That's a sign you're getting old."

"The remember part or the retirement part?"

"Both."

They arrived back at O'Mahern's car.

"I'll meet you back at the office," O'Mahern said. "Then we'll ride over to the coroner's office in my car."

"Sounds good to me."

Chapter 6

Illinois Territory, April 11, 1811

"George, wake up," Herman Strom whispered as he poked his friend. "It's time to go hunting."

"Right. Is it still dark?" Benjamin Washington asked as he rubbed the matter from his eyes.

"Yeah, but first light is coming soon."

"That's good. The deer should be down by the river getting a drink. I will meet you outside in a few minutes."

"I will be waiting."

Stepping out from the white tent, Strom walked over to the campfire to keep warm as his long-sleeved white cotton shirt and black pants weren't thick enough against the cool April morning; however, his raccoon hat kept his head warm and his long full black beard protected his face. He thought about what lay ahead that day after hunting. The group of ten settlers had decided the day before to start building a settlement on a hill overlooking the Mississippi River to avoid any flooding that might occur. The group had come from Vincennes in the Indiana Territory the week before.

A few minutes later, Washington came out of the tent ready to hunt. He was a little bit taller than Strom and wore a deerskin jacket over his white shirt and tan pants. He wore no hat like Strom but had a full head of brown hair and a short beard.

They walked a short distance to the mighty river and headed downstream along the bank, looking for deer or other animals. Their food supplies were dwindling, and they needed some meat.

The cloudy skies made the dawn come slowly while they walked along the river's edge. As they came around a bend in the river, Strom spotted a deer drinking out of the river. He tapped Washington on the shoulder and pointed out the young buck. Both stopped and lifted their muskets slowly, ready to shoot.

"Ready?" Strom whispered.

"Yeah."

"Fire."

Both fired about the same time. One shot hit the buck in the midsection, and he stumbled away. The settlers ran after the deer to finish it off. They saw the deer stumble and fall. They wouldn't need to reload their muskets and fire again. As they reached the deer, they heard some footsteps come running their way through the trees. They were shocked to see four Indians coming at them at full speed with tomahawks held high.

"Indians!" Strom yelled, hoping that the other settlers would hear them, but they were too far away from the camp.

The settlers ran for their lives back to the camp, but they were soon overtaken by the savages. One Indian struck Washington in the head with a war club, and he fell to the ground. Another savage finished him off with a knife to his kidney. Strom stopped and tried to help his friend, but he was outnumbered. He was able to knock down an Indian with a swing of his musket, but another savage got him in the head with a tomahawk, killing him almost instantly.

The Potawatomi warriors then scalped them to take trophies back home. They also took their muskets and the deer they had shot.

Chapter 7

Present Day

After the detectives arrived at the sheriff's office, they rode together in O'Mahern's car over to the Tippecanoe County Coroner's Office, located in a modern red-brick two-story government building on Sixth Street near downtown Lafayette, a building that looked like a government building from the outside, although it could be mistaken for an office building with not much flair. They entered the building and made their way to the autopsy room on the first floor. The room was very plain with blue tile walls, a linoleum floor for ease in cleaning up any messes that occurred, stainless-steel cabinets, and two stainless-steel tables for corpses. Another door from the room led to the cooler, where bodies were stored.

"You're here a little early," said Dr. John Jurgenson, the county coroner. "We're not quite done yet." He started to shake hands with the detectives but realized he still had gloves on. Dr. Kathy Acorn, a pathologist, continued to work on the victim although she stopped for a second to greet Palmer and O'Mahern with a simple hi. The doctor had her auburn hair in a ponytail to keep it out of her work. She had been performing autopsies for a couple of years. She did the work while Jurgenson supervised the operation as he trusted that she'd do a good job even if it was a very important autopsy. The somewhat attractive pathologist, who was in her midthirties, was a very thorough worker—nearly a perfectionist—something Jurgenson liked about her.

"We wanted to get the bullet as soon as we could so we could do some research on it and possibly get a hit off of it," replied O'Mahern. "What have you got so far, Doc?"

On the table, Patrick Daviess was laid open like a fish that had been gutted. The sight made Palmer squeamish, but it didn't bother her partner. O'Mahern had seen autopsies before, but she hadn't. The victim had two tattoos: a hawk on his left upper arm and a rose on the right forearm with the name Janice under it. O'Mahern wondered who Janice was; he figured it was some love in his life but not his ex-wife since her name was different.

"I don't think you're going to get much off of this bullet in your computer system since it's not a bullet. It's a lead shot," Jurgenson said.

Dr. Acorn lifted up the egg-shaped shot out of a metal tray. Dr. Jurgenson had been the county coroner for twenty years and dealt with murders before, so the lead shot was quite a surprise to him when Dr. Acorn found it in the body.

"Lead shot?" O'Mahern questioned.

"Yep. The bullet pierced the lower part of the heart and lodged in the backbone. He died quickly."

"That's the kind of bullet used in that muzzle-loader or flintlock pistol we saw at the victim's house," Palmer answered.

"Holy shit," O'Mahern said.

"Heck of a shot," added Palmer.

"Why do you say that?"

"Those weapons weren't the most accurate."

"We have some more work to do before my exam is complete," Dr. Jurgenson said.

"I think you got what we really need," O'Mahern said. "Send that lead shot over to ballistics for further examination . . . and thanks, Doc."

"You're welcome."

"Hold on a second," Palmer said and held out a hand. "Give me that bullet, please. I'll have a gun expert that I know examine it. He will know more than ballistics. He'll probably know exactly what type of gun it came from."

"Sure," the coroner said. Dr. Acorn flipped it to Palmer.

She caught it. "Thanks."

"That's not procedure," criticized O'Mahern.

"We'll just let him look at it first. Then we'll pass it on to ballistics tomorrow."

"But that would take it out of the normal chain of evidence."

"Yes, but it will stay in our custody, so it wouldn't be a problem later."

"Give it back to me tomorrow morning so it won't be a problem," Dr. Jurgenson said.

"I guess that would be okay since they don't work on Sunday, and the state police seem to take forever to get back to us on evidence we send them for analysis," O'Mahern said. "Just get it back here tomorrow morning. So who is this expert?"

"He's a man who collects artifacts from that time period and knows weapons. He has many authentic pieces that were used in that era. He should know exactly the weapon that was used by the size of this pellet. I'll call him when we get back to the office."

"Okay, oh wise one."

"You forgot to bow."

"Yeah right."

Chapter 8

Indiana Territory, July 1811

Tecumseh was down by the riverbank, sitting next to a Sycamore tree, trying to keep cool when his relaxation was interrupted by a canoe containing several white men coming up the Wabash River, a man in the front of the canoe waving a white flag to indicate that they came in peace. On his other hand, he held a paper rolled up and tied with a string. A couple of naked warriors greeted the canoe, and the white man handed one of the warriors the paper. "This is for Chief Tecumseh," he said.

As the warrior took the paper to Tecumseh, the white men turned their boat around and went back down the river, their mission accomplished.

Tecumseh could understand and speak English, but he was not proficient in reading it, so he took it back to the town to have his nephew translate the paper from Governor William Henry Harrison. Spemica Lawba read the paper and told him, "Governor Harrison wants you to come to Vincennes to explain why your warriors seized an entire boatload of salt instead of the five barrels the government was giving you as part of the settlement of the Fort Wayne Treaty."

"I did not sign that treaty, but I will go to the American capitol to speak with him. Then I will continue south to speak to more tribes to join us."

After a couple of days of preparation, Tecumseh was finally ready to leave for Vincennes. The weather was perfect—hot and dry—for leaving on the canoe trip down the Wabash River, lower than usual for this time of year and almost as calm as a lake. The trip would take a couple of days. Before he left Prophet's Town, he spoke to his brother that July morning.

"Brother, I'm leaving now for Vincennes to talk to the white chief," Tecumseh said and placed his left hand on Tenskwatawa's right shoulder. "Then I will go south to speak to more tribes about joining us. Do not cause any trouble with the white man while I am gone."

"I will not cause any trouble, brother," The Prophet said. "I will pray for your safe return."

"If the white man sends his army, leave this place and scatter to the wind. Send our brothers back to their tribes. I will deal with the white man myself."

"Yes, brother. I will do as you ask."

"I will be back before the snow flies."

"That is good."

They hugged, and Tecumseh left his brother's hut. He gathered up his followers, some three hundred of them, including thirty squaws to take care of cooking and other household duties while in Vincennes and down south.

When Tecumseh arrived in Vincennes three days later, his group was greeted by some American soldiers, who told them to camp at the same place they had camped the year before.

On the day the council with Harrison was to begin, a heavy thunderstorm canceled the meeting. Tecumseh considered this a bad omen.

The next day, Tecumseh and his party of one hundred and eighty came to the same meeting place they had met before near Grouseland Estate. His men painted themselves in red and white and were armed with knives, tomahawks, and war clubs, while the Americans had a small number of dragoons with pistols and knives. However, Harrison had hundreds of troops nearby in case hostilities arose.

Governor Harrison, who was dressed in his blue-and-gold uniform, sat behind a table with interpreters on one side and the armed soldiers off to the side. Tecumseh's party was arranged in a semicircle behind him.

This time, Harrison spoke first. "Earlier this year, two white men were killed by Indians on the Mississippi River. I understand they were of the Potawatami tribe, which have joined you at Prophet's Town. I am also concerned that you brought so many warriors with you to this conference when all I wanted was to speak to you."

Harrison went on to tell that he would not talk about the Fort Wayne Treaty as that was in the president's hands and not his. "I want to know why the entire salt shipment was seized by your brother." Harrison concluded.

"Last year, you were angry that we refused the salt. This year, you are displeased that it was taken. Those were not my men who stole the salt." Tecumseh lied to him about not knowing who stole the salt. Tecumseh himself had refused the salt in September 1810 in Fort Wayne. He had called the boat captain an "American dog" and handled him roughly. Then he told the captain, "Take it back to Harrison. Tell him we want nothing from him."

The governor continued, "Even if they were not your men, I want you to quit gathering the tribes together." He was afraid that an Indian nation would be a powerful foe.

"The Master of Life has appointed this place to light our fires. There we shall remain."

As darkness approached, the meeting was adjourned until the following day.

The next day, the chief of the Weas, Wawpawwawqua, opened the meeting with a speech lasting several hours. The five-foot-eight-inch Indian spoke about the treaties with the whites and how they had affected the Indians. At times, he would wave his hands around, which revealed the tomahawk on his belt under the gray blanket he had draped around his neck that hung down below his waist. On his head, he wore a turban over his graying hair with a single eagle feather sticking straight up, his wrinkled face showing he was much older than most of the Indians gathered there.

Harrison ignored much of what the Weas's chief said and turned his attention toward Tecumseh and the killing of the two white men again. "I want you to turn over the two Indians who killed the two white men in the Illinois Territory. If you do so, this will mend the damage done by your brothers."

"Brother, I will not deliver the warriors as I do not know who they are," Tecumseh replied. Again he lied; he knew who they were. "The two white men were trespassing on Indian lands. They should not have been there."

Then the chief went on to explain how he was going to travel to the south to gather more tribes for his nation. "I am going south to ask more Indians to join with me in Tippecanoe. I will be there until next spring. When I return, I and the other chiefs will be ready to visit your Great White Chief." He lied again. He actually planned to be back to Prophet's Town by the end of the year with his new recruits, but he didn't want to tell Harrison that as he didn't trust him.

The meeting dragged on until dark when Governor Harrison concluded it by saying, "The moon you see would sooner fall to the ground than the president would suffer his people to be murdered with impunity, and I will put petticoats on my soldiers sooner than give up a country I have bought fairly from its true owners!"

The next day, Tecumseh headed south to recruit more Indians for his nation from the Osage, Chickasaw, Choctaw, and Creek Nations.

Harrison was so delighted with Tecumseh's departure that he started planning his attack on Prophet's Town in his absence. He wrote a letter to Secretary of War Eustis and said in it, "I hope that if I can move against Prophet's Town before his return, then that part of the fabric which he considered complete will be demolished, and even its foundations rooted up."

Chapter 9

Present Day

The detectives proceeded to O'Mahern's car, which was parked in front of the building in a handicap spot, but it didn't matter since the office was closed on Sunday. As they got into the Mustang, O'Mahern said, "I'm going to stop on the way to the office and pick up some lunch. Are you hungry?"

"Yeah, I could eat some lunch," Palmer said.

He stopped at a small sandwich shop on their way back; they ordered sandwiches and took them back to the office to eat while they did research on the computer. Detective O'Mahern ordered a bacon, lettuce, and tomato on white toast while Palmer had a turkey and cheese on wheat.

On the drive back, O'Mahern lit up a cigarette before getting back to the office since smoking wasn't allowed there.

"Why don't you quit that nasty habit?" Palmer suggested.

"This job drove me to smoke. Maybe when I quit this job, I'll quit smoking."

"Or when you get lung cancer or emphysema."

"That too."

Palmer saw it was a useless topic, so she shut up and opened her bag of chips to munch on while she rode back to the office.

They arrived at the Tippecanoe County Law Enforcement Building on Duncan Road and parked in front of the modern two-tone building made of concrete block and other stones, one tone a light red and the other a clay color from the Bedford rock that was used. A large American flag waved on top of the pole from the stiff breeze that was blowing. At the back of the structure was the jail, a two-story structure.

They entered the secured entrance with a swipe of their cards and made their way to the empty office of the Special Response Team, a team that handled special crimes in the county, including drugs, gangs, murders, robbery, and whatever else the sheriff decided as special. Murders were rare in the county, so two detectives were always assigned to help out in the investigation unless more were needed. The sheriff thought two were all that was needed in this case, at least for the time being.

They took their seats at their respective desks, facing each other. The rather plain, stuffy office contained modern desks—Tuscany brown and black in finish, with a computer stand in the center and drawers on either side for files—set up so that four were put together facing one another in the open setting. Next to each desk was a plain wooden chair for suspects and witnesses, uncomfortable to sit on for a long time, a setting that provided no privacy, but none was needed as interview rooms off to the side provided the detectives all the privacy they needed to question a suspect. The walls were painted in off-white, like what the contractors usually used in new constructions, while the floor was covered in a speckled brown stain-resistant carpet. Fluorescent lighting in the ceiling provided light as there were few windows in the building.

Palmer shoved aside some paperwork to make room for her lunch in the Styrofoam takeout container. Although her desk was somewhat messy with stacks of paperwork, she knew where everything was located. She liked it that way. It sort of matched her apartment.

On the other hand, O'Mahern's desk was much cleaner. He liked setting up everything in trays as he worked on his cases. He was a lot more organized than his counterpart was. Under the glass that covered the top of his desk were some photos of the murder cases he had yet to solve. He put them there as a reminder and would work on the cold cases when he had some free time; unfortunately, he didn't get much free time to do just that. Usually, as soon as he finished a case, there was another case waiting for a detective. The department could use some more officers, but the budget hadn't allowed more to be hired in the last couple of years; however, the population continued to grow in the Lafayette area and in the county.

They ate their sandwiches as they scanned files on their computers, desktop models with flat screens that were all connected to a network. The two detectives continued looking at computer files and compiling information on the victim and his ex-wife.

"I'll check the gun registration file to see if that turns up anything," Palmer suggested. "Then I'll call my contact."

"You won't find anything in gun registration. Those types of weapons use gunpowder, and they aren't required to be registered," O'Mahern said.

"I didn't know that."

"Just call that so-called expert you know. What's his name?"

"His name is Bill Harrison."

"Don't know him. Check the background of the victim to see if that turns up anything too. I'll check into his ex's background and see if she's got any priors or guns registered."

"Right."

Palmer called Harrison, who was now a little like his forefather as he recently became president, although it was only president of the local historical society and not the country, an office he had taken about three weeks ago. Harrison said that the real expert was Jim Buchanan. She called Buchanan and set up a meeting for 3:00 p.m. at his house in Lafayette.

"Turns out I was wrong about Harrison. The real expert is Jim Buchanan, and we're to be at his place at three."

"Sounds good."

They both continued to check their computer files for more information. Palmer drummed the fingers of her right hand on the desk as she looked through files, using the mouse with her left hand, while O'Mahern's free left hand was still.

After about ten minutes, O'Mahern asked her, "What have you got so far?"

"Not much. Daviess has a record, but that was in his younger days. He was busted on a DUI at age twenty-three. Then he had an assault and battery as a result of a bar fight. The ex-wife we are going to go visit is his second wife. They were married twenty years and divorced in 2004. His financials show that he's come into some money recently. I don't know where it came from. He made a deposit recently of $25,000 in his money market account."

"Maybe he won the lottery?"

"I could check that."

"I was just kidding, but you never know. It's hard to track a cash transaction, but it does open a can of worms for us. Where did the cash come from?"

"Good question."

Sheriff Joshua Andrews came into the office still dressed in his church clothes, a dark blue suit contrasted by a light blue shirt and dark blue paisley tie, and shiny black shoes. "What do you guys have so far on this murder case?" he asked.

"Nothing much to report, Sheriff," O'Mahern said. "We're still in the researching stage of this baby. The only suspect we have is the ex-wife, but my partner thinks that an Indian or a ghost may be involved."

"Anything's possible. We do have an interesting development too," Palmer piped in.

"What's that, Palmer?"

"Turns out the bullet that killed the victim is a lead shot."

The sheriff had a puzzled look on his face. "Lead shot?"

"Yep, the kind used back in the 1800s."

"That's a bit unusual, I'd say. In all my years on the force, a weapon like that has never turned up in a case," Sheriff Andrews said. He had been in the Tippecanoe County Sheriff's Department for over thirty-four years, ten as the elected sheriff of the county, elected in 2000 over a fellow officer when the previous sheriff had retired. The six-foot officer was now in his early sixties, and his hair had turned gray from the stress of the job.

"And they aren't registered," she said.

"Right," the sheriff remembered. "Give me a report first thing tomorrow morning on your progress. Do you need any additional help with this one?"

"I think we can handle it," said O'Mahern. He really didn't love working with a rookie, but he preferred it over a task force of officers.

"Good, because I don't have much overtime in the budget with this budget crunch we are getting from the county," the sheriff explained. "Since today starts your work week, don't ask for overtime until you've reached forty hours. Then I might be able to give it to you, but I kind of doubt it. We only have so much money until the end of the calendar year."

"Right, sir."

"I got a call that might give you a lead," said Sheriff Andrews as he handed O'Mahern a piece of paper with a name and number to call. "She happens to be a psychic, and she's given us some credible information in the past, so I want you to go talk to her."

"Is she like that woman in that former TV show? You know, *Medium*?" said Palmer, who was standing nearby.

"Don't know. I've never seen the show."

"It was a good show for several years but got cancelled earlier this year."

"I hate cop shows. They're never realistic enough for me. Please contact her."

"May as well. We haven't got any hot leads yet," O'Mahern said.

"Thanks."

The sheriff turned around and went back to his office. O'Mahern picked up the phone and called the psychic, Sandra Barksley. She was at home and invited them to come over and talk to her.

"Let's go, Palmer. We're goin' to go see this psychic?"

"Okay. My car?"

"No, I'll drive." O'Mahern wanted to drive so he could enjoy a smoke on the way to the psychic's house on Ninth Street.

The weather had warmed up a little since the morning, so O'Mahern was able to open his window more to let the smoke out while he puffed away on a cigarette. On the way to the psychic's house, O'Mahern said, "I wonder if she'll do a séance to talk to the dead or something," he said.

"Or maybe she has a Ouija board that will spell out the killer's name."

"That would be convenient. Or she might have an eight ball to give us a lead."

"I don't think we could be that lucky with this case."

The psychic lived in an old large two-story Victorian house dating from the early 1900s, with lots of gingerbread trim, a bright yellow paint, and green-shingled roof, making it stand out from the other old homes on the block. O'Mahern took one look at the house and figured it fit the character of a clairvoyant.

They went up to the door and rang the doorbell. A short elderly woman answered the door. "Good afternoon, Officers. Come on in."

"Actually, we're detectives. I'm Jackson O'Mahern, and this is Julie Palmer."

"I'm very glad to meet you. I'll show you to the parlor. Do you want something to drink?"

"We're fine. Thanks."

The house smelled a little stuffy to the detectives, probably because she had closed all the windows some weeks before and the house was heated by the old-timey radiators. The parlor was surrounded by windows and contained several older chairs with small tables in between, small plants with flowers decorating every table; a cocktail table in the middle of the room held a shadow box that contained pictures and other memorabilia, the walls covered with family photos.

"Nice place you have here," Palmer said, trying to be as nice as she could.

"Oh thank you. It's an old house, but my husband is retired and has plenty of time to keep it up."

"So what have you got for us?" O'Mahern asked after he plopped down into a dark blue chair with dark-wood arms, the chair enveloping him.

"I had some visions over the last two days. The first was yesterday. I saw a man walking his dog by a monument. Then I saw an Indian take aim at him with a rifle and shoot him. Then the dog ran after the Indian, but the Indian jumped over a creek and the dog lost his scent."

"That's interesting," O'Mahern said.

"Then I had a vision just before you called me. I see a man getting attacked by an Indian with a tomahawk, but the vision ended before anything happened."

"Do you know where?" O'Mahern asked.

"The Indian came out of the woods. That's all I know. I wish I could help you more."

"Do you know when?"

"It will likely occur near dark since it was almost dark in my vision. Sometimes my visions come ahead of an event—a premonition."

"Could you identify these people?"

"Not really. They are too far away in my mind's eye for facial identification. The man in the second vision was wearing jeans, and the Indian had on deerskin. His face was painted."

O'Mahern looked at his watch and noticed their appointment with Daviess's ex-wife was quickly approaching. "Thanks for your time. We must go on to another appointment now, but please call me if you have any more premonitions."

"Oh, you're welcome, Detective."

He handed her a business card.

"Thank you, Sandra," Palmer said.

"You're welcome. I'll see you out."

As they walked down the hall to the front door, O'Mahern was thinking that she was interesting but a waste of time if she couldn't be more specific with her visions.

After some more cordial good-byes, the detectives left. On their way to his car, O'Mahern said, "I hope her vision for later today wasn't correct. We don't need another murder right now."

"That's for sure. Of course, we don't ever need them, but they do occur."

"Job security."

"I guess you could look at it that way, although I wouldn't mention that to the sheriff."

"Do you think we should put out some kind of bulletin about this upcoming murder?"

"We don't have enough information to warrant it right now. She didn't say where, so it could be anywhere. That's not much help."

O'Mahern drove to the ex-wife's apartment located in West Lafayette, close to Purdue University. The clear blue sky made it easy for Palmer to look over the information O'Mahern had gathered. She thought of a couple of questions she could ask her. They soon arrived at the address, a two-story modern duplex with red brick on the front and tan vinyl siding on the side. O'Mahern pulled in behind a dark green 2002 Ford Escort parked in the driveway.

"Have you got some questions now?" O'Mahern asked.

"I'm ready. I was born ready."

"Very well. You do the asking because she'll probably warm up to you more than me."

"Oh, woman on woman. I get it."

"Yeah."

O'Mahern knocked on the front door. They left their guns in their holsters as this would be a friendly visit to gather information—no need to be ready for any problems.

An elderly redheaded woman opened the door. "You must be the detectives."

"Yes, I'm Detective O'Mahern, and this is Detective Palmer."

"I'm Barbara Daviess. Come on in. Have a seat on the couch, please."

The small living room was decorated with an apple-colored couch and chair set with a cheap pine end table, separating the two in an L shape; a bronze lamp with a tan lamp shade sitting on the end table; and a coffee table matching the end table, on top of it a stack of women's magazines. The furniture was contrasted by a brown shag carpet and tan-painted walls.

Barbara wore a turquoise dress that had long sleeves with some white lace, a gold necklace with a cross, and plain gold stud earrings. She had worn the outfit to church and lunch. The only thing odd about her outfit was her red house slippers.

The detectives took a seat on the couch, both with notepads ready.

"First of all, my condolences to you," Palmer said.

"Is he dead?" Her face turned red, and some tears formed in her eyes.

"Yeah, I guess I forgot to tell you that when I called."

O'Mahern handed her a handkerchief from his pocket, and she wiped the tears from her eyes, but she wasn't hysterical about it.

"I heard on the news there was a murder in Battle Ground, but I never would have wished that it was him or anyone else for that matter. How was he killed?"

"That's still under investigation, so we aren't at liberty to say," O'Mahern said. "Can you tell me briefly why you two divorced?"

"Sure. He was cheating on me," she said frankly. "I was going to do a John Wayne Bobbitt procedure on him but thought better of it. So I divorced him."

O'Mahern cringed at the answer. Bobbitt had his penis severed by his wife in 1993 in Manassas, Virginia. "Yeah, that would have been drastic. How did the settlement go?"

"Oh, it went fine. I didn't want the house because I didn't want to fuss with the yard work at my age."

"Did you get any of his gun collection?" Palmer asked.

"No, I didn't want any of that stuff. He was a collector and a reenactor. I don't believe in guns."

"Where were you last night around dusk?" Palmer was probing for an alibi.

"I went out to dinner with a male friend of mine. We went to a restaurant out on Creasy Lane."

"What's his name?"

"Paul Simpson."

"Do you know if your ex had any enemies?"

"Not that I know of. Pat was pretty easygoing."

"You said he was a reenactor. What was his role?"

"A settler. He'd dress up like an old-time settler at the Feast of the Hunters' Moon. In fact, Pat was in a fake attack in which he was killed by an Indian last month as part of the reenactment. I never thought he'd ever be murdered for real."

"He recently wrote you a check for $500. What was that for?"

"He had agreed to give me $500 a year in compensation for him taking the house in the final settlement."

Palmer turned to her partner and said, "That's all I have."

Detective O'Mahern had more questions. "Barbara, were there any neighbors Pat had run-ins with?"

"No, not really. He got along with everyone."

"Anything strange about him?"

"He was in a ghost hunter's group in Lafayette. They'd go all around the state hunting for ghosts. He tried to get me to go along, but I was scared of that."

"Okay, we'll check into them. Thanks for your time."

"Yes, thank you too," added Palmer.

As soon as Palmer got in the car, O'Mahern asked her, "How do you like her for it?"

"No way. I don't see a motive."

"Very good. Yep, you have to have one."

Chapter 10

Indiana Territory, November 1811

In early November 1811, General William Henry Harrison's forces left Fort Harrison, a small fort they built along the Wabash River in western Indiana, and headed to Prophet's Town. He had decided to attack the Indian village and break up Tecumseh's confederacy after meeting with the chief in July, and that wish would come true in a few days. The general had been authorized to do so by Secretary of War William Eustis. The Wabash expedition had nine companies of United States Infantry, six companies of Indiana mounted riflemen, two companies of Indiana dragoons and Kentucky mounted riflemen, a company of Indiana riflemen, and a company of Indian scouts—a force of nearly a thousand men. However, some were green and had never seen battle.

Harrison's blue-coated army traveled along the Wabash River for a couple of days until they reached the Indian settlement by the confluence of the Tippecanoe and Wabash Rivers. They found a good ford to cross the Tippecanoe River and came upon a tall grass prairie. The mounted soldiers led the way so the foot soldiers could make it through the fields of weeds and wildflowers that were taller than a horse and rider in some places; the only thing the soldiers had to try to avoid was the smelly droppings by those horses in front of them. A cool autumn breeze on this mostly cloudy day, the sixth of November, helped to send those smells quickly away. After trekking a couple of miles, the prairies turned into farmland, and stalks of maize were stacked in upright piles as they came closer to Prophet's Town. They could see smoke rising from town and smell the wood fires as the west wind blew directly into their faces. Soon they were greeted by three Indians on horseback waving a white flag, carrying a note, and dressed in deerskin with no war paint on their faces.

"What does it say?" General Harrison asked the Indian scout who retrieved the paper.

"Tecumseh's brother, the Shawnee Prophet, is asking for a ceasefire until we can talk peace tomorrow," the scout said.

Harrison rubbed his chin and thought about the request for a few seconds. He already knew Tecumseh wouldn't be in the town because he was recruiting more warriors down south.

Harrison was right about Tecumseh being away recruiting more Indians to his confederacy. In fact, he was speaking to the Osage tribe at the time. They were located near the Missouri and the Little Osage Rivers.

Tecumseh told the Osage, "Brothers, we all belong to one family, we are all children of the Great Spirit. We walk in the same path, slake our thirst at the same spring, and now affairs of the greatest concern lead us to smoke the pipe around the same council fire!

"Brothers, we are friends. We must assist each other to bear our burdens. The blood of many of our fathers and brothers has run like water on the ground to satisfy the avarice of the white men. We ourselves are threatened with a great evil. Nothing will pacify them but the destruction of all the red men . . ."

He continued, "Brothers, the white men want more than our hunting grounds. They wish to kill our warriors. They would even kill our old men, women, and little ones.

"The red men have borne many and great injuries. They ought to suffer them no longer. My people will not, they are determined on vengeance. They will drink the blood of the white people."

He concluded, "Brothers, we must be united. We must smoke the same pipe. We must fight each other's battles. And more than all, we must love the Great Spirit. He is for us. He will destroy our enemies and make all his red children happy."

Harrison had met The Prophet the year before without his brother being present and was suspicious of the man, but he decided to hear him out instead of attacking right away.

"Tell him we will honor the request and meet with him tomorrow morning," General Harrison replied.

The general's reply was translated to the trio of warriors, who took the message back to the Shawnee Prophet. Tenskwatawa had asked for a peace talk because his scouts told him that the white man's army was more than twice the size of his force. Although Tippecanoe had grown to more than two thousand Indians, some good warriors had gone with Tecumseh, and others had gone home to visit their relatives in his absence. They would all likely return before winter, but that wouldn't do him any good. He remembered that Tecumseh had told him to leave if the white man's army showed up, but he wanted to speak to the white chief before he made that decision.

Harrison had to find a suitable camping ground for his army, so he continued marching his troops ahead toward Prophet's Town. About one hundred and fifty yards from the town, his troops were greeted by a number of Indians who were fearful that his army was attacking as the village was close by. Harrison's scouts asked them for a good place to camp, and they pointed northwest to a spot less than a mile away near the Catholic mission, where some Indians went to learn about the white man's religion. The general sent two officers and a quartermaster to examine the area. They returned a little while later and told the general that it was acceptable.

When the army arrived at the campsite, the general was afraid that it afforded a great approach for the savages. The site was a piece of dry oak land rising about ten feet above the marshy prairie in front and twice that height in the rear near a stream clothed in willows and other brushwood. Toward the left flank, this stretch of land widened considerably but is narrower in the opposite direction. Harrison decided to form an irregular parallelogram to protect his army from an attack on all four sides, some sides more open to attack than others.

The general met with his officers before setting up camp. "I don't trust this Indian leader, so I want sentries to stand post all night at various spots along our lines," he told them. "I think our most vulnerable position is to the south, so Captain Spencer, I want your Yellow Jackets to set up there."

"Yes, sir," Captain Spier Spencer replied.

"On the west side, I want you, Colonel Floyd, to put your militia groups. Make sure you set up with a clear view of that steep embankment, if some savages decided to come from that direction."

"Right, sir," confirmed Colonel Davis Floyd.

"Major Rodd, I want your troops to set up in reserve behind the lines, as well as your dragoons, Major Daviess."

"We will be ready, sir," said Major Joseph Daviess.

"I'm sure you will. I will put the Indiana Rangers along the creek on the east and the north, toward the mission. Are there any questions?"

"Do you think we should dig some trenches or barricade our positions more?" asked the colonel.

"I don't think that will be necessary. The men are tired from the long march here and need rest anyways. Get them fed and get them to bed, but tell them we still might be attacked."

"Yes, sir," the officers said together.

Just before dark, a former slave named Ben decided to go over to the other side to help the Indians. "I need to go in woods," the wagon driver told a sentry before leaving the camp. He spoke in broken English because he was born in Africa and was brought to America as a slave. The sentry waved his approval as trenches had not yet been dug for a latrine behind the line.

The African native wanted to get away from the white man. He had been a slave for more than a decade, but his master died and he was given his freedom. Afterward, the large black man in his early thirties went to work for the army and felt almost like a slave again as he was given some of the worst jobs to do, like digging trenches, cleaning up after the officers, and doing whatever he was ordered to do. He wanted to escape the oppression, so he ventured into the woods until he came upon some Indian warriors.

"Help me," he told them. They didn't understand him, so they grabbed his arms and took him to their leader, who was in his medicine lodge, keeping warm by the fire.

When Ben saw The Prophet, he was shocked to see him because of the missing eye the Shawnee chief displayed. The younger brother of Tecumseh, who became disfigured from losing an eye at ten years of age while fooling around with a bow and arrow, was quite capable of leading the camp. He had become the religious leader of the Shawnee. The Prophet was thought to be supreme and invincible. He earned that title years earlier. One day, he was smoking a pipe in his wigwam and went into a trance. Some thought he was dead. Afterward, he told of seeing the Great Spirit and began preaching to his tribe. He told the Shawnee they were the first creations of the Master of Life and greatest of all his children. "Pay the white traders only half of what you owe because they have cheated you," he told them. He wanted the Indians to go back to the old ways and give up the white man's clothing and wear traditional Indian clothing, not what the white man could provide. He wore soft deerskin leggings and moccasins decorated with dyed porcupine quills. The Prophet told them not to eat any meat from sheep or cows, only those from deer and buffalo, but the buffalo was becoming scarce in Indiana. He also told them not to drink firewater. "It is the drink of the evil spirit," he professed. "It makes you sick. It burns your insides." He preached to tribesmen that the white man was the scum of the earth and had stolen their land.

Ben was just what Tenskwatawa needed. The Indian leader had consulted with the spirits and decided to send a party to murder General Harrison in his tent to avoid a battle. The Prophet used visions, trances, and incantations to convince warriors that the bullets and swords of Americans wouldn't hurt them. Indians were very superstitious, and they believed the loud voice of the Shawnee Prophet.

The Prophet had disregarded what his brother Tecumseh told him to do before he had left to gather more Indians for his nation. Tecumseh had advised him to scatter into the forest if the Americans came toward the town. "If he (Harrison) attempts to destroy Tippecanoe, abandon it, move away, and let him have his will," Tecumseh had said. "Tippecanoe can be rebuilt."

The Prophet asked Ben, "Can you take us to the general's tent?"

"Sure, I can take you," he said nervously.

With Ben's help, a raiding party of three warriors stealthily headed toward the general's tent.

Chapter 11

Present Day

As the detectives left Barbara Daviess's house, O'Mahern asked Palmer, "Where's that gun expert's place that we have to go to?"

"It's over on Ninth Street, near the Historical Society. He lives in an old home."

"I figured that. Old collection, old home. Is he old too?"

"Depends on what you define old as. I think he's in his fifties, so more middle aged than old."

O'Mahern drove quickly to Ninth Street in Lafayette as the time was approaching three. "Right or left?" he asked.

"Right. Go to 923. That's on the left side of the street."

"Okay."

Up the hill he drove until he came to the old house with that address, a distinctive century-old Queen Anne home with a turret on one side and wrap-around porch on the other. The three-story structure was painted all white, except for the gingerbread trim painted in a contrasting dark blue. He pulled into the long driveway that led to the rear of the home and parked.

Palmer did the honors and knocked on the door. She knew him but didn't know if he would remember her. A few seconds later, he answered.

"Hi, Julie. I remember you now," Jim Buchanan said.

"Hi to you too. This is my partner, Jackson O'Mahern."

"Glad to meet you."

"The same to you."

Palmer took the lead ball out of the plastic evidence bag she had it in and handed it to him as they walked down the floral wallpapered hallway, a hallway full of large old pictures of people from the 1800s, a hallway full of memories for the owner to walk through. The smell of broccoli filled their nostrils as Buchanan had broccoli soup for lunch and stunk up the whole house with the vegetable smell.

"Here's the bullet we recovered from the body."

"We'll go to my exhibit room to make a comparison of this."

"Pretty place you have here," she said.

"Thank you. It's taken me some time to restore the old place, but I think I'm about done with it. Now it's time to redecorate, according to my wife. She watches all those home improvement shows and wants to make changes to the house now that we've had it a few years."

He showed them into a room that looked more like a museum than a normal room in a house as one wall was lined with rifles, another with swords, and another with spears, all of Indian origin, all original. Glass cases were arranged in the center of the room, containing pistols, knives, other weapons, and artifacts. A case in the corner contained Native American artifacts, such as Indian arrowheads, bows, tomahawks, pottery, spears, and other items.

"Wow, you have quite a collection," O'Mahern said as his eyes whirled around the room and took in all the antiques.

"Thank you. It's been years in the making. My father started the collection and passed it on to me. Then I started collecting, so this room has filled up accordingly. They are all original Indian artifacts. I don't buy copies or reproductions."

Buchanan took the lead ball and put it on a small scale. Then he picked up a ball from a nearby bowl and put it on the other scale. The two weighed about the same.

"I see this lead ball lost a little from its original shape after entering the body. I'd say it came from a muzzle-loader like those in this rack." He pointed to a nearby rack of six rifles, all were long rifles.

"Like this one," Palmer said and put a hand on one that wasn't in the rack but leaning against it. "May I?"

"Oh sure. You can handle it."

She picked up the rifle and started examining it. She took a whiff of the end of the rifle, and it smelled of gunpowder. "This one's been recently fired, hasn't it?"

That remark made him a suspect in O'Mahern's mind because he had the means available. O'Mahern stayed silent though because he didn't want to interrupt the conversation.

"Yes, I was demonstrating it to some friends yesterday afternoon in my gun range in the basement. I haven't got around to cleaning it. That's why I had it leaning against the rack. A lead ball like this could have been used in any of those rifles. Do you know how far it traveled?"

"We don't know exactly, but I think about a hundred feet," Palmer said.

"And where was the victim struck?"

"In the abdomen, just below the heart." Palmer pointed to the spot on her own body.

"That's a pretty accurate shot, so I'd say it came from a long-barrel musket like the one you're handling. The longer the barrel, the farther a shot would sail and the more accurate it would be."

"Can it be matched to the gun that fired it?" asked O'Mahern.

"Yes, if it came from a reproduction of a musket. They have rifling and are more accurate than those muskets originally used. If an older musket was used, your ballistics department wouldn't be able to match the bullet to it. These old rifles aren't like the newer ones. They didn't have any rifling and weren't as accurate as the ones today." He closely examined the lead shot again. Buchanan was a gun expert and a military veteran as he spent a tour in Vietnam in the early 1970s when the war was winding down, but he saw some action and killed a few Vietnamese in his time with the US Marine Corp. "I don't see any rifling on this lead shot, so I'd say it came from an original musket or shotgun."

"I never knew a shotgun could fire a lead ball," O'Mahern said.

"Yep, it sure can be designed that way."

"Who has these types of rifles around here?" Palmer queried.

"There are only a few collectors around here like myself, but the reenactors would have a real one or a reproduction that could fire a lead shot if they wanted to do so. They normally fire blanks that cause a lot of smoke for effect."

"Could you give us some names?"

"Sure. I have that information on my computer in my home office. Can I get you something to drink?"

Both detectives answered no. He left and went to his office down the hallway. While he was gone, Palmer and O'Mahern looked more closely at his impressive collection, which was more extensive than some museums.

"Interesting stuff," O'Mahern said.

"Yeah, he's got a large collection."

"I'll say. He must be rich."

"Yeah, he's got some money. A lot of it is from an inheritance though."

A few minutes later, Buchanan returned to the exhibit room and handed Palmer the list.

"Here you go. As you can see, there's quite a few reenactors, but not all of them live around here. They come from all over the Midwest and Canada for the Feast of the Hunters' Moon. The list has addresses and phone numbers for all of them."

"Yeah, looks like we've got our work cut out for us. Did you know Patrick Daviess?" Palmer asked.

"Yes, I knew him. He played a settler last month who was 'killed' by an Indian during a reenactment. Quite ironic that someone would kill him like that in real life."

"In the reenactment, where was he shot?"

"In the chest like you showed me."

"That may not be ironic. It may be a copycat who has changed fake to reality."

"So you're saying the Indians used muskets too?" O'Mahern asked.

"Of course."

"Oh, I thought they only used bows and arrows."

"They used those too. And they also used tomahawks, knives, clubs, spears, and other weapons."

"I guess I've been watching too much television where they show the Indians using bows and arrows instead of muskets."

"Television and the movies aren't always accurate. They don't show the gore that really occurred, like someone actually being scalped."

"They can't get that gross. I think we're done here," O'Mahern said. He wanted to get back to the office to start researching the list of reenactors. "Thanks for the history lesson and your assistance. We'll contact you if we need anything else."

"I was glad to help you, Detectives. Call on me anytime."

They shook hands, and Buchanan showed them to the front door.

The cooler air hit them when they left Buchanan's warm home as the sun was starting to set. Palmer noticed the beginning of a brilliant sunset on the horizon, like some painter brushing strokes of pink on the bottom of the clouds.

On the drive back to the office, O'Mahern fired up another cigarette and started to think about the interview they had with Buchanan. He realized he should have asked him another question. "I forgot to ask him what he was doing last night around dark."

"No, I don't think that was necessary," Julie Palmer decided. "He's not a suspect. He's a resource."

"Everyone is a suspect in my book. What were you doing last night at that time?"

"Very funny. That's none of your business."

"Oh, you were out with your boyfriend?"

"Brilliant deduction, Sherlock." She was dating a lawyer who practiced family law. He had nothing to do with criminals.

"No, seriously, what were you doing?"

"About that time, we were finishing our dessert at that new restaurant out on Creasy Lane. What were you doing?"

"Sitting in my apartment, watching a college football game."

"You and your sports. Do you watch anything else on television other than sports?"

"No."

"Weren't you a former jock?"

"Yeah, I played three sports in high school but just football in college for Purdue."

"That's right. Did you ever go to a bowl game?"

"Yes. The team made one bowl game in the four years I was with them. I played in the Peach Bowl in 1984, and we lost to Virginia."

"What position did you play?"

"I was one of those special team's guys. You know, covering kickoffs and punts. I played some defense as well. I was mainly a backup guy at defensive end. It was fun."

Chapter 12

Indiana Territory, November 7, 1811

T he night became pitch-black as the clouds moved into the area, and a cold drizzling rain fell at intervals on General William Henry Harrison's camp as his men settled in for the night. Campfires gave the men a little warmth, but the Indians from the nearby town gave them little comfort, creating fear for their lives and making sleep hard to come by even after a long day of marching.

"Do you think they're going to attack us tonight, Sergeant?" asked Private Daniel Pettit, who was sitting against a large oak tree to provide himself some protection from the rain and from any bullets coming from the nearby woods. The large oak tree had shed most of its leaves already, so it didn't provide much protection. He put his wool blanket over his legs to keep them warm and drier.

"You never know with these Injuns," replied Sergeant James Martin. Martin had been with the militia for eight years now and was recently promoted to sergeant because of his experience, experience that included a surprise attack in the middle of the night by some Indians a few years before, so he knew they could attack at any time. "Just be ready. Is your rifle loaded?"

"Yes, sir, it is."

"You need to put that bayonet on it as well. Now get some shut-eye. I will wake you when it's your turn for sentry duty."

"I'll try to get some sleep. I just wish it would stop raining." Pettit had never seen any action against the Indians, so he was as nervous as an expectant mother. He was new to the local militia near Vincennes, not a trained military man like some of those in the force. Pettit had family back home: a wife and two children.

Meanwhile in the Indian camp, Shabonee of the Ottawa went to the Shawnee Prophet around midnight and asked him, "Brother, my warriors want to attack the white men now while they are sleeping."

"No, my brother, we should wait until dawn to attack so we can see the white man better," The Prophet replied as he put another log on his fire inside his medicine lodge.

"If we attack now, we will surprise them."

"I have sent the black man with three of my warriors to kill the white chief. If they kill him, there will be no need to attack them. They will probably retreat back to Vincennes. If they do not succeed, I will send the chiefs tomorrow morning to speak with the white chief. The Winnebagos will surprise the white chief. They will kill him with their tomahawks. That will start the battle."

"Yes, brother, that would be good."

Not long after midnight, Ben led the raiding party toward the American camp to Harrison's tent. In the dark, he slipped and fell, breaking some branches and causing enough commotion that he was heard by two American sentries, who quickly took him into custody. The three Indian companions got spooked by the sentries and returned back to Prophet's Town. Ben was taken back into the camp and bound. The Prophet's first plan to kill Harrison had failed.

When the raiding party returned to tell the Shawnee Prophet they had failed, he prayed to the spirits in his medicine lodge. A couple of hours later, he had a change of heart after consulting with the Master of Life and emerged from the medicine lodge, wearing a scarlet turban around his head, huge earrings, a necklace of bear claws, and a large silver gorget—a piece of armor that protected the throat—and dozens of silver and bronze bracelets around his wrists. The Prophet had painted large white circles around his eyes; across his chest was a pair of scarlet sashes and around his neck, a hip-length ermine cape. And his buckskin blouse and leggings were decorated in designs with painted porcupine quills.

"We cannot wait!" the Shawnee Prophet declared to a large group of warriors. "We must attack now while it is dark." He gathered his warriors on the west side of the valley and stood on a rock the shape of a mushroom on the side of a hill to address them further, singing songs and making them promises of victory. "The enemy is sleeping and will be easy targets in their beds!" he said loudly so the hundreds of warriors could hear him. "His powder will turn to sand, and their bullets will be harmless! They cannot hurt you! They will be

71

asleep or drunk! After you are victorious, I will give every warrior a horse load of scalps, a rifle, and many horses."

The Prophet picked out his best warriors. "I want you to crawl through the brush like snakes and kill the sentinels. Then go after Harrison. He will be on a white horse. Kill him and the Americans will be confused."

Then the Shawnee Prophet turned to all his warriors again and said, "When you hear the rattling of deer hoofs, you will yell and attack the white man. Some of them will run, and you will have possession of their camp and their equipage. Then you can shoot them with their own rifles. But above all else, you must kill the great chief. Now go."

The Prophet stayed behind with his wife.

A dream about an Indian attack woke up General Harrison in the middle of the night. He looked at his gold watch and it read 3:45 a.m. He started to get ready as the troops would be rousted at 4:00 a.m. to prepare for the day's activities. He started thinking about how the Indians would respond to his request to return to their tribes and break up Prophet's Town. If they refused, he planned to attack them and send them back running.

A few minutes later, a Kentuckian sentry by the name of Corporal Stephen Moss heard some branches break. He looked in the direction of the noise and saw some Indians advancing on his position at the northwest corner of the camp near the creek. He fired the first shot of the night. A warrior cried out in pain. Other warriors yelled out like wolves. The frightened sentry ran toward the camp as quickly as his legs would carry him, but he was shot in the back and fell to the wet ground before getting back to the American lines. His mind raced as his body slowed, and he died seconds later.

Private Pettit also made a dash back to the camp from his forward sentry position, cocking his rifle as he ran. When he got the musket cocked and ready to fire, he stopped and turned around to fire at an Indian chasing him. He fired, but the Indian was already on top of him. The Indian fired his musket about the same time, but he was almost past Pettit and the flash of the musket set fire to the private's handkerchief that was tied to his head. Pettit ran back to the line, swatting the fire on the back of his head as if it were bees stinging him. He finally got back to the line and put out the fire.

General Harrison was putting on his boots when he heard the first shots, so he hurried the process. "Get my horse, private!" he yelled to one of his aides.

Private Isaac Jones ran to get the general's horse, but the gray stallion broke away from the tether it was tied to and ran off into the nearby woods, so White grabbed a nearby brown bay horse and brought it to the general. The general mounted the horse and joined Colonel Abraham Owen, who was riding a white horse. As they rode to the area where the first attack came, Owen became a target for the Indians, who thought he was Harrison. They fired shots and arrows at the colonel and hit Owen several times, unseating him from the horse and killing him almost instantly. Owen was behind the general, so Harrison didn't know he went down and continued to ride in the direction of the first shots. Harrison also had a close call as a bullet passed through his hat and grazed his head.

The savages yelled horridly as they started attacking the camp from several directions.

"Fire at will!" ordered Captain William Baen. His company of men began firing and reloading their muskets as fast as they could do.

"Return fire!" Captain Fredrick Geiger ordered his men to start firing as well.

The Indians assaulted in a furious fashion, some managing to penetrate the American lines. A couple of savages made their way through the lines and went to a tent to steal what they could.

One of Captain Geiger's men lost his gun and reported that to him, so the captain made his way to his tent to give the man a replacement. When Geiger opened the tent, he found two Indians already in the tent, so he pulled out his sword and thrust it through one of the savages, killing him. The other Indian ran past him out the tent opening, retreating hastily back to his own lines.

Geiger and Baen quickly put their companies together and put out the night fires that were blazing so that they wouldn't be easy marks. Despite the yells from the Indians, the soldiers reacted with coolness and held their ground, firing their muskets or using their bayonets.

The warriors had intended to attack the American camp at the same time, but it didn't turn out that way. Some Indians didn't hear the attack signal, the rattling of strings of dried deer hoofs. Once the shooting started though, they joined in.

When Harrison arrived at the spot where the attack began, he saw that Barton's company had suffered severely and Geiger's company had been broken badly. He ordered Cook's and Captain Wentworth's company under Lieutenant Peters to form a line at an angle to defend the corner. They did so and held the Indians back.

Then an attack came at the northeast angle to the camp against the Indiana militia and army regulars, so General Harrison rode a short distance to that corner. He was approached by Washington Johns, a quartermaster of the dragoons who were behind the lines in reserve. "Major Daviess wants to charge the Indians on foot," Johns said.

"Tell Major Daviess to be patient," the general responded. "He shall have an honorable position before the battle is over."

A couple of minutes later, a private from the dragoons asked the general again about the major attacking. The answer was still no.

Then a minute later, Lieutenant Davis Floyd made the same request.

"Tell Major Daviess he has heard my opinion twice. He may now use his own discretion. There are some Indians behind a log over there," the general said, pointing to the area. "We will open a space in the line when he is ready to charge."

Daviess, a tall man with a vigorous frame, picked twenty soldiers and charged beyond the lines on foot in a single file. The major carried a sword on his right hand and a pistol on his left. Almost at once, he was wounded. He fell to the ground, and his white blanket coat showed a red bloodstain on his right side, where he had been struck by a bullet. After he went down, two of his men carried him back to the safety of the American lines.

General Harrison then promoted Captain Benjamin Park to take his place to command the dragoons.

On the Indian side of the battle, some of the warriors were made so confident by the Shawnee Prophet's promises that night that they became easy targets. One warrior, a Delaware, had trouble with his musket and went over to a fire to repair it; he was shot to death by a regular soldier by the name of Dexter Earll. When Earll rushed over to take his scalp as a trophy, he became a victim as well with an arrow in the back.

After many Indians were killed, Chief Shabonee sent a runner to the Prophet, who was still by the rock where they had first gathered.

"Our brothers are dying from the white man's bullets," said the Ottawa warrior.

"I will speak to the spirits," said the Shawnee Prophet. "Fight on!"

"Yes, brother." The warrior returned to the battlefield to urge on his kind.

The Prophet continued pounding his drum and letting out war cries from his position near the battlefield.

Meanwhile, Captain Josiah Snelling with his company of regulars drove the enemy back from their location on the south side of the formation with a heavy loss.

On the west end of the camp, Captain Spier Spencer's mounted riflemen silenced several of the screaming warriors before taking losses themselves. Spencer was first shot in the head. He told his men to keep fighting. Then he was shot in both thighs and went tumbling down from his horse. He continued to encourage his men to fight until a lead shot went through his body to silence him.

Although Captain Spencer and Lieutenant Warrick went down, their men held their positions and continued to fight. Harrison had Captain David Robb's Indiana militia reinforce their positions.

"Huzzah! My sons of gold, a few more fires and victory will be ours!" General Harrison yelled.

The general rode from point to point in the camp to monitor the lines and reinforce weak areas with his reserve forces. Upon arrival, Harrison's aide-de-camp Thomas Randolph took a bullet to his torso and fell to the ground. The general got down from his horse and bent over to ask him, "Is there anything I can do for you?"

"Watch over my children," Randolph requested. They were the last words he spoke.

As daylight approached and the Indians came into better view, Harrison ordered Major Parke to have his dragoons charge the warriors on the left flank. However, Major Wells misunderstood the orders and led his Kentuckians to execute the order. They performed so gallantly and effectively that they drove the Indians from their positions. Then when the dragoons arrived on horseback, they drove them into the wet prairie and back to their town.

While this was happening, the troops on the right flank rushed their foes and drove them into the marshy ground, while others disappeared into the willows and bushes by the creek and beyond gunshot.

The battle had gone on for about two hours.

As the Indians retreated to their town, the Shawnee Prophet joined them there. The dismayed warriors approached him.

"You did not protect us!" a warrior complained.

"My wife touched the sacred vessel and broke the charm," The Prophet explained.

Not believing him, the warriors left the village in fear of an attack by the Americans. The Prophet went to his medicine lodge and placed a curse on Harrison and the Great White Chief, President James Madison. Then he left his town with a small band of Wyandotts in canoes on a creek that led to the Wabash. Within minutes, Prophet's Town was nearly empty. The Indians headed back to their own villages.

Meantime, Harrison decided not to counterattack. The daylight showed him that his army had suffered many losses. One hundred eighty-eight soldiers, almost one fifth of his force, were either killed or wounded. Thirty-nine lay dead on the battlefield. And some died soon after the battle. Such was the case of Major Daviess, who died by early afternoon.

Chief Surgeon Josiah D. Foster and his assistant, Dr. Hosea Blood, had set up a hospital in the middle of the camp and had more injured men than they could handle. Some died before they ever got any assistance from the physicians. And those who were severely injured didn't stand a chance of recovering anyway.

After breakfast, some soldiers ventured out of the camp to check for wounded savages and take scalps. Private Joseph Miller came across an Indian who was wounded in the leg. The bullet had penetrated the Indian's knee and passed down the leg, breaking it. Miller put his foot against the injured leg of the warrior. The Indian raised up his head and said in his native tongue, "Don't kill me, don't kill me!" But the soldiers didn't understand a word he uttered.

Several other soldiers came up and tried to shoot the Indian, but their muskets misfired as their powder was wet. Then Major Davis Floyd rode up on his black horse. "Let me show you how to kill an Indian," the major said and dismounted.

He was about to shove his sword into the savage's body when a messenger rode up and said, "Don't kill him. The general wants all Indians still alive to be taken as prisoner."

When the major returned to the camp with the injured Indian, General Harrison told him through an interpreter, "Tell your people that if they return to their own camps, we will not harm them."

The Indian told the general that the Indians were planning another attack. He didn't know that his comrades had fled in fear of the counterattack. The general ordered him to be taken to the surgeons to have his leg removed. The Indian refused treatment. He preferred death to dismemberment. Indians wanted to go to their grave with all their limbs intact like a warrior.

Another soldier, Private Henry Huckleberry, never heard the order about taking injured Indians as prisoners. He saw an Indian get up in the prairie and walk toward the woods. The private aimed his musket and fired. The Indian dropped over and died immediately. Some Kentucky volunteers saw what happened and hurried over to the Indian. They found him dead, so one of them pulled out his knife and scalped him. Then he cut the scalp into four quarters so each of his comrades would have a piece of the scalp. The remaining Indians were dead, and the soldiers scalped them as well.

Instead of attacking, Harrison had his healthy soldiers fortify their positions in case the Indians attacked again. His men retrieved downed trees from the surrounding forests and threw up log breastworks to defend the camp from another attack.

Because the cattle in the camp scattered during the attack, no rations were available for the men. Instead, a meal of broiled horseflesh was cooked from the four-legged friends they had lost in the battle.

The lost men were buried in a mass grave. Then dead wood and logs from the forest were put over them and burned to conceal the graves from the Indians.

When night fell on the camp, every man was on their guard, without food or fire in a drizzling, cold rain. "Have the men sleep fully clothed opposite their line of defense and be ready for an attack," General Harrison ordered. Every five minutes, the men had to pass the words *wide awake* from right to left in order to assure none of them would sleep. And Indian dogs provided frequent alarms during the night as they prowled the woods looking for food. Several privates who had been injured during the battle fell to a final sleep during the night. No attack came during the night, so General Harrison ordered his dragoons and other mounted troops to take possession of Prophet's Town the next morning. He also told them to take the Indian chief they had found wounded to the town.

The contingent arrived after a few minutes as the town was only about a mile away from the battlefield. They found only one old squaw in the town, but plenty of food was left behind by the fleeing Indians. They confiscated all the beans, corn, and peas they could carry and then torched the buildings. Some of the cattle that had abandoned their camp were also found, so the army had all the rations they would need for their trek back to Vincennes.

The next day, General Harrison's army packed up twenty-two wagons with the provisions and the injured and left the camp. By night, they had passed the dangerous ground where they could have been attacked again but were not.

A few days later, some of the Indians returned to Prophet's Town and found a charred community, the squaw, and the injured chief. A couple of days after that, the warriors returned to the battlefield to find some of their dead who had been scalped and mutilated. In reprisal, they dug up the soldiers and did the same undignified acts, scattering their remains in the battlefield like throwing out the trash. The turkey vultures and other animals of the forest got a feast.

Chapter 13

Present Day

The sun was quickly diving into the horizon as sunset was arriving when Battle Ground resident George Baen went for an evening walk before retiring for the night, except he didn't know that he wouldn't be returning. He walked every morning, afternoon, and evening to stay healthy in his retirement years, forced on by the termination of his job due to his company moving to Mexico like many other American companies; however, he did get a severance check from the company. Since the company move, he decided not to go back to work but sit back and collect unemployment. He was going to be receiving his first Social Security check soon.

Baen left his 1980s single-level home on Battleview Drive about a half hour before dark and was greeted by his neighbor as he began his trek. "Hi, Sam."

"Going for your evening stroll, George?" Sam said as he continued raking leaves. He had on a Purdue sweatshirt and black pants to go along with the school colors, black and gold.

"Yeah, got to do it. My doctor said it's good for my health, so I'm making it a habit."

"What are you going to do in the winter?"

"I think I'll go to the Tippecanoe Mall and walk there."

"That sounds like a good idea. Have a good walk."

Baen headed south toward Prophets Rock Road. A frost was expected overnight, and the temperature was already down to forty, so the former auto mechanic wore jeans with a long-sleeved jean shirt and matching jean jacket.

The only items in his outfit that weren't denim were his sneakers and his black baseball cap with white lettering—*Sox*, standing for the Chicago White Sox, a team he had loved all his life. He had come to Indiana from South Chicago some twenty years before to work at an automotive plant. The middle-income worker decided to move to a house in Battle Ground because it was cheaper than Lafayette. Being a bachelor, the two-bedroom house gave him plenty of room. Under the hat, the tan he got golfing during the summer was now fading, and his long beard was now all gray from aging. The beard could come in handy if he decided to play Santa Claus during his retirement years.

The six-foot Baen had walked all the way to the battlefield, then turned around, and came back through the town center before returning back home right at dusk, a trek of about two miles. He returned on Prophets Rock Road, making his route look like a triangle with a handle from a hawk's point of view, and there were plenty of them in the area.

As he came close to the historical marker identifying Prophet's Rock to visitors, he heard something stirring up by the historic rock, but it was dark in the shadows of the trees and the cave-like structure. So he walked up to the edge of the woods to see what had made the noise. Then he heard a branch break and saw a shadow among the trees. "Somebody there?" Baen asked.

Then he saw something flying at him. Before he could even get his hands up in defense, the object hit him in the chest. He looked down at what he thought was an ax. He grabbed it and tried pulling it out, but he was too weak to do so. "What did I do," those were his last words. He fell to the ground in agony. His heart stopped beating. He was dead.

Chapter 14

Moraviantown, October 5, 1813

Not long after the sun lifted above the horizon, British commander Major General Henry Proctor, wearing his scarlet coat and gray pants, was notified by his Indian scouts that American forces were quickly approaching his position near the Moravian Indian village of Fairfield, Ontario. The general ordered his still-hungry British regulars to retreat two miles to form a defensive position. He arranged his eight hundred regulars in a loose line of battle so the force would look larger than it really was, much like a bird spreading its wings to make it look more impressive. He also had his only artillery, a six pounder, moved there as well, but the cannon was virtually useless because they had just about run out of ammunition for it.

His left flank was protected by the narrow Thames River with a high and precipitous bank. On his right was a marsh running almost parallel for about two miles. He chose to position some of his troops with Tecumseh's Indian force along the marsh to flank the American forces coming down the road from Detroit. He hoped to trap the Americans on the banks of the Thames by driving them off the road with cannon fire. He had no fortifications or protection except for some scattered beech, sugar maple, and oak trees along the riverbank. His demoralized troops were tired from marching and a diet of half rations. They had been retreating from Detroit for several days now. Tecumseh had wanted to attack the Americans sooner. After seeing the destruction at Prophet's Town, he was determined to fight the Americans and General William Henry Harrison to the death.

Harrison had ordered his force of about thirty-five hundred Americans and Indians to advance on General Proctor's position after receiving a note from Master Commandant Oliver Hazard Perry that read, "We have met the enemy and they are ours." Perry had gained a complete victory in the Battle of Lake Erie three weeks before.

Tecumseh was almost exuberant that the British general was finally making a stand to fight the Americans although they were outnumbered. He had little faith in the British general. A couple of days before the battle, he had told some other British officers, "General Brock very brave man, great general. He say, 'Tecumseh, come,' we go. General Proctor say, 'Tecumseh, you go.' Proctor no Brock."

Tecumseh positioned his warriors in the black ash swamp. He didn't know how many warriors he had until he collected the sticks he had given them. Only then did he know the size of his force, about five hundred warriors. That was half of what Tecumseh had started with when the War of 1812 began.

Before going to the swamp to lead his men, the confident and exuberant Tecumseh rode along the British line and shook hands with each officer. He was dressed in his usual deer skin clothing with a red turban wrapped over his brow and a handsome ostrich feather tucked in. Around his neck, he wore a medal the British had given him. Tecumseh's outfit blended in with his own warriors, except for that shiny medal. He didn't want to dress differently than them. He made some remark in Shawnee to each officer as he shook their hand, so he was not understood. When he got to Proctor, he remarked in Shawnee, "Father! Have a big heart!"

Tecumseh once told General Proctor that he reminded him of a frightened dog who runs away with his tail tucked under his belly. He felt the general had no heart or stomach for fighting and couldn't understand why he was leading men.

When the great warrior arrived at the swamp, he spoke to his men several times. He told them in his native tongue, "Ki la wa wishi ga tui!" In English, "Be brave and strong." Tecumseh placed his weapons—a pair of pistols, a tomahawk, and three war clubs—in the bushy swamp area around his position for quick availability. He carried his loaded musket, a knife, and his war club Thunder by his side. He sprinkled a bit of tobacco on the ground, put his pipe back into its bag, and laid it on the ground. Then he prayed to the Indian god.

Meanwhile, Colonel Richard Mentor Johnson readied his command of a thousand cavalry, mostly from Kentucky and some from the River Raisin

Massacre, a massacre that occurred earlier in the year when some Indians slaughtered wounded Kentuckians. The Kentuckians wanted revenge.

General Harrison addressed the troops in the middle of the afternoon as he was preparing for them to attack. "Remember the River Raisin, but remember it whilst victory is suspended. The revenge of a soldier cannot be gratified on a fallen enemy." Harrison wanted to warn the Kentuckians that they should only fight the enemy and not mutilate the dead.

After their Indian scouts viewed the battlefield for the American forces, Colonel Johnson reported back to General Harrison. "Tecumseh's strength is partially concealed by the thick growth that overshades the field. We should bring them into the open ground," he told the general.

General Harrison ordered, "Form your regiment on the left against the Indians, and I will bring up the infantry and attack the British on the right." Harrison was dressed for the battle in his dark blue uniform, with brass epaulets that matched the gold handle on his sword and other gold features of his uniform, including his buttons.

Johnson then sent his lieutenants to check over the swamp before attacking it blindly. They did so and returned to him with the results of their scouting.

"General, the swamp is impassable," he told the general.

As Harrison contemplated some new strategy, he hand-combed his black hair back off his forehead on his hatless head. "Then pull back your men and act as my reserve," the general remarked.

The dismayed Colonel Johnson put his hands on his hips, puckered his lips, and said, "General Harrison, permit me to charge the enemy. The battle will be won in thirty minutes." The colonel was not taking no for an answer.

"Then you must charge them!" Harrison demanded of the almost-insubordinate officer. "Lead forth your men in files of ten." The general almost wished he was by their side to personally fight Tecumseh and his warriors on horseback, but he had to lead his more than two thousand infantry militiamen into the battle. They consisted of two small regular infantry brigades under the command of Generals Duncan McArthur and Lewis Cass and five brigades of Kentucky militia led by General Isaac Shelby, the sixty-three-year-old governor of Kentucky and hero of the American Revolutionary War. Harrison would move his battalions along the road by the Thames River to attack the British infantry. Harrison rode away on his white horse to inform Shelby about the change in the battle plan.

Before Johnson made his move against the Indians, he sent more Indian scouts to check the marsh again before proceeding. One of the scouts reported back to him of a place to cross through the small swamp to attack the Indians in the larger marsh. The colonel turned to his brother, James, and asked him, "Would you lead the first battalion and charge the British? I will cross the swamp with the second battalion and attack the Indians. Brother, you have a family and I have none." Richard knew he would be facing a tougher foe—Tecumseh.

"I will do as you wish, brother," James replied.

Then Colonel Johnson turned to his men, garbed in their dark blue coats, gray trousers, and black top hats with a feather protruding from it, and ordered with his booming voice, "Kentuckians! Press them with unwearied might!"

Colonel Johnson first tested the British defense by sending a group of twenty volunteer riders to form a forlorn hope, an advance party designed to draw enemy fire. They found that opposition was more than ready for them as fifteen riders were cut down and four others returned injured. However, those five remaining were able to report their findings back to the American force.

The sounding bugles broke the silence of the midafternoon air and summoned the advance. The Johnsons led their battalions like red flames toward the British troops and warriors. As they swept through, they yelled, "Remember the Raisin!"

Tecumseh saw the advancing troops. He turned to his men and said with conviction, "No death we face! Each chose his sheltering oak. Give ground no more. Let every heart be rock."

Riding a white horse, Colonel Johnson shouted at his men, "Battalions! Rush them!"

His men rode into battle armed with a musket, hatchet, and knife. And each man rode with another soldier mounted behind him as there weren't enough horses for them.

Meanwhile, Tecumseh was resolute in his stand. "Warriors! Draw blood till every heart be dry! Stand in strife!" he yelled loud enough in his Shawnee language that most could hear him.

The Indian warriors fired away at the oncoming Kentucky riflemen, and several fell from their horses. Johnson himself was hit several times, but he stayed on his horse.

Tecumseh's shoulder-length black locks waved in the troubled air. Smoke from gunfire clouded the swampy area. As the Kentuckians fired, many Indians around Tecumseh fell to their death, including his brother-in-law, Wahsikegaboe.

About a half hour into the struggle, a lead ball ripped through Tecumseh's shoulder, creating a gory wound. He raised his axe to throw it, but suddenly he was hit by another bullet in his sixth rib. The Shawnee native dropped the axe as if it weighed a ton and fell to the ground. Suddenly, he saw himself as a little boy . . . a young warrior . . . a young war chief . . . a father . . . a war veteran. The Shawnee chief was now on his way through the twelve levels of heaven to the Kohkumthena's Lodge.

Colonel Johnson took five bullets himself, and his horse fell into the branches of a fallen tree. He was able to kill a warrior who came at him with a tomahawk. Then his horse broke free and carried him to safety to treat his wounds. Some said he was responsible for killing Tecumseh, but he could not verify that.

Meanwhile, Johnson's brother was busy blazing through the redcoat lines as if it wasn't even there. The redcoats got off only two volleys from their Brown Bess smoothbore flintlocks before they were overrun by the Kentuckians at full gallop. It took James Johnson only ten minutes to defeat the British and force most of them into surrender, although his brother had predicted thirty minutes to seize the victory. However, General Proctor escaped into the woods and took refuge in the swamp, escaping certain death at the hands of the Kentuckians.

The word of Tecumseh's death spread quickly through the Indian ranks, and their resistance quickly faded. Shabbona ordered a retreat into the woods behind the marsh. Indian squaws were so fearful that the Kentuckians would butcher their infants, they drowned them in the swamp instead.

When General Harrison heard of Tecumseh's demise, he gave a sigh of relief. He wanted his scalp, but nobody had brought it to him. The warrior who had haunted him for nearly two decades was finally dead.

A group of Shawnee warriors, who hadn't heard about Tecumseh's death, noticed he was missing when they sat down to eat supper, so they returned to the battlefield to find his body as dusk was ending the day. It took them awhile to find their brother war chief, but they finally did among twenty other dead warriors. Tecumseh's scalp was still intact, but his chest and thighs had been skinned by the Kentuckians. Undoubtedly, they didn't realize he was the Shawnee chief, but that was because he dressed so much like the other warriors.

The warriors carried him back to their camp on a wooden litter. The next morning, they cleaned and prepared his body for burial. The medicine man performed a ceremony and did a dance. Then he struck the body with a ramrod four times. When Tecumseh didn't respond, they took him far into the woods and buried him in a secret place.

The next day, American forces entered Fairfield Village, stole provisions, and torched it. They even set fire to the Moravian Church.

With the death of Tecumseh, the British's hopes of winning the War of 1812 were severely damaged. The American victory would go down in history as the Battle of the Thames to the Americans. The British called it the Battle of Moraviantown. The Native Americans remembered it as Tecumseh's final battle.

Chapter 15

Present Day

Detective O'Mahern quit talking as he concentrated on parking. The sun was now low in the sky, and sunset was approaching in less than an hour, but their day was not going to end yet as he wanted to do some research on that list of reenactors before calling it a night. He knew the sheriff wanted some results before his meeting with the commissioners the next morning, and that the first forty-eight hours of any murder case was the most important.

On their way into the office, O'Mahern barked out an instruction like some drill sergeant, "Make a copy of that roster you have."

"Will do."

After Palmer made a copy and handed it to him, he told her, "We'll split it up to research these reenactors to see what kind of suspects we can get out of this. You take *A-L*. I'll take *M-Z*. See if anyone has a record. Check driver's records and court records as well. That's it for now."

"Right, boss man," she said sarcastically.

He ignored the comeback.

They scanned records on the reenactors from several different databases. It took them about an hour before they finished researching their lists. Palmer found five good suspects, and O'Mahern found a few. Palmer printed out suspect sheets and put them up on an evidence board.

"Tell me about your guys," O'Mahern said to her when she finished taping them up.

"It turns out one guy had a couple of domestic violence charges that were dismissed against him a few years ago."

"Let me rephrase that question. What about likelys with actual felonies?"

"Yeah, I sure do. Two as a matter of fact. One guy is Jeremiah Smithson. He has a few—assault and battery, petty theft, and a public intox. The other guy is Jason Whybrew. He's a Native American. He has a DUI, and he fired a weapon in Battle Ground illegally."

"Why was it illegal?"

"Well, according to the police report, a neighbor reported him after he shot a hole in his window, so Battle Ground Police charged him with that offense."

O'Mahern nodded. "Okay, he sounds like a good possibility."

"And guess who else is an Indian reenactor?"

"Daniel Day-Lewis," he said, referring to the actor who played as an Indian in *The Last of the Mohicans*. "Hell, I don't have a clue."

"None other than Marshal Redbird. I knew he had Indian heritage, but I didn't know he was a reenactor."

"Then I guess he's a suspect in this case too."

"Right . . . I doubt that. He's a teammate, if anything."

"Why didn't he help us more then?"

"Because we didn't ask for it. Plus, he had that ceremony this morning to celebrate the two hundredth anniversary of the battle."

"Whatever. Let's go through that list. You take the Indian reenactors, and I'll look at the others."

"I was hoping for more serious stuff, not a bunch of minor nonsense, but I guess we'll go with that. I'll print my guys, and you paste them up since you're done and I'm not quite finished."

"Sure."

He printed out three pieces of paper, and she stuck them up on the whiteboard. Then she went off to the restroom while he finished his research. When she returned, he had two more suspects to put up on the board. The board now had a total of ten suspects, whom they wanted to interview.

O'Mahern looked over the suspects that Palmer had uncovered and scratched his growing beard as he did so. "I think we should go pay a visit to this guy first," he said and pointed to a picture on the murder board. The picture was of one of the suspects he developed from his list of reenactors.

"Tonight?"

"Yeah, tonight. It's only about eight. We'll interview him and call it a night after that."

"Whatever you say. I'll have to call my boyfriend and tell him to forget about dinner."

"Yeah, and tomorrow we have to be here by seven-thirty to get a fresh start."

"Right."

On the way out of the office, Palmer pulled out her cell phone and called her boyfriend to give him the news. She was supposed to meet him at the La Scala restaurant in downtown Lafayette at eight-thirty for some Italian cuisine. He was used to cancellations from her as her job made her work some strange hours at times. As an attorney, his hours were more nine to five. She was afraid that canceling dinner would strain their relationship even further, but he said he understood.

On the way to the suspect's home, Palmer asked as she drove, "So who is this guy we're going to see?"

"His name is Justin Lahti. He's forty years old and has been in trouble with the law a few times."

"Like what?"

"Oh, he has a felony conviction for marijuana possession. He had an assault charge a few years ago, and he had a domestic violence charge dismissed. That tells me he's capable of murder."

"That's a stretch if you ask me."

"I didn't ask you, but it's better than nothing."

"I guess so. Does he play a soldier or pioneer?"

"He plays a French soldier at the feast."

She pulled up to his apartment building located on Forest Drive. It was now about 8:30 p.m., and a cold breeze blew out of the west, dropping the temperature to around freezing.

O'Mahern knocked on the door.

A few seconds later, a man answered the door dressed in a T-shirt and sweat pants with no shoes. "Can I help you?" he asked.

Detective O'Mahern introduced himself and Palmer and asked, "Can we come in and talk to you?"

"What's this about?"

"It's about a crime."

"Oh, come on in."

As they entered the apartment, they were greeted by cigarette smoke and the pungent smell it gives off, so Palmer didn't like the place immediately, but it didn't bother O'Mahern, of course. The large forty-six-inch flat-screen high-definition television was showing a National Football League game. The Chicago Bears were playing the Indianapolis Colts, and the score was tied at seven each. The living room was scantily decorated with one large framed picture of Napoleon, the famed French general. Lahti took a seat in a red recliner, which matched the color of the couch. In between the couch and recliner was a round end table with a clock set inside it. On top of it was a large silver lamp with tan shade. It was all the light in the room. The walls were painted white. Lahti grabbed the television controller, turned off the game, then took a sip of a locally brewed beer, which he was drinking out of a tall beer mug. "Have a seat," he said, directing them to a sofa.

"No, thanks. Where were you last night?" O'Mahern started the interview.

"I was at a movie with a buddy of mine. I got home around seven-thirty and watched television after that."

"Name of your buddy?"

"George Wittbold."

"Number I can reach him at?"

"Let me look it up on my cell." Lahti opened his phone and searched for the number. "Here it is."

Palmer went over to him. "Let me give him a call."

"Go right ahead." He handed her the phone.

She turned around and walked away from them while she was calling Wittbold. Her partner continued the questioning.

"Do you know Patrick Daviess?"

"Yeah, he plays one of the settlers at our reenactments."

O'Mahern got up from his recliner and went over to Lahti. He got in his face and said, "So why did you kill him?"

"I did nothing of the sort!" Lahti said. O'Mahern was so close to him that Lahti could smell his bad breath. "I hardly knew the guy."

"Do you own a musket?" O'Mahern released the grip he had on him and backed off.

"Yeah, it's a reproduction musket that we use at reenactments, but I don't fire real bullets. All I have are blanks, which puff a lot of smoke when fired."

"Can I see it?"

"Sure, it's in the bedroom."

Palmer finished the call and turned back to the pair. "Nobody home. I left a message for him to call us."

"Let's go see this musket you have," O'Mahern said.

They all walked to a bedroom down the hallway. Lahti was using the spare bedroom for different purposes—a treadmill sat by the window and pointed at a television, a cheap wooden desk had a computer on it.

"Here it is, and these are the kind of blanks we use."

"Can't be the gun," Palmer said.

"Why's that?" O'Mahern asked.

"It would be traceable because it's a reproduction. We're looking for an authentic musket."

"Oh yeah," O'Mahern said. He then turned to Lahti and said, "Well, I guess we're done here. Thanks for your time."

"Sure enough. I hope you catch the guy. Pat was a good guy."

"We'll try our best."

With that, the two detectives left Lahti's place and drove back to the office. On the way back, O'Mahern said, "I think it's time to call it a night. We can get a fresh start tomorrow morning."

"I agree with that."

"Wanna get a nightcap?"

"Not tonight. I just want to get some sleep."

"Very well. Be at the office at seven-thirty."

"I will."

It was now almost 9:00 p.m. By the time she got home, it would be closer to ten, and she would go to bed if she could sleep since she would have to get up at 6:00 a.m. She thought about calling her lawyer friend but decided against it. She wasn't happy that he was so disappointed about her canceling dinner plans. She felt her job came first though.

Chapter 16

Indiana, August 30, 1838

General John Tipton, along with his mounted militia of a hundred men, arrived at Chief Menominee's log cabin chapel in northcentral Indiana around the hottest time of the day, in the midafternoon. The chief and a dozen of his closest Potawatomi followers were sitting under a shade tree next to the chapel, trying to keep cool on the hot August day while they awaited the general, who had sent out a notice to meet him there that day. Most were clad in nothing but a loincloth. The chief had on a headdress of eagle feathers. They knew not what the white man wanted of them, but they suspected he was up to no good.

"Take them," the general ordered as they dismounted their horses. The men herded the Indians together using their rifles.

"We have done nothing," the chief responded.

"That's why we're taking you prisoner. You were supposed to have gone to Kansas last year."

"I did not sign the white man's treaty," Chief Menominee said as a militia man grabbed his arms and put them behind his back while another started to tie him with rope.

"You should have. Now we have to take you there as a prisoner along with your men and any other Potawatomi in this state. Governor's orders! Put them in the cabin and guard them," the general ordered the men.

After the Indians were shoved and pushed into the log cabin, the general ordered his militia to gather with him under the shade tree, a large oak that provided plenty of cover. The general took off his hat, unbuttoned his blue coat, and took a white handkerchief from his blue trousers to wipe the sweat from his forehead.

"You four men," he said, pointing to a small group of men in the rear of the gathering, "you guard those Indians. I'm going to send the rest of you to scour the area for more Indians. The governor wants them all rounded up. Come back here by nightfall, and we will camp here for dinner. We will do the same for the next couple of days until we have rounded them all up. After you take them into custody, burn their homes and destroy their crops. We want to discourage them from returning from Kansas once we let them go there. Any questions?"

"What if they resist?" said one of the militiamen.

"Tie them up and bring them back forcefully. I don't want you to hurt any of them though. Let's get to it then."

The general picked out groups of about twenty men to head in all directions from the Twin Lakes village of Chief Memominee. Then he closed Father Benjamin Marie Petit's chapel as he was away on business. The French priest had been trying to bring religion to the Indians and had baptized many of the Potawatomi. The Indians called him Chichipe-Outipe, little duck in Potawataomi, as he was a short man in stature who often wore a black strawhat to go along with his black stole.

Within four days, the militia had gathered up more than eight hundred Indians in all. Father Petit returned as well, and the Indians begged their Father Black Robe to accompany them. He did.

On September 4, the march of the captive Indians to Kansas began from Twin Lakes. Leading the forced march was a mounted soldier carrying the United States flag: twenty-six white stars graced the field of dark blue. The dragoon holding the flag was dressed in a dark blue uniform that nearly matched the blue used in the flag. Behind him was a long line of Indians and soldiers. First were staff baggage carts in single file, followed by a horse-drawn jail wagon carrying Chief Menominee and two other chiefs, Black Wolf and Pepinawa. The other Indians followed in single file on their horses—about three hundred of them—with the sick and old riding in forty baggage wagons behind them. Flanking the long line were armed dragoons and volunteer militia to hasten the stragglers and discourage anyone from trying to escape, having orders to shoot if necessary. They also harassed the Indians with severe gestures and bitter words if they slowed up.

The wagon train headed south and passed through Chippewa-Nung Village on the Tippecanoe River the first day. The next day, it reached Rochester. The day after that, they traveled to Logansport and the Wabash River, where the wagon train stopped to rest, resupply, and care for the sick. Many of the Indians were sick, and four children died during the four days they camped there as the weather was hot and unforgiving to the sick. Father Petit and Bishop Brute of Vincennes conducted a mass for the Indians who had died on Sunday. Then they were buried. At Logansport, more Potawatomi joined the march, including a warrior chief by the name of Cardinal. They tossed him in the jail wagon with the other chiefs.

"Where did they find you?" asked Chief Menominee.

"I was in a small village on the Tippecanoe near Monticello," replied Chief Cardinal.

"How many were with you?"

"About fifty of us there. Where are they taking us?"

"Kansas Territory. It is many days away from here."

"They may take me there, but I will return someday to this place."

"Then they will punish you if you do."

"Let them punish me then. I will not go where the white man wants me to go. I will go where I want to go."

"I agree with you, but this is now the white man's land."

The march continued on the seventh day and followed the Wabash River on its northern bank. They passed by what used to be Prophet's Town. Chief Menominee remembered the days he spent there as a young warrior. Now it was just a field of long grass and a few decaying log cabins.

On September 21, they arrived in Perrysville, Indiana, and were joined again by Father Petit, who had received permission from his superiors to travel with the group the rest of the way. He came upon some newly born Indians and baptized them. He also buried several dead ones. They had died from the heat and travel.

When the caravan arrived in Danville, Illinois, it rested and was resupplied. General Tipton and his fifteen dragoon soldiers handed over the task of marching them the rest of the way to Judge William Polke, an Indian agent in Illinois.

The wagon train continued across Illinois past Decatur, Springfield, Jacksonville, and Naples. On October 10, the train crossed the mighty Mississippi into Missouri. In Missouri, the train passed by Quincy, Palmyra, Clinton, Paris, Huntsville, and finally Keatsville, where it rested for a week. On November 1, the train started up again and arrived four days later in Osawatomie, Kansas, its destination.

On arrival, the Indians were counted, and fewer than seven hundred were still around. Forty-two had died along the route, mostly women, children, and the elderly. One little child died when he fell off a wagon and was run over by the back wheel. Some others either escaped or were left behind along the way due to illness or age. Father Petit stayed with the Indians a few more weeks, but he became sick with a fever and died soon after that in Saint Louis. Chief Cardinal stayed in Kansas until the following spring, then returned to live out his life in Indiana near the town of Battle Ground.

Chapter 17

Present Day

The Tippecanoe County detectives arrived at their office the next morning around 7:30 a.m. Julie Palmer was first to get to the office, wearing a dark red sweater over a pair of black slacks. Jackson O'Mahern dressed more casually in a long-sleeved blue shirt and a pair of blue jeans. He had stopped at his favorite coffee shop before arriving for his usual morning wake-up call—a Venti vanilla latte and a donut. This time he had chosen an apple fritter, and it melted in his mouth as they studied the board again.

"Who do you like for the murder?" O'Mahern asked after he devoured the fritter.

"Oh, I like the tall, handsome one over there," she quipped.

"I said for murder, not for a date."

"This guy that plays a pioneer has the longest list of priors. His worst offenses were against his ex-wife."

"That's not much, but if he's got the worst record of the bunch, we should start with him. Let's start there."

"Sounds good."

Just as the detectives were headed out the door, Sheriff Joshua Andrews yelled from his office door, "O'Mahern! Palmer! Stop! Come here!"

Both detectives halted dead in their tracks and turned around with almost military precision. They hurriedly went to him at the door of his office.

"We have another murder in Battle Ground, and the MO looks to be about the same as yesterday," he told them.

"What happened?" O'Mahern asked.

"Well, it seems the victim was killed over by Prophet's Rock."

"That's close to the battlefield," Palmer added. "I'll drive."

"I know you will," O'Mahern said. "And grab that stack of suspect folders we have so I can look them over more carefully on the way there."

"I'm putting another pair of detectives on this case since it looks like we may have a serial killer at large. You'll still be the lead on this case. I'll send them to help at the crime scene as soon as I figure out who to send."

"Right, Sheriff. We have our hands already full with the first murder."

"I know. Not a word about this to the media. I don't want people thinking we have a serial killer out there just yet. I don't want them panicking."

"Sure enough, Chief. Handling the press is your job. I don't even like talking to the media."

On the way out, Palmer said, "I need to run that lead shot over to the coroner's office."

"No, you don't. He'll be at the crime scene. Just give it to him there."

"Oh yeah. You're right."

"I know. I'm always right."

She rolled her eyes at that comment. As she drove to Battle Ground on that bright chilly day, O'Mahern examined the files of the suspects again. He didn't find any hardened criminals that he liked for the murder. "Not much here," he commented.

"That's for sure," she agreed. "We may be looking in the wrong place."

"Perhaps, but it's all we have for now."

"Maybe it's a ghost."

"Do you also believe in Santa Claus?" he said sarcastically.

"Yeah, as a matter of fact. Seriously, there are a couple of ghost stories about the rock that I heard about when I was growing up there. In one story, these teenagers were sitting on top of the rock one day, and they swear they saw an Indian ghost from up there."

"And what were they smoking?"

"I don't know, but it scared them enough to go home immediately and not pass go."

"So it was the Monopoly ghost."

"Very funny. The other involved a group of girls who were walking up the path from the rock to the top of the hill. As they were walking, one girl saw an Indian running in the woods. When the Indian turned and started running at her, she screamed, and the Indian changed directions and ran back down the path. The group was so shook up that they left."

"What's the history of this rock?" O'Mahern said seriously.

"It is where the Shawnee Prophet rallied his followers before attacking the soldiers, who were encamped for the night on the other side of a stream not far from the rock. The Prophet stood on top of this large mushroom-shaped rock and drove them into a frenzy before the attack."

"That reminds me of Hitler or Mussolini."

"Sort of, but they were in World War II."

When the two arrived, the county road had been blocked off to traffic, making it easy for them to park. The crime scene looked much like the first murder, with brown-toned sheriff vehicles, a state police car, an ambulance, crime scene unit, and the coroner's car blocking the street. A film crew from the local television station was there again but behind the tape that blocked their access to the crime scene. The crisp air greeted the detectives as they exited their vehicle.

A reporter from the local television station called out to them, "Detective, can we talk to you?"

"No comment," O'Mahern said and ducked under the yellow police tape.

Not far from the road was the body next to the plaque giving the history of the rock, the plaque reading,

WHERE THE PROPHET SAT AND SANG TO ENCOURAGE
THE INDIANS IN BATTLE OF NOV 7, 1811, ERECTED 1929
BY GENERAL DELAFAYETTE CHAPTER D.A.R.

Crime scene technicians were looking around Prophet's Rock. The coroner was standing over the body, which was covered by a white sheet, as the detectives approached. The film crew from Real TV was catching the action again.

The detectives walked up to where the body was located, O'Mahern keeping his hands in his pockets to keep them warm on that chilly fall morning.

"You're not going to believe this one," Dr. John Jurgenson said and reached down to uncover the body for the detectives to see. Part of the man's skull had been removed.

"Scalped," said Palmer.

"Wow," O'Mahern said.

"Right, Detective. He was scalped. It was done postmortem," said the coroner, who was attired mostly in black as he wore a black leather trench coat with black polyester trousers and black boots, boots that protected him whenever he went out to the field. He learned a long time ago that field conditions weren't always ideal, like today's frost on the ground.

"So the chest wound killed him?" Palmer asked.

"I'm pretty sure the large gash in his chest is responsible for his death. It probably came from some sharp object, like an axe."

"Or could it be a tomahawk?" Palmer said. She asked that because she thought of what the psychic had told them the day before.

"I'll know more when I get him back to the lab. I'll tell Dr. Acorn to do impressions for a better idea. Okay?"

"Yeah, yeah. I was just wondering because someone told us that somebody would die after being attacked by an Indian with a tomahawk."

The coroner had a puzzled look on his face. "You mean like a psychic?"

O'Mahern jumped in. "That's right, Doc. A psychic gave us a lead on a murder yesterday. Do you have a time of death?"

"I think about dusk last night, according to rigor mortis."

"That has a familiar tone to it. Just like the last one."

"You're right," Palmer added.

"Do you know who he is?" O'Mahern asked.

"Yeah, the local marshal was here earlier and identified him as George Baen, who lives a couple of blocks from here.

"Do you know his address?"

Jurgenson shrugged. "What do I look like, the Yellow Pages?"

"Sorry, I'll check his wallet once you're done."

"I'm done, have at him?"

"Here's that lead shot from the first murder." She handed him a plastic evidence bag with the shot inside it.

"I'll get to the state police as soon as I get back."

While the film crew from Real TV focused on O'Mahern, he checked the pockets of the victim's jeans and found a brown leather wallet, a small black cell phone, and house keys and then handed them to Palmer. He didn't find anything in his denim shirt pockets or the pockets of his denim jacket. He checked the driver's license for the address of the victim.

Then the detectives stepped back out of the way as the body was about to be picked up and carried away. O'Mahern handed the phone to Palmer while he looked through the wallet's contents.

Palmer flipped opened the phone and started looking at it. A picture of a wind turbine, like the ones being built in the county, appeared on the screen. She first went to his text messages and looked at the most recent ones. None of the messages gave her any leads as most were cryptic or advertising from a telemarketing firm for medical insurance for seniors.

"This is going to take some research," Palmer said.

"Yeah."

"So let's see. Mr. Baen went for an evening walk, and as he got here, he heard a noise in the woods and went closer to investigate. When he got close enough, the murderer jumped out of the woods and killed him."

"Maybe. I think Baen got a call from someone who told him to meet him here at this spot to exchange something. Baen showed up, but he didn't want to do what the man asked of him, so he was killed."

"Perhaps. Or a Cubs fan came by and saw he had on a Sox hat, so he killed him."

"Oh, so you're a Cubs fan."

"Die-hard fan. 'Maybe next year' seems to be their motto."

"Detective O'Mahern, can I ask you a couple of questions?" asked Real TV's Jeff Shortridge.

"Sure, go ahead, make my day," O'Mahern said, adding a little saying from the Dirty Harry movie *Sudden Impact*.

"Since this is the second murder in two days, do you think it's the work of a serial killer?"

"Wow, that's a little difficult to answer at this point. I can only say it's a possibility, but I sure hope not."

"Do you know how the second person was killed?"

"We don't know exactly what the murder weapon is at this point, but the coroner thinks it may have been an axe. He'll know more once he completes the autopsy."

"Do you have any suspects for the first murder yet?"

"We have plenty of suspects, but we don't have a murderer."

"Do—"

O'Mahern cut him off when two more detectives arrived on the scene. "That's enough questions for now."

One of the detectives was Russ Whitmore, wearing a long black trench coat with dark blue pants underneath, making him look a little thinner than the three hundred pounds he actually weighed. On the other hand, his partner, Bo Stinson, was much taller in height and slimmer in weight; so the two looked like Mutt and Jeff standing next to each other.

O'Mahern was glad to see them. "I was hoping the sheriff would assign you two birds to this case."

"Why's that?" Whitmore questioned.

"Because Bo knows."

"Very funny, Flash," Bo Stinson said. "That joke went out with the new century."

"So what do you want us to do?" Whitmore asked.

"We got this latest vic by the name of George Baen. I want you guys to go over to his house and check it out for any leads. Here's his wallet."

"Okay," Stinson said.

"Then proceed to investigate it, and we'll get our heads together later."

"At the end of the shift?" Whitmore added.

"Yeah. The sheriff thinks we have a serial killer loose here in Battle Ground, but I'll have you guys concentrate on this second murder and we'll see if they really do connect later."

"Sounds good to me," Whitmore agreed.

"Here's the stuff we found on his body," said Palmer, handing the items to Whitmore.

"We'll check it out."

O'Mahern thought it was better to have them do the legwork on the second murder, and he could concentrate on the first. Plus, they had only just begun interviewing suspects. He wanted to focus on that rather than getting wrapped up in investigating two murders at the same time, which he felt was like opening a can of snakes.

As Whitmore and Stinson walked away, Palmer asked O'Mahern, "So why did he call you Flash?"

"Oh, I picked that up when I was a deputy sheriff. Nobody who ever ran from me got away because I was so fast. Comes from my football days."

"That's better than the other meaning of the term."

"Oh yeah, when you add *er.*" He chuckled. "I did that in college too."

O'Mahern's cell phone rang. He didn't recognize the number calling him, so he opened it and answered, "Detective O'Mahern."

Stinson and Whitmore got into a new black Dodge Challenger, a sheriff's department car they used instead of their own cars. Stinson looked up the address from the victim's driver's license and typed it into the laptop computer of the car to direct them to the house because neither knew the roads well in Battle Ground. In seconds, they had the address and proceeded to the house. They arrived at George Baen's house in less than a minute, a single-story ranch-style home built in the 1950s, small in comparison with some of the homes in the same neighborhood.

Stinson took the lead and knocked on the front door. "Police," he shouted out. No response. He turned the doorknob and found the door was unlocked, so they proceeded inside with their Glocks drawn. They found nobody in the home, except for a black cat that scurried under a king-sized bed when it got one look at the football-sized Whitmore.

"A black cat just crossed my path, so I guess we're not going to have much luck with this one either," declared Whitmore. He said that to his partner because the last murder they investigated together ended up not being solved, a case involving a farmer who was shot to death in his field while plowing. They had decided in the end that the shooting could have been accidental, but the sheriff wasn't happy with an unsolved murder. They both hoped that they could make up their shortcomings by solving this one.

After putting on latex gloves, the two detectives started to comb through Baen's belongings to find out more about him. While Whitmore looked in the living room, Stinson went through the bedroom turned into an office, containing a large walnut desk, a desktop computer sitting on top along with some paperwork, and a large bookcase displaying hardback books and some golf, bowling, dart, and baseball trophies. On the wall was a degree certificate from Purdue University declaring that Baen had a bachelor's degree in engineering. The detective looked through the papers on the desk and many referred to Social Security, retirement, and an engineering company, so Stinson came to the conclusion that Baen was a retired engineer. He looked at his checkbook, but nothing jumped out at him as suspicious.

In the living room, Whitmore found a personal phone directory, so he grabbed it up in order to notify the next of kin of his death later when they got back to the office. He also found a shadow box with old photos and a fob watch, so he pulled out the gold watch to take a closer look.

Stinson grabbed the hard drive of the computer and joined Whitmore in the living room when he was done. "Find anything interesting?"

"No, not really," Whitmore replied. "This watch was made in 1895."

"That makes it an antique."

Whitmore nodded.

"I think the guy's a retired engineer from a local company in Lafayette, according to the paperwork I found on his desk."

"That doesn't help us much, but it's a good place to start, I guess."

"Yeah, we can call the company to find out more about him. Maybe he pissed off someone and they are getting payback."

"That's extreme payback."

"It's better than going into your workplace and killing a bunch of people like that guy did the other day in Pennsylvania."

"I saw that on the news last night too. Shame."

"Let's go back to the office to do more research."

"I'm right behind you. There's nothing here that looks promising."

Chapter 18

A cold, wet day in early March greeted the residents who gathered in the nation's capital to see William Henry Harrison take the office of president of the United States, the ninth to do so. He would become the Great White Chief in Chief Tecumseh's words.

Harrison was now sixty-eight years old, and his dark hair had turned gray, his large nose had grown even larger, and his haggard face had a lot more wrinkles. The Whig candidate, who came out of retirement to run again—he ran in 1836 and lost—used the famed Battle of Tippecanoe for his campaign slogan: "Tippecanoe and Tyler, too." John Tyler was his running mate. The Whig Party also used another chant: "Old Tip he wore a homespun coat, he had no ruffled shirt: wirt-wirt, but Jackson he has the golden plate, and he's a little squirt: wirt-wirt!" The Democrats countered by calling Harrison "Granny Harrison, the petticoat general," because he resigned from the army before the end of the War of 1812. However, the Whigs boasted of Harrison's military record. In the end, Harrison won the presidential election over the diminutive Democratic candidate Martin Van Buren by a landslide in the electoral college, although the popular vote was much closer. He became the oldest president to take the office.

Despite the nasty March weather, Harrison decided not to shorten the long inaugural address he had planned, so he spoke for an hour and forty minutes. He was dressed in a black suit for the occasion without a hat, gloves, or overcoat in the brisk March wind. His graying hair was combed forward into a point on his forehead as he had always done. During the longest presidential address ever, one of the things he said was, "The freedom of the press is the greatest bulwark of civil and religious liberty. Our citizens must be content with the exercise of the powers with which the Constitution clothes them." He also made some promises during the speech, one promise being the return of the Bank of the United States and another promise was to use patronage to create a qualified staff, not enhance his own standing in government. By the time he was done speaking, some people had already left and some wondered if he was ever going to finish. After the speech, he rode in an open carriage to the White House so that he could wave at the people who had gathered.

Harrison had an open-door policy to people wanting to work for the government, so they flocked to the White House like pigeons to speak to the president about a job. They would wait for hours to see him. Then on March 16, a group arrived at the Executive Mansion demanding that the president remove all the Democrats applying for any appointed office.

"Mr. President, you shouldn't be interviewing any Democrats for office," a gentleman in a gray suit with a top hat demanded.

"So help me God, I will resign my office before I can be guilty of such an iniquity," Harrison responded.

Ten days later, Harrison got drenched in a downpour while out strolling. He came down with a cold as a result. After the cold got worse, Dr. Thomas Miller was called to treat the president. He diagnosed his condition as bilious pleurisy, a lung disorder. Dr. Miller and other doctors began treating the president with opium, castor oil, leeches, and even Virginia snakeweed. He seemed to be getting better before he turned for the worse and came down with pneumonia.

As he was near death, he said his last words to his doctor: "I wish you to understand the true principles of the government. I wish them carried out. I ask nothing more." Those words were directed at Tyler. He died at 12:30 a.m. on April 4. He had served as president for only thirty-one days, twelve hours, and thirty minutes. For some, it was hard to believe he was dead. He was a man who had survived several battles with the Indians and other hardships only to succumb to a disease soon after he was at the pinnacle of his career.

His body was laid in state at the Capitol while an Episcopal funeral service was held in the East Room. Then twenty-six pallbearers and a procession of some ten thousand people followed the funeral wagon to his temporary grave in Washington. His remains would be moved to North Bend, Ohio, later for permanent burial.

The Prophet had put a curse against Harrison and the presidents of the United States after his defeat at Prophet's Town. The curse against the Great White Chiefs was put on presidents elected in a year ending in zero, and they would die in office. Little did the Shawnee Prophet know that Harrison would be the first to die from the curse because he died in 1836. After Harrison died, the Indians called the curse Tecumseh's Curse or the Curse of the Tippecanoe. The next election ending in a zero would not be held until 1860.

Chapter 19

Present Day

In the Tippecanoe County Courthouse at about 10:15 a.m., the secretary called Sheriff Joshua Andrews to the podium to address the three commissioners at their monthly meeting. The sheriff tucked in his brown uniform shirt as he got up from his seat and wandered over to the podium.

"Where are you on this string of murders in Battle Ground?" asked Commissioner Jeff Sandusky as he rolled up the long sleeves of his white shirt. The room, a large room with about a hundred chairs for spectators and a long table up front where the three commissioners and secretary sat, had become a little warmer now that it was nearly full of citizens, many of whom were concerned over the two murders and other matters facing the commissioners that day, matters like the wind turbines making too much noise for some people and matters like the county schools making teacher cuts.

"Nowhere so far, but I have four detectives working diligently on the cases. They are being supported by several other deputies as well."

Sandusky scratched his gray-haired head and asked, "Are we dealing with a serial killer?" That question brought some chatter among the audience.

"Quiet, please," the secretary asked of the crowd.

"We don't know that for sure at this point, but it is under our consideration since the crimes are similar and held in the same town."

"I think you should call in the state police and the FBI to help."

"I think my men can handle it for now. I can bring those agencies in if we don't solve it soon. I'd like to give them a little more time. I'd like to give them forty-eight hours at least," he said, almost begging for more time.

"Well, it's been twenty-four hours already, so you have until tomorrow morning. Then I want you to bring in the other agencies,"

"As you wish, commissioner." The sheriff didn't have to do what the commissioner requested as he was an elected official by the people, but he didn't want to anger the commissioners since they approved his budget and allocated money to his agency. They could make his life miserable, and he knew it.

"Detective, this is Sandra Barksley. I've seen another murder."

"The other vision you told us about yesterday came true last night," O'Mahern replied into his cell phone. "A man was killed, and the murder weapon could have been a tomahawk, like you envisioned. So what have you seen for the next murder?"

"I saw a man getting hit by an arrow in the river and falling dead into his boat."

"Can you tell me when?"

"Well, it is during daylight as far as I can tell."

"Do you know where?"

"No idea."

"Can you identify the man or who shot the arrow?"

"No, I only saw the man hit by the arrow, and it's too far away to see his face very well."

"Thanks, Sandy. Call me anytime you have another vision."

"Will do, Detective."

Detective O'Mahern turned to his partner. "That was the psychic. She's seen another vision. A man gets killed by an arrow in a river, but that's all she saw. I don't know how that's going to help us."

"It doesn't sound like it will."

"Since we're in Battle Ground, why don't we go over to Ivan Smulski's house near here?"

"Sure, I have the addresses in the car."

After they got into the car, Palmer looked up the address. "It's over on North Street. I know where that is."

"I'm glad you do. I'd have to look it up on my TomTom if I were driving."

As she drove the short distance to the street, O'Mahern asked, "Do you know this guy?"

"No. I think he's lived here just a short while. Came from Chicago, I believe," she informed him.

"Wanted to get away from the big city, I suppose."

"Undoubtedly, we have a few like that around here."

They arrived at the house, a three-story home that was over a century old, painted all white with sky-blue trim. In the front yard was a small pond with a bird bath and feeder next to it. A couple of robins were getting a drink. They were staying for the winter and hung around the house as they were always being fed by the owner.

Palmer knocked on the front door instead of ringing the doorbell.

A few seconds later, an older woman with her hair in rollers and wearing a dark pink robe answered the door. "Can I help you?" she said.

"I'm Detective O'Mahern, and this is Detective Palmer from the Tippecanoe County Sheriff's Office. Are you Mrs. Smulski?"

"Yes."

"Is your husband home?"

"He's laid up in his bed with the flu. I can take you to him if you like," she offered.

They nodded, entered the house and followed his wife up the stairs to the second floor, the staircase wall containing many family photos that the detectives glanced at while they climbed up the stairs. O'Mahern got a whiff of cat smell in the place as they walked into the bedroom and saw that Ivan Smulski was sitting up in the king-sized bed adorned with a dark magenta quilt, his wrinkled face pale with tired brown eyes and a red-tinged nose from blowing it so much. He was wearing brown pajamas and reading the *Journal Courier* newspaper while watching a television newscast coming from a thirty-two-inch flat-screen television located on a dark-walnut dresser nearby. He reached over and hit the power button on the remote control to turn off the television. The master bedroom was painted a light green with a pinecone border at the top of the walls. The sun was shining in the windows on one side of the room, but the lighting was helped out with an overhead chandelier containing four lights.

"Honey, these two detectives wanted to speak to you. Can I get you something to drink?" his wife said, turning to the detectives.

"No, we aren't going to be that long," said O'Mahern. He then turned to Ivan and began his questions. "How long have you been laid up in bed?"

"Since Friday. I came down with the flu, and it threw me for a loop for a couple of days, but I'm better now." He looked like he hadn't shaved since then as his wrinkled face was sporting a short gray beard, his balding head showing he was up in age.

"Did you know Patrick Daviess?" O'Mahern asked.

"Yeah, I knew Pat. Terrible thing him getting killed like that right here in Battle Ground. How'd he die?"

"I can't tell you that. The case is still under investigation. Did you know a George Baen?"

"No."

"Well, he's dead too. Someone killed him last night."

"Oh my god," said Mrs. Smulski.

"I hope I'm not next," Ivan added.

"As long as you stay inside, you probably won't have to worry about that. Do you know anyone who had something against Daviess?"

"I do remember there was an Indian at the feast who seemed to take his role a bit too serious and had an argument with Pat after a staged attack," Ivan recalled.

"Do you know his name?" Palmer asked.

"No, I sure don't. I'm fairly new to the group and know only a few of the reenactors, like the settlers I play along with."

"Do you think you could identify him from pictures?"

"I don't know unless they were in their outfits and had on war paint like they do at the feast. My memory's not so good anymore."

"We'll try and get some photos of them and bring them by later for you to look at," O'Mahern said.

"That would be fine. Maybe by then, I'll be up and around."

"It will probably be a day or two, I imagine," Palmer interjected.

"Yeah," O'Mahern agreed. "Thanks for your time and get better."

"You're welcome, Detectives. Any way I can help."

"You've already been a big help, but if you can ID him, that would be great," O'Mahern said.

Before they left, Palmer got the Smulskis' phone number to call later.

When they got to the car, O'Mahern said, "I think we can concentrate more on the Indian reenactors first based on what he said."

"For sure."

"I'll look at them and decide where we should go next. Is there a place we can get a cup of coffee in this town?"

"No, not really. We'll have to drive up to the interstate exit."

"Okay."

She drove the short distance to Interstate 65 and pulled into a McDonald's. He ordered his favorite, a French vanilla latte, and she ordered straight coffee with cream. They sat in a booth and started looking through the files.

After a couple of minutes, O'Mahern said, "We'll start with this one, a Jason Whybrew. He's located near here and he's got a record, although not a long one. Of course none of them do."

"Then we could talk to the ghost hunter's group," said Palmer.

"No, I think that's a waste of our good time."

"Okay. It's up to you, boss."

106

Palmer drove into the country to get to Whybrew's house. They passed by a hog farm, and the smell was similar to a backed-up septic system, but worse. She made a turn and thought she was lost.

"Why are you stopping?" O'Mahern asked.

"Because I'm lost. Please hand me the county map from my glove box."

O'Mahern looked in the glove box and found it. "That's why you should go buy a navigational system, like I have."

"I'm waiting for Santa to buy me one."

"That's not far away."

Chapter 20

Washington DC, April 14, 1865

*B*am! A single gunshot and some screams in the middle of a humorous scene during the third act of *Our American Cousin* confused the audience at Ford's Theatre this night around 10:15 p.m. They didn't know whether it was part of the play or something else was wrong.

Suddenly, actor John Wilkes Booth appeared at the opening to the presidential box. The curly black-haired Booth, with a moustache that curved down around his mouth, held a Philadelphia derringer in one hand and a bloody dagger in the other, held high over his head. He yelled, "Sic semper tyrannus," the Latin Virginia State motto meaning "Thus always to tyrants."

As he leaped the fifteen feet down to the stage, the spur on his right riding boot caught the fold of the Stars-and-Stripes bunting, and he fell awkwardly onto the stage, fracturing his left fibula just above the ankle; however, he painfully got right back up on his feet.

"They have shot the president!" cried Mary Todd Lincoln from the presidential box. "They have shot the president!"

"Stop that man," Clara Harris yelled from the box, pointing at Booth.

Pandemonium broke out, and people started running from the theater as if it was on fire. Several men from the crowd came running down the aisle after Booth though.

While running across the stage to the back door as best as he could, Booth yelled, "The South is avenged." He went out the back door and mounted an awaiting horse. One man was right behind him and tried to stop him, but Booth hit him with the handle of his knife. Then the dark-suited actor rode off in a black horse and quickly disappeared into the dark, foggy night.

Charles Leale, a young army surgeon on liberty, was near the presidential box and arrived there first, finding President Abraham Lincoln slumped over in his chair and his wife with her arms around her husband, sobbing. On the floor was Major Henry R. Rathbone, bleeding profusely from a knife wound in his upper left arm. Leale ignored the wounded soldier and treated the president instead. Lincoln was still alive, but he was hardly breathing. Leale cut away the bloodstained collar of his white shirt to examine the wound. The doctor felt around the back of his left ear, finding a bullet hole and a blood clot, so he removed the clot and Lincoln's breathing improved.

Then Dr. Charles Sabin Taft and Dr. Albert Kin, both of whom had been watching the play, arrived at the booth to help out. The three doctors consulted on what to do next with the president.

"We shouldn't take him to the White House as the ride would probably kill him," King commented.

"I agree," Dr. Taft said.

"I don't think it matters," Leale said, lending his opinion. "His wound is mortal."

"I think we should take him to a bed to be more comfortable," said Dr. Kin.

"Yeah, I agree," Leale agreed. "We could take him over to the Star Saloon. They have some rooms there."

Several Union soldiers carried the sixteenth president of the United States from the theater. As they got out into the street, a man holding a lantern across the street yelled to them, "Bring him here!" They did as Henry Safford asked and carried the president to Petersen's boardinghouse across the street from. The soldiers carried the president into a first-floor bedroom and laid him diagonally on a bed as the tall president was longer than the bed. Blood was splattered all over the president's black coat and white shirt. His craggy, bearded thin face looked almost as white as his shirt.

Meanwhile across town, a tall, broad-shouldered young man named Lewis Powell knocked on the door of Secretary of State William H. Seward's home in Lafayette Park, not far from the White House. The baby-faced Powell had been given the duty of killing the secretary at the same time Booth was killing the president. Accompanying Powell was David Herold, who stayed outside by the horses.

"May I help you?" one of Seward's black servants, William Bell, asked Powell, who was dressed in a dark overcoat and beaver hat. Bell was much smaller and dressed in black pants, a white shirt, and black bow tie.

"Yes, I have some medicine for Mr. William Seward from Dr. Verdi," he said. Powell knew that Seward had a carriage accident on April 5 and was suffering from a broken jaw and broken right arm.

"Okay. You can give it to me. I will pass it to Mr. Seward, who has retired for the evening."

"No, I need to give it personally to him and explain how to take the medicine."

"No one is to see him," insisted the servant.

"The doctor wanted me to personally give it to him and make sure he takes it as prescribed."

Tired of arguing with the towering man, the servant said, "Very well, sir. Mr. Seward is on the third floor."

Powell climbed the staircase and came to the third floor, where he was greeted by Frederick Seward, the son of William and the assistant secretary of state. "I have some medicine here for Mr. William Seward."

"I'll take it to him," insisted Frederick.

"I'm sorry, but I have doctor's orders to take it to Mr. Seward himself so that I can instruct him on how to take it."

Frederick became suspicious of the intruder and told him, "I'm sorry, my father, William, is asleep and is not to be disturbed under any circumstance."

Powell reluctantly handed the medicine to Frederick. Then he turned and started back down the stairs.

Just then, the door to William's bedroom opened and Seward's daughter, Fanny, said, "Fred, father is awake now."

Powell saw where the room was located and ran back up the stairs. He drew his gun, a large and heavy 1858 Whitney revolver used by the navy during the Civil War. He also carried a silver-handled bowie knife hidden under his black wool coat. When Powell got to the top of the stairs, he pointed the revolver at Frederick's forehead and pulled the trigger, but the gun misfired. Powell then smashed the gun over Frederick's head, exposing his brain from the crushing blow. Frederick collapsed unconscious in a pool of blood.

Fanny heard the commotion, looked out the door, and screamed in horror. Powell hit her with the broken gun, and she fell to the floor. Powell then came upon Sergeant George Robinson, who had been assigned as Seward's nurse. The tall Powell swiped him across the forehead with the gun, and Robinson fell to the floor.

Herold heard the screaming, got on his horse, and rode off, leaving his accomplice to fend for himself.

Powell saw the secretary in his bed in the dimly lit room and went after him with his large knife. He slashed William's right cheek so long that the cheek flipped down to his neck. William rolled to his side. Powell tried then to cut his neck, but it was protected by a metal neck brace.

Seward's son, Augusta, heard the commotion and came running into the room. He and Robinson managed to pull Powell off the bed, but Powell slashed Robinson across the shoulder and Gus in the forehead and right hand. When he saw Robinson going for a pistol, he ran from the room. As Powell got to the front door, a State Department messenger had arrived with a telegram for Seward. He stabbed the defenseless messenger in the back and yelled, "I'm mad! I'm mad." Then he ran to his horse, untied it, and rode away into the night, confident he had accomplished his part in the plot.

"Oh my god, father's dead!" cried Fanny.

The bleeding Robinson lifted the secretary back into bed. "Staunch the blood with cloth and water," Robinson ordered her.

William spat out the blood from his mouth and said, "I'm not dead. Send for a doctor. Send for the police. Close the house." Blood was splattered all over the bed, and the room looked like it had rained red.

At the same time this was happening, George Atzerodt was supposed to kill Vice President Andrew Johnson at the Kirkwood Hotel in another part of Washington. He had rented room 126, directly above the suite where Johnson was staying. Before the appointed time, he went downstairs to the bar. The German immigrant looked the part of an assassin, a sinister-looking face featuring a dark mustache and beard, long black hair hanging down below his ears. The short thickset man was armed with a large bowie knife although he had a pistol back in his room.

"I hear the vice president is staying here," Atzerodt said to the bartender after ordering a whiskey.

"Yeah, he was down here earlier for dinner and a drink."

"How's he doin'?"

"Oh, he's doing just fine. He retired about a half hour ago."

"Give me another," Atzerodt said after swigging down the previous order in one big gulp.

Atzerodt left the hotel just before the time he was supposed to kill the vice president. He decided he wasn't going to kill him as instructed by Booth. He threw his knife away in the bushes. When he arrived at the Pennsylvania House Hotel around 2:00 a.m., he checked into a room there and went off to sleep.

Booth and Herold made their way across the Navy Yard Bridge and into Maryland. They met up in Surattsville, where they had weapons and supplies stored. They then went to a local doctor to treat Booth's leg. Dr. Samuel A. Mudd determined that Booth had a broken leg and splinted it for him. Booth and Herold stayed at the doctor's house for a day. Then they went on the run.

Back across the street from Ford's Theatre, the doctors cared for Lincoln throughout the night, but there was nothing they could really do to save the man who had led the nation through its bloodiest war. Lincoln succumbed at 7:22 a.m. the next morning. The crowd of men around his bed knelt and said a prayer. "Now he belongs to the angels," said Secretary of War Edwin M. Stanton.

Wanted posters went up all around Washington and the surrounding states. A $100,000 reward was put on Booth's head, while $25,000 was offered for Harold and the others.

Eleven days after the president died, Union soldiers tracked down Booth and Harold to Richard Garrett's farm at 2:00 a.m. on a Wednesday morning. They were held up in a tobacco barn.

"Come out of the barn," an officer from the Sixteenth New York Cavalry requested.

Harold came out of the barn and surrendered, but Booth refused to come out. Armed with three pistols and a carbine, Booth asked the soldiers, "Why don't you come get me?"

The standoff lasted a couple of hours. Finally, a federal detective had waited long enough and said, "This is your final warning. Come out now, or we're striking the barn."

Booth stayed put, so the soldiers set fire to the barn.

Boston Corbett, an enterprising soldier, crept up to the barn and saw Booth through a gap in the barn. The soldier shot Booth in the back. Booth fell to the ground, not able to move.

The soldiers rushed in and dragged him out to the steps of the barn. Another soldier dribbled water onto his mouth.

"Tell my mother I died for my country," Booth said, unable to move. "What's wrong with my arms?"

A soldier lifted his arms as Booth could not. "Useless," Booth said. He lay there, a quadriplegic, for a couple of hours before he finally bled out and died.

Herold, Powell, Atzerodt, Mudd, and four others were convicted by a military tribunal. Herold, Powell, and Atzerodt were hanged to death. Mudd was given a life sentence.

First elected to the office of the presidency in 1860, Lincoln was destined to die while in office according to Tecumseh's Curse. He became the second victim of the dreaded curse from the Shawnee Prophet. Lincoln also became one of the most famous presidents as he issued his Emancipation Proclamation and promoted the passage of the Thirteenth Amendment to abolish slavery; he successfully led the country through Civil War as well. He was fifty-six years old.

Chapter 21

Present Day

"I did it," said the man into the black wall phone at the receptionist's window, a bulletproof window made to protect the attendant from anyone at the Tippecanoe Sheriff's Office, a window that was put in as a security measure after the attack on the nation on September 11, 2001.

"Did what, sir?" replied Rusta Coulter. She had no idea what the man was talking about. To her, he looked like he had just walked out of the homeless shelter, his tattered jeans showing years of wear, his holey sweatshirt bearing dirt streaks, his pockmarked face dirty and unshaven.

"Kill that guy in Battle Ground the other day."

That startled her. "One moment, sir." The redheaded middle-aged receptionist hung up the phone, swiveled around on her chair with the greatest ease as she had done thousands of times before, picked up another phone, and punched the sheriff's direct line. "Sheriff, I have a man out here who says he killed that guy in Battle Ground."

"I'll be right there," Sheriff Joshua Andrews said.

Rusta swiveled back around to the window, picked up the phone, and said, "The sheriff will be with you shortly. Just have a seat in the lobby." She swiveled back around to her desk to continue playing her game of solitaire on her computer, although her thoughts were about the man and what he said he had done.

O'Mahern's cell phone rang as they were just about to arrive at the next suspect's house. "O'Mahern," he answered.

"Jackson, this is Sheriff Andrews. I want you to come back to the office and question this guy who just confessed to the first murder," the sheriff requested, but it was more of an order than a request.

"We're about to question another suspect."

"Don't bother with him until you talk to this guy!"

"We're on our way, Chief."

"Thanks. We'll put him on ice until you get here. See me when you're done questioning him."

"Okay." O'Mahern turned to Palmer and said, "Turn around, we have to go back to the office."

"Why's that?"

"Seems that somebody confessed, and the sheriff wants us to talk to him right away. We'll have to come back here later."

Palmer slowed down to make a U-turn on the gravel country road. She didn't quite make the full turn and had to stop and back up to make it successfully. Then she was on her way.

The detectives arrived back at the station about a half hour later. The suspect was sitting patiently in an interview room.

"Who's this guy?" O'Mahern asked Sheriff Andrews, who was sitting in his office, searching for information on his computer.

"His name is Robert Nesius. He goes by Bobby. Here's a rap sheet on him."

"Thank you, sir."

"Sure."

O'Mahern started looking over the information on Nesius, who had been previously arrested for petty theft, drunk and disorderly, disturbing the peace, and trespassing. Nothing serious. He was a Vietnam veteran, spent four years in the army, single, and lived in an apartment near downtown Lafayette. He had no registered firearms.

"I want you to record the interview from the computer room next to the interview room while I take his confession," O'Mahern told Palmer. "Do you know how to run the equipment?"

"Yeah, I've done it before."

Palmer looked over the man on the computer screen as she got ready to tape the interview.

Detective O'Mahern entered the plain room, which had a table and two chairs. The walls were empty and painted white. The floor was covered with a dark gray carpet. Up in the corner away from the door was the camera recording the interviews in the room.

"Good morning, Bobby," O'Mahern said. "I understand you have something to tell us."

"Yeah, can I have a cup of coffee?" Nesius asked.

"As soon as you tell us why you're here."

"Like I told the other officer, I killed that guy in Battle Ground."

"Let me first read your rights,"

"They already did that."

"Yeah, but I want to make sure you understand them." O'Mahern also wanted to get it on camera so there was no doubt about obtaining the confession properly. He liked to move his interview in steps, and reading Miranda rights was always his first step so that anything obtained wouldn't get thrown out of case for not reading someone their rights.

"Okay."

O'Mahern read him his rights, then asked, "Why did you kill him?"

"He owed me some money, so I killed him."

"That's not a great way to collect what you're owed."

"He wasn't going to pay me so that's why I killed him. So where's my coffee?"

"Just hold on. How did you kill him?" O'Mahern asked.

"I shot him to death."

The media had broadcasted that fact to everyone, but the type of gun used was not released to the media by the sheriff's department.

"What gun did you use?"

"I used a .38 that I have."

"You should have brought in the gun."

"I don't like to carry it around. It's back at my apartment."

"Okay, we'll get you a cup of coffee now. What do you like in your coffee?"

"Cream and sugar. Thanks."

O'Mahern left the room and peeked in on Julie in the next room.

"He's not our guy, obviously. Give him a cup of coffee and then let him go," O'Mahern said.

"Yeah, wrong weapon. Why did he confess?"

"Who knows? We sometimes get a crackpot after a murder occurs. He probably just wanted some free food. In any case, he's not our man. I need to take a break. Release him after you get him a cup of coffee and throw in a donut." Someone usually brought in a dozen donuts every morning. They all took their turn doing that.

"Okay."

Palmer got the man a cup of coffee and took it to him. "Here's your coffee. You can drink it here or on your way home. You're free to go."

"But I killed that guy!" he insisted.

"No, you didn't. The gun you described doesn't match the weapon used. Why did you confess to something you didn't do?"

"I don't know. It just seemed the right thing to do."

"We don't like putting innocent people in jail for something they didn't do. Now get outta here."

"Okay. Do you have a couple of dollars you could spare?"

"Not on me. If you need some assistance, talk to the sergeant at the front desk. He can tell you where to go for help."

"Oh, thanks so much. I'm fresh out of money and food."

Palmer thought that Neisus may be suffering from posttraumatic stress syndrome, a common affliction suffered by soldiers after seeing action. She went back to her desk and called Jim Buchanan to get photos of the reenactors so she could show them to Smulski to see if he could identify the Indian he spoke about. Buchanan told her that he'd be glad to e-mail her the photos since they were in digital form. Palmer liked that idea. She could then have Smulski come into the office and look at the photos on the computer.

Meanwhile, O'Mahern went to speak to the sheriff liked he had asked.

"Yeah, boss. You wanted to see me."

"Was that guy the murderer?"

"No, he's one of those constant confessors or something like that."

"That's what I thought, but I wanted you to talk to him right away since we are suddenly pressed for time."

"Why's that?"

"The commissioners want this case solved yesterday. You have until tomorrow morning before I call in the cavalry."

"I'd like to say I'll have it solved by then, but the case is going nowhere right now."

"I'd give you more men if I had them, but I don't. Expect the state police and FBI in the morning. I'll set up a meeting, but you'll be in charge of the investigation."

"Okay, I'll do the best I can."

"I know you will. Get on with it," the sheriff said, giving him signal to go with the back of his hand as he looked down at his desk at his next problem.

Chapter 22

Washington DC, July 2, 1881

On a sunny, hot July morning, President James A. Garfield finished packing his bags and headed to the Sixth Street Station of the Baltimore and Potomac Railroad to catch a train for Williams College, his alma mater, in Williamstown, Massachusetts. He was going there to give a speech, then take a much-needed vacation. Accompanying him on the trip was Secretary of State James G. Blaine, Secretary of War Robert Todd Lincoln (the son of Abraham Lincoln), and two of his sons, James and Harry.

Meanwhile at the three-story train station marked with a tall clock tower at one end, Charles J. Guiteau waited patiently for the president. He had been stalking the nation's leader now for weeks, looking for a good time to kill him. The lawyer figured the train station was a good place since he knew the president was going to leave by train that morning. He was dressed like a lawyer of that period with a dark suit, vest, and black bow tie over a white shirt. His dark brown beard was neatly trimmed; and his hair, which came to a point at the front, was cut short. While waiting for the president, he had his black shoes shined and then nervously paced the lobby. At one point, he went outside and told a cab driver who had a horse and wagon waiting, "I will need your service later to take me to jail."

"Right," the driver said and walked away from him. The cab driver with the chestnut brown horse and black buggy thought he was drunk as he smelled liquor on his breath.

As the full-bearded president walked through the crowded terminal waiting room with his entourage, Guiteau came up from behind him; pulled out his revolver, a .44 Webley British Bulldog revolver with an ivory handle, from under his black coat; and shot the president. The first bullet grazed the president's arm. The second went through his black coat near the spine. Garfield moaned and fell to the ground. Several men in the station grabbed hold of Guiteau and took the gun away from him. Garfield lay on the station floor in agony from the bullet, but he was still alive.

When the police arrived to arrest Guiteau, he said, "I am a Stalwart of the Stalwarts! I did it and I want to be arrested! Arthur is president now!"

The Stalwarts were a faction of the Republican Party that was in favor of Ulysses S. Grant running for a third term. The Stalwarts strongly opposed Garfield's Half-Breeds, who were moderates.

Chester A. Arthur, the vice president, would take office if President Garfield died; however, Guiteau's shots didn't kill the president initially. Garfield was severely injured though.

Doctors tried to find the bullet that entered his spine but could not. Instead, one of them managed to puncture his liver when he tried to find the bullet. Inventor Alexander Graham Bell was called upon to find the bullet. He built a metal detector to find the bullet, but his machine read only the metal bed springs in the bed beneath him.

Garfield became increasingly worse as the summer progressed. He was in extreme pain much of the time and suffered from fevers in the White House. Doctors gave him smelling salts.

On September 6, the president was moved to Jersey Shore and stayed in the Elberon section of Long Branch, New Jersey, not far from New York City. The two-story house he stayed in was located not far from the Atlantic Ocean. Doctors hoped that the fresh air would do him some good. It did not. His condition just got worse.

On the evening of September 19, the first lady, Lucretia Rudolph Garfield, turned to his chief doctor, Dr. Willard Bliss, and asked, "Will he ever recover from this?"

"I think not, my lady," he said frankly. "Mrs. Garfield, the president is dying."

She leaned over her husband's body and kissed him on the forehead. "Why am I made to suffer this cruel wrong?" Then she left the bedroom.

At 10:35 p.m., the president's body jolted, and Dr. Bliss could not find a pulse. "It's over," he said to Mrs. Garfield and the other doctors in the room. They filed out, leaving her alone with her husband. She cried.

A few months later, the deranged Guiteau was tried for killing the president. His attorneys tried in vain to use an insanity defense. At one point in the trial, Guiteau told the judge, "The doctors killed Garfield, I just shot him."

Also, during the ten-week trial, Guiteau once informed the jury, "God told me to kill Garfield. It was the Deity's act, not mine."

The jury found him guilty of killing the president on January 25, 1882. "You are all low, consummate jackasses!" he told the jury.

On June 30, 1882, he was given his last meal and taken to the gallows.

"What are your last words?" the hangman said.

Dressed in a black-and-white striped prisoner's uniform, Guiteau read off a poem he had memorized: "I am going to the Lordy, so glad . . . I saved my party and my land; glory, hallelujah. But they have murdered me for it, and that is the reason I am going to the Lordy . . ."

The hangman put the black hood over his head and sprang the trap as Guiteau said, "Glory, glory, glory . . ."

The Republican had been elected president in 1880. He died two-hundred days after taking office on March 4, 1881. Tecumseh's Curse had struck for the third time in a row.

Chapter 23

Present Day

While Palmer was taking care of the confessor, who was a waste of time, O'Mahern received a call from the detectives investigating the second murder. He told them that they would go to the coroner's office to see what they had to offer on the latest murder. He then asked them to concentrate on trying to find any connections to the first murder and develop a suspect list.

Then O'Mahern told Palmer, "I'm going to call a profiler who lives in Carmel and see what he can tell us about serial killers. We'll go into the conference room so we can talk to him on speaker phone."

"Sounds like a good idea."

O'Mahern made the call to Clay Downing in the plain conference room that contained only a long oval black table with a dozen straight-back chairs, which was more reminiscent of a dining room than a conference room. The room was painted off-white, had no windows, and had a few pictures of county officials on the walls.

"Downing," he answered.

"Hi. This is Detective Sergeant Jackson O'Mahern of the Tippecanoe Sheriff's Department. I wanted to speak to you about a serial killer we might have here in Battle Ground. Do you have a couple of minutes?"

"Oh sure. How many victims, and how were they killed?"

"Let me put you on speakerphone so my partner, Julie Palmer, can hear you."

"Sure."

He put the phone on speaker and hung up the receiver.

"There were two victims so far. One of the victims was shot with a long-barrel musket," O'Mahern continued. "The other was killed with a tomahawk or axe."

"You want to look for a single white male who's probably above average in intelligence," he explained with a voice that was a little scratchy. "He may have had trouble holding down a job. He's probably come from an unstable family. His father may have left, and he was stuck with a domineering mother. They often come from abused families as well. Do you have any suspects like that?"

"Our main suspects on the first murder are reenactors," O'Mahern said. "Do you think we are on the right track?"

"A reenactor might just be acting out for real what he does when he is in character, so that's a possibility. Then again, it could be a psychopath on the loose in the town you're talking about. By the way, he probably lives in that town. Do you have any other evidence?"

"No."

"How about witnesses?"

"None."

"How about forensic evidence?"

"Not much at all there, either."

"Timewise, how far apart were the murders?"

"Two days in a row."

"Typically, serial killers don't kill that often. They sometimes take years between murders. Are you certain it is the same killer?"

"The time of death, location, and similarity of the antiquated weapons leads us to believe that it's a serial killer."

"Your situation may be a little different. Your killer may have just reached a boiling point or is hinging the murders on some event and decided to kill these men now. It's highly possible that he may strike again soon then."

"Just what we don't need. Anything else?"

"Not that I can think of right now. Call me back if he strikes again, if you wish. I'm retired and have plenty of time. I just do consulting work now. If you want, I can come up there and give you a hand, but it will cost."

"I don't handle the budget. I just know we are in somewhat of a budget crunch right now. I'll let you know."

"Sure, see you later."

"Bye."

Chapter 24

Buffalo, New York, September 5, 1901

The bright sun was beginning to fall to the horizon, and the temperature was finally turning cooler by the time the presidential special train reached the outskirts of Buffalo, New York. President William McKinley was overjoyed to see thousands of people waving their hats and handkerchiefs and cheering his arrival as the train went by the train stations on his way to the Pan-American Exposition. Factory and locomotive whistles sounded, church bells rang, and automobile drivers beeped their horns.

Suddenly, a thunderous boom shook the train and broke the glass in the front coach of the train. When the smoke cleared, the crowd could see that all the windows on one side of the coach were blown away. A cannon used to greet the president had been placed too close to the tracks. The explosion shook up McKinley and his party, but they were quickly assured by the train staff that it was all an accident and nobody was hurt. His wife, Ida Saxton McKinley, became outwardly upset with the accident, her face turning red and contrasting sharply with her white blouse. Perhaps the accident was an omen of what was to come.

The presidential train pulled into the exposition station at 6:25 p.m., slowing down easily and stopping smoothly in sharp contrast to the jar from the cannon. The president stepped off the train and was greeted by thousands that had gathered near the station, but the platform was only occupied by a double row of blue-coated soldiers, who stood at attention as he passed by them. He tipped his large black top hat to the crowd and received an even louder cheer. "Thank you, thank you," he said.

The next morning, under a bright sun with moderate temperatures, the president and first lady crossed the Triumphal Causeway and entered the fairgrounds in an open carriage preceded by troops, military bands, and a mounted honor guard. They proceeded to a covered stage on the Esplande, the stage elaborately decorated with bunting and American flags, with seating for about a hundred dignitaries. The black-tuxedoed president took off his top hat to address the sea of several thousand people wearing white strawhats, black bolos, and a variety of colorful bonnets. The president began his speech around 10:00 a.m. under the warm September sun. Near the end of his short speech, he said, "Let us ever remember that our interest is in concord, not conflict, and that our real eminence rests in the victories of peace, not those of war." His comments about peace stemmed from his experience with war. McKinley, a captain during the Civil War, was the president during the Spanish-American War, a short conflict that was easily won by America in 1898. His success in the war helped lead him to his reelection over Democrat William Jennings Bryan in the 1900 presidential election.

After his speech, the president and the first lady toured the grounds. They were amazed at what people called the Rainbow City because of its use of colors like the rainbow. Upon entering the exposition grounds, the president was treated to a sight of splendid domes, attractive minarets, towers, and pavilions in a variety of pleasing hues of red, blue, green, and gold. Regal statues—some five hundred in all—also adorned the grounds. The architecture of the Pan-American Exposition was appropriately a free treatment of Spanish Renaissance style to complement the Latin American countries at the fair. The smell of freshly brewed coffee lured them to stopping in for a cup with the Latin American commissioners at the Porto Rican Building.

The following day, the presidential party took a train to Niagara Falls to view the marvelous falls. Upon their return that afternoon, President McKinley, dressed neatly in a black suit with a silver-colored vest and matching tie over a white shirt, went to the Temple of Music around 3:30 p.m. to meet and greet visitors of the fair. He proceeded to a reception hall that was adorned with several large American flags in his honor. Accompanying him was a security force containing several members of the Secret Service, a couple of Buffalo police detectives, and a squad of eleven army servicemen, who kept an eye on a long line of people who had been waiting to shake hands with the president. The fifty-eight-year-old McKinley, a heavyset short man at five foot seven inches, combed his thinning gray hair to the right to try and cover the baldness on the top of his head. He was a handsome fellow with an oval face, a crease in his chin, and bushy eyebrows.

The president had been shaking hands for about ten minutes when a dark-haired man of average height wearing a dark brown suit with a dark brown vest and open-collared white shirt approached him with what looked like a handkerchief-bandaged hand to the security personnel. As the president reached out to shake hands with the man, the man slapped his hand to the side and shot the president twice in the abdomen with a small gun hidden under the handkerchief. The first bullet hit him in the ribs and bounced off. The second one entered the president's stomach.

"I done my duty!" the man shouted.

A couple of people behind him grabbed hold of the man before Agent James Parker punched him in the face, then tackled him to the ground. Agent George Foster jumped on the man as well and shouted to fellow agent Albert Gallagher, "Al, get the gun! Get the gun!"

Gallagher grabbed the burning handkerchief, but the gun wasn't there. One of the army privates spotted it and picked up the gun, a .32-caliber Iver Johnson Safety Automatic revolver that the man had purchased for $4.50 a couple of days before.

Parker punched the man again.

"Don't let them hurt him," said President McKinley, who remained standing despite being shot. He showed more concern for the man than for himself.

Buffalo Police took the dark-haired man into custody and hauled him off to jail. They found out he was Leon Czolgosz, the son of a Polish immigrant. The unemployed factory worker told police, "I killed President McKinley because I done my duty. I didn't believe one man should have so much service and another man should have none." However, the president was not yet dead; he was still unconscious from the ether that the doctors had given him.

Someone called for an ambulance, and it arrived soon after the shooting to take the president to the hospital on the exposition grounds. One of the doctors suggested that they use a new x-ray machine invented by Thomas Edison on display at the exposition to find the bullet inside the president, but the other doctors were afraid the machine would do more harm than good, and the idea died. The doctors then decided to do an exploratory surgery on the president to find the bullet and remove it before the president bled out; however, the hospital had no electric lighting although the exposition had thousands of lights elsewhere on the grounds. So nurses held up silver pans to reflect light onto the president as doctors opened him up. They couldn't use candles because the president was given ether to put him asleep before operating on him, and that gas was very flammable. They opened the president up and began looking for the bullets. One bullet had deflected off his ribs and gave him a superficial wound, while the other buried itself into the president's large interior, traveling through his stomach, hitting one of his kidneys and damaging his pancreas; but the doctors were unable to find it. They closed him up; he was taken to Exposition Director John Milburn's home to recuperate.

Eight days after the shooting, the president showed some signs of recovery as he sat up in his bed and ate toast with his coffee for breakfast. By that afternoon, his condition rapidly got worse. His last words to his wife, Ida, and those in attendance were, "It is God's way, His will be done, not ours." He succumbed at 2:15 a.m. the next morning. Doctors told his wife that her husband died from gangrene around the wound and other complications. Theodore Roosevelt took over the office of presidency.

Swift justice came to the president's murderer. Czologosz was tried and found guilty a month later; he was sentenced to death. Before his execution, his last words were, "I killed the president because he was the enemy of the good people—the good working people. I am not sorry for my crime. I am sorry I could not see my father."

Then he was strapped into the electric chair on October 29—a month and a half after the president died—at the Auburn Prison in New York and executed.

The twenty-fifth president, who had first taken office in 1897 and was reelected in 1900, became the fourth consecutive victim of Tecumseh's curse.

Chapter 25

Present Day

After O'Mahern disconnected the call with the profiler, Palmer said, "Maybe it's possible the murderer waited until the anniversary of the battle to make his move. He struck the night before the anniversary, which is when the Indians gathered before the attack. So perhaps we're on the right track and should be looking for an Indian reenactor. Or it could be a ghost."

"I'll buy your Indian theory but not a ghost. We'll concentrate on the Indian reenactors first before we look at the others. Who's the first on the list for Indian suspects?"

She glanced down at the list. "Jason Whybrew."

"The answer would be beer." O'Mahern liked beer himself and preferred it when he was out celebrating. On the other hand, Palmer liked the more fancy drinks, like a margarita.

"Very funny. We have a serial killer running around town, and all you can think about is making puns."

"I don't take this job so seriously that I can't make jokes."

"Even if they're bad ones."

"Whatever. Let's go pay Mr. Whybrew a visit. Where does he live?"

"Remember, we were on our way to his house when we got called to the guy who confessed."

"Yeah, and you got lost."

"As if you never get lost."

"No, I don't, now that I have TomTom on my side. So where does he live?"

"He lives right in rural West Lafayette, but he's probably at work. Let me call and check first," she offered.

"Fine, do that. I'm going to get another cup of coffee."

Palmer called his home, an apartment near downtown. There was no answer, only an answering machine. She called his workplace, and the receptionist said he was there working.

"Did you find him?" O'Mahern asked as he returned to his desk.

"Yeah, he's at work."

"Okay, you drive so I can finish my coffee."

"I figured so."

On their way to Whybrew's workplace on the west side of Lafayette, O'Mahern asked, "So why are we going to see Mr. Whybrew first?"

"He's got a record, but not much. Of course, none of the reenactors have much of a record. They are all pretty much upstanding citizens."

"That's what makes this case a difficult one. We haven't got any good suspects for the murders."

"Is it ever easy?"

"I once had a murder that was a piece of cake. I captured the guy fleeing the murder scene. We had him dead to rights, so he confessed. Easiest case I ever had."

"And your hardest case?"

"I've had a few that have never been solved and probably won't be. There was this retired schoolteacher who was murdered in her home. Never did find anyone for that one, even though we put out a reward of $10,000."

"I think I recall that one. I had just come on the force."

On the way there, Palmer noticed that all the fields were barren now that harvest was almost over, fields that carried mostly corn and soybeans in this part of the country. Farmers would be turning their attention toward Christmas. Both detectives got a whiff of a dead skunk as they neared their destination. "Phew," Palmer commented. She swung her car into the parking lot of the Columbia Manufacturing Company and pulled into a slot marked Visitors. The large warehouse building was an older one made of red bricks down by the Wabash River. They headed to the two-story building in the middle of the warehouse, where they had spotted an Office sign. They went inside and were greeted by a lovely young redheaded receptionist, the same one Palmer had talked to on the phone.

"We need to speak to Jason Whybrew," O'Mahern said, flashing his shiny gold badge by pulling his black leather jacket to the side.

A large man by the doorway saw the detectives show their badges and ran toward the back of the warehouse. It was Whybrew.

"That's him," the receptionist said.

Detective O'Mahern took off after him as if he was some kind of running back for the Indianapolis Colts. Palmer was not far behind.

"Stop! Police!" O'Mahern ordered.

Whybrew ran past an assembly line of people who were putting together chairs that came down a conveyor belt. O'Mahern closed in on the Native American as he was much faster than the heavyset man, who was dressed in a plaid shirt and jeans. When Whybrew slowed to turn in between rows of stock, O'Mahern dove after him and tackled him, the two sliding into a stack of dining chairs, which tumbled down around them. The two rolled over, and Whybrew ended up on top of O'Mahern. The Indian grabbed a chair and was about to hit him with it when Palmer put her gun to the back of his head.

"Drop the chair or I'll drop you!" she demanded.

Whybrew did what she asked and dropped the chair over to the side. O'Mahern pulled out his revolver and pointed it at Whybrew; he wanted to pop him one but knew that wouldn't be procedure.

"Now get up slowly and put your hands behind your back," Palmer said.

Whybrew did as she ordered, and she cuffed him.

"You're under arrest," O'Mahern said and put his gun back in his shoulder holster under his jacket. "Now read him his rights."

Palmer read him his rights from memory as they made their way out of the factory. The workers stopped what they were doing and gaped at the cops who had taken one of their own. Palmer stuffed him in the backseat of the car and drove back to police headquarters. Whybrew shook his head to get his long black hair out of his dark brown smooth face, the hair he wore long like his Potawatomi ancestors. His family had returned from Kansas to live in Indiana when he was just a child.

On the way back, Whybrew asked, "What are you arresting me for?"

"Resisting arrest for one thing. The other would be murder."

"I didn't murder anyone."

"Then why did you run?"

"Oh, I thought you were after me for something else."

"What would that be?"

"I'm not saying. In fact, I'm not saying anything more until I get an attorney."

That silenced the detectives from asking him any questions.

"You earned your nickname of Flash back there."

"He wasn't exactly fast."

"Perhaps, but you're quick."

"Drive on, Rook."

When they arrived back at headquarters, they put Whybrew into an interview room and allowed him to call his attorney.

"Get a search warrant for his house," O'Mahern told Palmer out in the hallway. "Let's see if the murder weapon or other incriminating evidence is there."

She nodded. "Will do."

By the time Whybrew's attorney showed up, Palmer had the search warrant in hand.

"Ask the sheriff if he can send some officers to search the house while we question him," O'Mahern said.

"Why don't I go with a deputy and you question the man?" she suggested.

"You're right. You know what we're looking for. You go. Call me and let me know what you find so I can either charge this guy or let him go."

"Thanks. I'll be calling you soon."

Palmer rode with a uniformed deputy sheriff in a sheriff's car to Whybrew's apartment, which was only a couple of miles away.

While she went to search, O'Mahern started an interview with Whybrew, whose attorney, Gordon Cooper, sat next to him. O'Mahern knew Cooper from a previous case. He wasn't impressed; however, O'Mahern didn't have much use for lawyers who represented criminals.

"Where were you on Saturday night about dusk?" O'Mahern asked.

"Watching college football at Clancy's Bar. I was there with about a hundred other people."

"Okay. Where were you Sunday night about dusk?"

"Clancy's again. I was watching the Colts whip the Bears. What a game that was."

"Did you know Patrick Daviess or George Baen?"

"No."

"You're a reenactor, I understand."

He nodded. "Yeah."

"Did you kill any settlers at the Feast of the Hunters' Moon during a reenactment?"

"Don't answer that," Cooper said.

"Why not?"

"He doesn't have to answer any of your questions, and I don't want him to incriminate himself. Ask me the questions."

"It was only a fake killing that I'm asking about."

"Doesn't matter. I don't want him answering it."

"Okay. Do you want anything to drink?" O'Mahern was stalling. He had run out of questions and wanted to hear from Palmer before he proceeded.

"I'd like some coffee," said the attorney.

"I'd like a Coke," Whybrew said.

"We have water or coffee."

"Water then."

"I'll be back in a few minutes."

On the way to fill the beverage order like some waiter, O'Mahern called Palmer. "Find anything yet?"

"No. I don't see any weapons here that match the murder weapons we're looking for. And I didn't find anything else that would link Whybrew to the victims or any other crime for that matter."

"Okay. Go over to Clancy's Bar and see if they remember Whybrew being there on Saturday and Sunday night around dusk, when the murders occurred. That's his alibi."

"I'm on my way."

O'Mahern returned to the interview room with their drinks. "Here you go. I'm going to charge your client with resisting arrest since he ran from us."

"Running from you is no ground for charging my client with resisting arrest," Cooper said.

"Okay, I'll charge him with resisting law enforcement."

"Perhaps."

"I'll be back in a few." O'Mahern got up and left the room. He went to the bathroom. He really wanted a smoke after that little confrontation. He didn't like smart-ass lawyers.

A couple of minutes later, Palmer called him with the news. "The bartender verified Whybrew's alibi. He was here during those murders."

"Then I'm going to cut him loose. He's not our guy."

"Are you going to charge him with resisting law enforcement?"

"I don't want to bother with that. You should have let the jerk hit me with that chair. Then we could charge him with something a lot more serious."

"I wouldn't do that. You know I have your back."

"I was just kidding. Come back home. I'm letting Whybrew go. I guess we're back to square one." O'Mahern had a frown on his face after he hung up. This case was getting to him. His frustration level was going up. He decided he'd let the suspect go, then go out and have a smoke.

Chapter 26

San Francisco, September 1923

President Warren Gamaliel Harding left the White House in Washington DC in June 1923 to take a cross-country trip and meet ordinary people to explain his policies during his Voyage of Understanding. He hoped to revive the Republican Party after it had taken a beating in the 1922 congressional election. The fifty-seven-year-old politician was feeling rundown; and his doctor, Dr. Charles E. Sawyer, thought he would feel better if he got away from the stresses of the Capitol. His trip across the country led him all the way to Alaska, where he became the first president to visit the Alaskan Territory. America had purchased Alaska from Russia in 1867 for about two cents an acre; it became an organized territory in 1912. While there, Harding received a secret telegram telling him about an impending scandal for his administration concerning a Senate investigation of oil leases.

On the way back to the continental United States, the president made a stop in Vancouver, Canada, where he took in a round of golf. After playing six holes, he turned to his group and said, "I'm not feeling very good. How about we cut this round short?"

"Certainly, Mr. President," said a local Canadian politician. "Do you want to go over to the seventeenth hole right over there and play from there or go directly back to the clubhouse?"

"Let's go to the seventeenth hole. I think I can play two more holes since it's on the way to the clubhouse."

"Fine, let's go tee off over there," the Canadian said and pointed at the tee box.

The president finished his round, then went back to his hotel room to rest.

The next day, he went on to Seattle and rested a couple of days before giving a speech at the University of Washington to a jubilant large crowd in the auditorium.

"Our most dangerous tendency is to expect too much of government, and at the same time do for it too little," he said during his oratory. "My god, this is a hell of a job! I have no trouble with my enemies . . . But my damn friends, they're the ones that keep me walking the floor nights." That comment got a laugh and an applause.

He looked a little worn during the speech, his face displaying a few more dark circles under his eyes than normal, his skin tone was pasty. After the speech, he went back to his hotel room, where he got sick to his stomach and threw up several times. He called for Surgeon General Charles Sawyer to come to Seattle to treat him. By the time Sawyer arrived a few days later by train, the president was getting better. The doctor felt the president may have suffered food poisoning.

A day later, President Harding left Seattle to continue his trip down the West Coast, stopping at Portland, Oregon, to speak; but when he arrived there, he decided he wasn't feeling well enough to give a speech. He proceeded on to San Francisco to rest until his scheduled speech. When he arrived in San Francisco on July 29, Harding checked into Palace Hotel, where a presidential suite was awaiting him. He was feeling feverish, and his red face contrasted with his nearly white thinning hair. Dr. Sawyer examined him and thought he had come down with pneumonia as his temperature rose to 102 degrees.

A couple of days later, his temperature broke and he was feeling better. "What do you say we go fishing off Catalina Island tomorrow?" he asked his wife, Florence Kling Harding.

"I'd like that," replied his wife. The sixty-four-year-old woman knew all about not feeling well sometimes as she suffered from chronic kidney problems in the past, losing a kidney in 1905. Then in 1922, she developed a urinary tract illness in her remaining kidney. Consultant doctors Charles Mayo and John Finney recommended an operation, but Dr. Sawyer disagreed. Luckily, she recovered from the illness.

In the early evening of August 2, Warren was resting in his pajamas in the king-sized bed in the suite when his wife asked him, "Can I read you a story?"

"Oh, I like bedtime stories."

She read him "A Calm View of a Calm Man," a profile of him that had appeared in the *Saturday Evening Post*.

About halfway through, the president commented, "That's good. Go on, read some more."

When Mrs. Harding finished the article, she looked over and saw that her husband's brown eyes were closed. He had fallen asleep while she was reading. She left him alone and went downstairs to have some dinner.

During her absence, his nurse, Ruth Powderly, checked in on the president. As she approached his bed, the president's face twitched, his mouth dropped open, and his head dropped to the side. Powderly went over to him and felt no pulse. She called Doctor Sawyer and said, "I think the president is dead."

The surgeon general and a couple of other doctors went to the suite and confirmed that he was indeed dead, concluding the president must have suffered a stroke.

Harding's body was examined the next day by naval medical consultants, who determined he had suffered a massive heart attack, but the first lady refused to give them permission to do an autopsy as she saw no need for the procedure since he died from natural causes. The *New York Times* reported it as, "A stroke of apoplexy (stroke) was the cause of death." Harding had been a newspaper publisher early in his career before politics.

On the long train ride back to Washington, the First Lady began to learn of the major scandals facing her husband's former administration.

Years later, author Gaston Means wrote a sensational book, *The Strange Death of President Harding*, and suggested that he was poisoned by his wife. Since an autopsy had never been performed, his charge could not be disproved, but it was ignored. It didn't matter what he thought because Mrs. Harding had passed away a year after her husband. The president's body was not exhumed. It was a dead issue.

Harding beat Democratic Ohio Governor James M. Cox in the 1920 election and became the twenty-ninth president of the United States, taking office on March 4, 1921; thus, he became the fifth consecutive victim of the Tecumseh's curse.

Chapter 27

Present Day

After telling Detectives Stinson and Whitmore that they would visit with the coroner, Detectives O'Mahern and Palmer arrived at the Coroner's Office just after 3:00 p.m., the place smelling as if it had been freshly cleaned. County coroner Dr. John Jurgenson, still dressed in whites, was typing some information into his computer at his desk when the detectives entered the morgue.

"So what's the verdict, Doc?" O'Mahern asked.

"Guilty as charged," the white-coated coroner responded. "Oh, I guess you're asking about the murder weapon?"

O'Mahern nodded. "Yeah."

"I think the murder weapon on the second victim was an axe or maybe a tomahawk."

"Tomahawk. Now that's interesting."

"That proves my Indian theory is right on," said Palmer.

"But not the ghost theory."

"What?" Jurgenson asked. He had a quizzical look on his face.

"She thinks a ghost could have killed these people," explained O'Mahern.

"I don't think so," Jurgenson said in agreement with O'Mahern.

"So why do you think an axe was the murder weapon?" O'Mahern dug deeper for a reason. He didn't think it could be a tomahawk.

"The curvature of the fatal wound tells us that. The killer could have either thrown it or come up upon him and hit him with it. In either case, the killer then pulled it out and probably watched the poor guy bleed to death. God only knows."

"Can't you narrow it down to one or the other?"

"No, because an axe and tomahawk are really shaped the same way." Jurgenson was now getting annoyed with the third degree he was getting from O'Mahern. "Without the actual murder weapon, I can't make an exact match. If you find it, I can probably see if it matches. It's just like finding a gun for a bullet that was fired."

"Find anything else that could help us?"

"The hawk tattoo on his left arm is the same one we found on the first victim."

"Let's see it," O'Mahern said.

"The body is in the cooler, so follow me and I'll show you."

"I'll take a photo of it with my phone," Palmer said.

"You can also research that as well," O'Mahern added.

The trio walked into the cooler, temperature set at forty degrees. The room contained four other corpses. Jurgenson directed them over to Baen's body. Palmer took a photo of the tattoo with her phone, and they quickly left because it was too cold in the cooler to stay for long. However, they had their coats on, so it was much like they were outside. When they got back into his office, Palmer asked, "How about the time of the murder?"

"Like I told you at the crime scene, I think about dusk last night. Now could I get on with my work?" Jurgenson made a deep sigh, and his face reddened.

"Okay, Doc. You don't have to get upset," O'Mahern said. "We'll get out of your hair."

"I've got this report to turn in before I can call it a day. Good-bye." Jurgenson turned his head back to the computer and returned to typing up a report.

"So long," Palmer said.

As they exited out into the parking lot to go to Palmer's car, she said, "I think that confirms that we are on the right trail—that the murderer could be an Indian or one that portrays an Indian."

"Or it could be someone with an axe to grind," he said and chuckled.

She rolled her eyes. "Very funny."

"Oh, I forgot to add 'no pun intended.' We better go back to the office to meet with Bo and Russ since I told them we'd meet later. Their shift is up at four unless they're planning on working later."

"Fine."

A half an hour later, the four detectives met in the conference room. "Were you able to make any connections between your vic and ours?" O'Mahern said to start the meeting.

"Nothing yet. We didn't come across Daviess anywhere while looking through Baen's stuff," said Bo Stinson. "We haven't looked at some things yet, like phone records, e-mails, and financials. We're still waiting on an e-mail from the phone company as the techs couldn't figure out his password."

"Has the sheriff given you any overtime to work on the case?"

"We didn't ask. I have an appointment after work that I must go to," Russ Whitmore explained.

"I was hoping you'd work as long as you could tonight in order to solve it by tomorrow morning because that's our deadline, before the state police and the FBI will be called into these cases."

"Who decided that?"

"The county commissioners gave the sheriff until tomorrow morning to solve the murders."

"That's ridiculous. I guess they been watching too much television. There's that show called *48 Hours*."

"I'll stick around if you want," Stinson said.

"That's fine. You can work as much time as you want until you reach forty hours, then you have to ask the sheriff for overtime," O'Mahern pointed out.

"Okay," Stinson said.

"I'll come back after my appointment," Whitmore said.

"Great."

"Have you got any likelys to interview?"

"We did find out from one of his friends that he gambles a lot and might owe some bookie in town a lot of money," Stinson said.

"I don't think that would be a motive to kill him because the bookie wouldn't get his money then," O'Mahern said.

"Good point. We have some other people we want to talk to but nobody as a real good suspect yet." Stinson continued, "This guy was a Christian, and he had no enemies according to people we've talked to so far."

"What did he do for a living?" O'Mahern said.

"Oh, he's retired," Whitmore said.

"Hey, Palmer. Check your reenactor list and see if he's on it," O'Mahern said.

Palmer nodded. "Okay." She left the room to check the list on her desk.

"Is he married?" O'Mahern continued asking questions.

"No. His wife passed away last year, so he lives by himself."

"Did he have a dog by any chance?"

"No, but he had a black cat."

Palmer returned with the list. "I don't see his name on here anywhere."

"What'd you find out from the coroner, Flash?" Stinson asked.

"He thinks an axe or tomahawk was the murder weapon," O'Mahern said. "I think it was more of an axe than a tomahawk, but he won't be able to match

137

the wound with the weapon until we find the murder weapon. So you didn't come across anyone with an axe to grind against Baen?"

Stinson chuckled. "Funny. No."

"Well, I think we're done here for now. Let me know the minute you find anything that connects these two murders. Perhaps they aren't related although the MO seems to be about the same, except for the strange choice of murder weapons."

"Will do," Stinson said.

The detectives went back to their desks to figure out their next steps in the cases, except for Whitmore, who went off to his appointment.

"Palmer, who's next on your list of Indian suspects to go interview?" O'Mahern asked.

"We could go talk to a guy by the name of Corey Goodman, who I think may have Indian heritage. It's hard to say, but he's not such a good man. He's got a record."

"Sounds good. Where does he live?"

"In Monticello."

"Call the White County Sheriff's Department to get them to meet up with us."

"Right."

"I'll drive so we can use my TomTom for directions to his house." O'Mahern also wanted to smoke for the half-hour drive to the small city just north of Battle Ground. "What's the address so I can put it in?"

"It's 405 Lutz Drive."

"Okay."

Before they left for Monticello, Palmer called the White County sheriff, and they gave them permission to interview the suspect. They'd also meet them at the cottage to act as a backup unit.

As they headed up Indiana 43 toward Monticello, O'Mahern asked, "So what kind of priors does this guy have?"

Palmer looked up his information on the laptop. "He has an assault and battery, public intox, and a DUI."

"Not the worst record, but he still has a record. Sounds good."

On the way to Monticello, Palmer's cell phone rang, and she saw it was her lawyer boyfriend, so she answered it. "Yeah, hon."

"Can you make it to dinner tonight?" asked Fred Schultz.

"No, I don't know what time I'm getting off, so you'll have to have dinner by yourself," she said.

"Another late one, huh?"

"Yeah, this murder case keeps us going."

"Okay. I'll give you a call tomorrow."

"You bet. Love ya."

"You too."

"That must have been your boyfriend," O'Mahern said.

"Yeah. He wanted to go to dinner, but I told him I couldn't."

"Police business will do that to a relationship." O'Mahern had dated some since he became a cop but never got serious about anyone because of the job, as he had seen his share of marriages break up because of the job, so he decided a long time ago that it wasn't worth getting married over. To him, it was either do the job or get married. He didn't think the two mixed together so well.

"Yeah, I know. He knows too, but he's not very happy about it."

"Too bad."

There was silence in the car as Palmer thought about her relationship with the lawyer, a relationship that had been going on for some six months after she had become a detective. They had met each other on the job when Schultz was representing a burglar she had busted. She was impressed by the debonair, handsome lawyer, who was about her age. Then they met at a country-western bar of all places on a Saturday night, and he asked her for a dance. They danced the rest of the night and started seeing each other on a regular basis after that; however, neither had thought about taking the relationship to the next step just yet. He was a young lawyer, and she was a young detective. They both wanted to get their feet on the ground solidly in their careers before they decided to spend the rest of their lives together. They were having sex together, but he was very careful not to get her pregnant and force the issue. He always wore protection.

O'Mahern turned on the radio to a local Lafayette station to hear the broadcast of the local television station. The lead story was the latest murder: "Could the two murders be the work of a serial killer? Police aren't sure at this point whether the two murders occurring the last two days are the work of a serial killer or just random acts of violence by two other individuals. The FBI and state police may be called in on the cases if they are not solved soon . . ."

"I just knew the media would put the 'serial killer' twist on these two murders," O'Mahern said. "They always look for the worse angle in a story."

"Yeah, they always do," she agreed.

O'Mahern followed the navigational driving system closely as he approached Lake Shafer, just north of the city. The streets around the lake were very curvy, with lots of dead ends to the lake. "Turn right," the soft female voice told him. He turned on the street where the suspect lived. "You have reached your destination." Sure enough, they arrived exactly where the TomTom told him to go. That wasn't always the case, however. Once in a while the device was wrong—not this time. A deputy from the White County Sheriff's Department was there to meet them.

"Detectives O'Mahern and Palmer," O'Mahern introduced them.

"Deputy Wiltfong. So I hear this guy's a suspect in those murders in your county."

"Yeah, that's right," O'Mahern said. "We wanted to interview him."

"You go right ahead. I'll wait here and act as your backup if you want or go in with you."

"You can just act as our backup. We aren't expecting any problems, but you never know."

"That's for sure."

They cautiously approached the old cottage on the lake, the stucco walls painted brown, the smell of a wood-burning stove reefing the area. They could hear loud music seeping out of the place, rap music playing. With one hand on his pistol, O'Mahern knocked on the door with a sharp rapping to try and make a dent in the noise coming from the place.

"Who's there?" a voice inside yelled at them.

"Sheriff's department!"

"Just a minute." A few seconds later, the music stopped.

About fifteen seconds later, O'Mahern became impatient and knocked on the door again. "We haven't got all day."

Some more time passed before the door opened up to reveal Corey Goodman in a T-shirt and jeans with bare feet.

"What took you so long?" O'Mahern asked as he flashed his badge on his belt.

"I had to get some clothes on, if you don't mind."

"Oh. Can we come in?"

"Not unless you got a warrant."

"Then you can come with us for a trip to the White County Sheriff's for questioning."

"Fine. Can I get some shoes on?"

"Do it. You have a minute."

Goodman closed the door.

"Marijuana," said Palmer, who knew the distinct smell it gives off.

"Right. That's why he didn't want us to come in."

"Guy knows his rights."

"I guess."

Goodman returned to the front porch fully dressed, with a brown suede jacket as well.

"You get to ride with that gentleman," said O'Mahern, pointing to the deputy sheriff standing next to his two-tone brown sheriff's car.

"Okay."

"He didn't want us in his house, so we'll have to take him down to your station for questioning."

"Right. See you there."

O'Mahern and Palmer followed the sheriff's car back to the station house on Sixth Street in Monticello, a modern one-story gray stone building that had the county jail inside of it with about a hundred prisoners.

They followed the deputy sheriff and Goodman into the corrections building and down a hallway to some rooms. The deputy put Goodman into an interview room. "He's all yours."

"Thanks, Deputy Wiltfong."

"You're welcome. Need anything to drink?"

"No, we're fine."

"If you need anything, I'll be in the office on the left."

"Right."

After they all sat down, Goodman asked, "So what did you want to talk to me about?"

"Your name came up in a case we're working on, so we wanted to chat with you," O'Mahern said. "That's why you're in handcuffs."

"Right."

"Where were you on Saturday night about dusk?"

"At home watching a movie I rented from Redbox."

"Were you with anyone?"

"No."

"How about Sunday night about dusk?"

"Same place. I don't go out much because I was laid off a few months ago and can't afford it."

O'Mahern was getting more suspicious now that he didn't have an alibi. He was looking for a telltale from the suspect, the tell showing him that the suspect was lying. As a detective, he was used to people bullshitting him from time to time. "Do you own a musket?"

"Sure, I do reenactments and play an Indian because I'm half Potawatomi."

"Is it an authentic one or a reproduction?"

"Reproduction."

"How about a tomahawk?"

"Sure. Like I said, I portray an Indian. They all had them." Goodman flipped his eyes to the ceiling and acted as if it's a dumb question to ask.

"Do you know Patrick Daviess or George Baen?"

"No."

"Then why did you kill them?"

"What? You're accusing me of murder?"

"Yeah."

"I'd never kill anyone. I'm a Christian and go to church on Sundays. I follow the Ten Commandments."

Palmer jumped into the mix. "And you smoke pot!"

"I'm not going to answer that question."

"That wasn't a question. That's a fact. I smelled it coming from your house. Now why did you kill those guys?"

"I didn't kill anyone. I don't have to take this harassment. I want a lawyer."

That remark ended the interview. "You're free to go," said O'Mahern.

"Can you give me a ride back to my place?"

"I'll get the deputy to give you a ride."

Palmer and O'Mahern left the room. "I don't think he's our guy," Palmer said.

"He hasn't got an alibi."

"Yeah, but his musket is a reproduction. We're looking for the real thing."

"Right. Oh well. Let's get back to Lafayette."

On the way back to Lafayette, O'Mahern lit up a cigarette and puffed away while Palmer was content to listen to a radio station giving the latest news about the murders they were investigating. It wasn't much different than the one they heard on the way to Monticello, but nothing had changed in the way of the case anyway, so she didn't really expect something different.

As they arrived at the sheriff's station, O'Mahern said, "I'm hungry. I don't think there's much more we can do tonight. Why don't we go to dinner together and talk about the case before we call in a night?"

"Nah, I need to go home and shower and wash my hair. Then get some sleep." She lied. She wanted to do some more research on her own without O'Mahern present.

"Okay. I'll see you twelve hours from now at 7:30 a.m. then."

"Sounds good. See you then."

"Night."

When Palmer got to her car, she called the head of the ghost hunters, Rich Nyland. She didn't want her partner to know what she was doing since he didn't believe in ghosts as she did, but she thought there might be something there that could help them in some way. Nothing ventured, nothing gained.

Nyland answered the call and told her to stop by his house in nearby Dayton off Interstate 65, not far from her own apartment, located on the south side of Lafayette near the Subaru Automotive Plant. She arrived at his home about a half hour later. He lived in a plain-white modular home in a subdivision of the small town, a suburb of Lafayette. She knocked on the front door, and he answered.

"Detective Palmer."

"Glad to meet you, come on in. Why don't we sit here in the living room." The living room was simply decorated with a couch, an easy chair with a light pine cocktail table next to it, and a beanbag. The dark brown furniture was contrasted by the off-white walls and tan carpet. The walls contained pictures of local scenes taken by the owner.

"Fine." She sat down in the easy chair. She could hear the sound of television coming from another room. The place had the odor of a freshly baked pie—pumpkin, she presumed.

"So how can I help you?" asked Nyland, a large man in his early forties, with dark brown hair cut short. He sat down in the couch and brushed some crumbs from his jeans. He wore a dark blue sweatshirt with an American flag on it and the words *God's Country*.

"Was Patrick Daviess part of your group?"

"Yeah, he sure was. We are all planning to go to his funeral to pay our respects."

"Did he have any enemies that you know of?"

"No, he got along with everyone in our group."

"I wanted to hear about the ghost stories you know from Battle Ground. I understand there were some stories near the monument."

"I've heard a couple of stories. There's one in which an Indian is spotted near the front gate. He's carrying a musket and then he runs away toward the creek."

"I've heard that one, but I didn't know he ran toward the creek."

"Did you hear about the one where a soldier was seen?"

"No."

"It's another residual haunting. A local group went to the battlefield a few years ago with a Ouija board. They went there at night, which was not allowed as the park was closed. They sat down around the monument with their board. They first asked the board if anyone else was with them. The board spelled out *Yes*. Then they asked it who it was. The board spelled out *Go*. They kept asking it questions, and the answer was always *Go*."

Palmer leaned forward in her seat as the story really interested her. "Interesting. Don't stop, go on."

"Then the cursor moved by itself, and that really scared the shit out of them. Some screamed and ran to their cars, except for one guy. He froze. Then he heard the sound of horses and wagons, as well as some muffled voices. He could even smell horses, but there isn't a horse for miles. Then in the darkness, he saw shadows moving along. What he saw was a residual haunting from the hundreds of Indians that passed through here on their way to Kansas during the trek there. You know, the Trail of Death."

Palmer nodded. "Un-huh. I know all about that story. I just hadn't heard any ghost stories about it. Any others?"

"Not about the battleground."

"How about Prophet's Rock?"

"Yeah, there have been some sightings there too. One was seen by some Purdue students who were sitting on top of the Prophet's Rock. They saw an Indian running up the hill from the rock."

"I wonder what they were smoking or drinking."

"Pot probably. The other involved a Girl Scout troop that had come to the site."

"Haven't heard about that one."

"It's a recent sighting."

"How did that go?"

"The scouts were climbing up the hill from the rock when suddenly they heard someone running behind them. A young girl at the back of the pack let out a piercing scream, which scared everyone else in the group. They all started screaming then. She told the scout leader that she saw an Indian ghost running right past her and down the hill. Nobody else saw anything, but they all heard the steps before she screamed. Anyways, that scared them enough to head back down the trail to their car."

"Did your group go there to hunt ghosts?"

"Not yet. It's on our list, though. Do you think a ghost could have done these murders?"

"Not really, but I wouldn't want to rule it out. My partner won't even consider it a possibility."

"He doesn't believe in ghosts?"

"No."

"His loss. There are a lot of unexplained things that need further investigation—even ghosts."

"Thanks for your time. I need to get some rest."

"You're welcome." He saw her out the door.

On the way home, she thought about the conversation she had with Nyland. She didn't think the crime scene techs went down by the creek to look for evidence, so she decided she would call Forensics and ask them to go back to the crime scene to look for footprints by the creek. It was worth a shot. Perhaps there may be a footprint there or something else that could help them with the case.

When she arrived home, she saw her karate outfit hanging on the closet doorknob. She remembered that she was going to fill in tomorrow night for her karate instructor, so she called him and told him that she couldn't be there. Duty called. Palmer had earned a black belt in karate and could now teach the class. The training she did in her teen years helped her a lot when she decided to become a police officer instead of a lawyer. Karate moves came in handy in a fight with someone.

Chapter 28

Warm Springs, Georgia, April 12, 1945

In late March, President Franklin D. Roosevelt traveled to Georgia to rest and recuperate at the Little White House, a little house made from Georgia pine that looked a little bit like the large White House in Washington DC, with four columns gracing the front entrance of the home, but the resemblance stopped there. Painted all white with black shutters, the little house had three bedrooms, two bathrooms, a living room, kitchen, and sundeck and was built on Pine Mountain in 1932.

Roosevelt had started visiting a nearby health spa there twenty years earlier to find relief for his paralyzed lower body, which had been stricken with polio in 1921 at age thirty-nine. With the war winding down in Europe and the Pacific, his family and friends thought he deserved a rest; and he looked like he needed one, his complexion ashen gray, dark circles and deep bags under his eyes.

Around 2:00 p.m., he was sitting comfortably in the living room of his cottage, wearing a short-sleeved dark blue shirt and tan shorts, talking with some friends and family while he signed letters and documents on a card table in front of a stone fireplace. On the stone mantle above the fireplace sat a picture of a large white sailing ship, and above that was another sailing ship with a black hull. FDR loved sailing, and he had once been the secretary of the navy. A couple of other photos of ships adorned the pine-paneled walls of the cottage-style living room. There was even a photo of his wife, Eleanor, who was not there as she was back in Washington DC attending to some business. A fancy carpet covered the wood flooring.

As Roosevelt was sitting in the office-type chair, he felt a headache coming on. He removed his glasses and turned to an artist who was painting his portrait and said, "We have only fifteen minutes."

"Yes, sir," Elizabeth Shoumatoff replied. She was doing an oil painting of the president. Although he was dressed in a short-sleeved shirt, she had given him a brown suit coat and red tie with a white shirt. The artist had already captured the president's oval face with green eyes and silver-gray hair. Although Roosevelt's complexion was very white this time of year after being inside during winter, the artist added a little pink to it to make it stand out more. She also added the major wrinkles of the president's old face in the portrait.

Suddenly, the president grabbed his head of thinning hair. "Oh, I have a sharp pain in my head," he proclaimed. Then he slumped over, and his hands dropped to his side; the chair's arms saved him from falling to the floor.

"Get the doctor!" the artist yelled.

"Oh my god!" a relative screamed. The congenial atmosphere had suddenly turned chaotic.

A Filipino houseboy and one of Roosevelt's cousins carried the president into his bedroom and laid his six-foot-one-inch frame on his bed. Two doctors arrived within a few minutes, but there was nothing they could do for the president, who was nonresponsive. All they could do was take his vitals. A heart specialist, Dr. James E. Paulin, from Atlanta was summoned; he was given a police escort to the Little White House. Paulin arrived and was directed to the president's bedroom. The telephone rang.

"President's suite," one of the president's cousins answered the phone. She turned toward the bedroom and said, "Dr. Bruenn, it's for you."

Bruenn came out of the bedroom and took the phone from her. "Yes," he answered. As he was talking to Dr. McIntire from Washington DC, someone from the bedroom called out to him. "Dr. Bruenn, we need you now!"

"I'm wanted," he said and put the phone back down.

When he entered the bedroom, he saw that Dr. Paulin was doing chest compressions on the president, whose heart had stopped. After a minute or so with no response, Roosevelt's death was called; FDR had died of a cerebral hemorrhage.

A couple of hours later, Vice President Harry S. Truman was at the office of House Speaker Sam Rayburn when a call came in for him.

"You need to come to the White House immediately," he was told. After he hung up, he wondered about the urgency of the call. He figured it must be war related.

When he arrived, he was greeted by the first lady, Mrs. Eleanor Roosevelt. She had a concerned look on her face and said, "Harry, Franklin is dead."

"Is there anything I can do for you?" Truman asked.

"Is there anything we can do for you?" she replied. "For you're the one in trouble now."

At 7:09 p.m., Truman was administered the presidential oath by Chief Justice Harlan Fiske Stone beneath the portrait of President Woodrow Wilson in the White House Cabinet Room.

Tecumseh's curse had claimed its sixth president in a row. President Roosevelt was elected to his third term on November 5, 1940, and died during his fourth term in office. The thirty-second president of the United States went down as the longest-serving president in United States history.

The portrait that Elizabeth Shoumatoff was painting of the president at the time of his death became famous and known as the *Unfinished Portrait of FDR*.

Chapter 29

Present Day

The dawning of a new day brought a brilliant sun to brighten up the chilly start to the November morning, one of those mornings that the air was so crisp it was exhilarating. Aerial photographers loved this kind of day to take photos of buildings or anything else for that matter from an aircraft. The sun would warm the temperature up to the sixties later, warm enough to go fishing or golfing outside.

Shortly after dawn, Monty Wentworth arrived at his boat dock along the Wabash River near Battle Ground to do some fishing for the last time of the year. He planned to winterize and put his dark green bass boat away for the winter afterward. Wentworth had the day off from his job as the manager of an auto parts store in Lafayette; he wanted to take advantage of the nice weather to do some serious fishing. His wife had to work, so he had the day to himself, something he relished once in a while.

He pushed the boat out from his wooden dock into the slow-moving Wabash. He planned to just drift downriver and fish until he got to Lafayette. Then he would turn around, use his motor, and come back upstream to the dock. After putting his favorite scientific fishing lure called a diver on his fishing rod, he tossed the line out toward the middle of the river. He eased back on his seat and relaxed. Suddenly, the line pulled. He snagged a fish, probably a bass. The fish fought when Wentworth pulled the pole back quickly to set the hook in its mouth. The fight went on for a few minutes before he hauled the fish into his boat. He took the hook from the smallmouth bass, which wasn't big enough to be a keeper, so he tossed it back into the river.

All of a sudden, he felt a sharp pain in his back and yelled loudly, disturbing some ducks floating peacefully by the boat. The pain was much worse than the agonizing kidney stones he had experienced in the past. He looked over his shoulder and saw an arrow sticking out from his back. Suddenly, he felt faint and fell facedown in the boat, hitting his head on a seat and losing consciousness.

A half hour later, a Purdue University student, dressed in a black-and-yellow jacket with Purdue on the back of it, left his apartment in downtown Lafayette to walk to the university on the other side of the Wabash River. As he strolled across Tapawingo Bridge, a large, wide expanse used only by pedestrians, he looked down and saw a bass boat approaching the bridge. He could hardly believe what he saw—a man lying facedown with an arrow protruding from his back, like a mast without a sail! The college freshman nervously pulled his Blackberry out of his pants pocket and dialed 911.

"This is 911. What is your emergency?"

"I'm on the Tapawingo Bridge, and a small fishing boat just passed under me with a dead man in it."

"How do you know that he's dead?"

"Well, I don't know, but he's not moving and he's got an arrow sticking out of his back," the nineteen-year-old student said with panic in his voice.

"We will get a unit there right away."

"You better send it farther down the river because the boat is floating away."

"We have a patrol boat that we'll send downriver to catch up with it. What is your name, sir?"

"Clyde Wesler, but I can't wait around. I need to get to class."

"That's okay, you can go to class. I have your number, and a detective may call you later. Thanks for your help."

"You're welcome." Clyde put the phone back into his black-and-yellow jacket pocket with his trembling hand. His stomach was so queasy, he felt like tossing his breakfast into the river below as he had never seen a dead body before.

O'Mahern and Palmer were on their way to interview a suspect when dispatch called them and diverted them to the boat launch on the Wabash River. They got into the patrol boat and headed downriver to capture the bass boat and bring it back.

When they arrived at the boat dock, O'Mahern commented, "At least there's no film crew here this time."

"You miss them like you miss the dentist, don't you?"

"You got that right."

On the way to the boat carrying the third murder victim in as many days, Palmer got a call from her boyfriend, but she ignored it. She figured she wouldn't be able to speak to him as the patrol boat with its roaring engines would make it impossible for her to hear him. She sent him a text message instead. He replied quickly and asked her out to dinner. She replied that she wouldn't be able to make it because of yet another murder.

About a half hour later, the sheriff's department patrol boat caught up to the silver bass boat, snagged it, and pulled it over to their boat. By then, several other people had called 911 to report a fisherman slumped over in a boat with an arrow sticking out of his back.

Detectives O'Mahern and Palmer jumped into the boat and started looking around. O'Mahern searched the man's pockets and retrieved a cell phone, wallet, and comb. He handed Palmer the phone while he examined the wallet.

Just then, a boat pulled up alongside their boat with the film crew from Real TV.

"I guess I spoke too soon about the TV crew not joining us. They're running just a little bit late."

Palmer nodded. "Yeah."

O'Mahern continued checking the body. "Check his arms to see if he has the same tattoo as the other victims?" Palmer asked.

"Right." O'Mahern concurred and checked his left shoulder first. Lo and behold, the tattoo on the other two victims was on this victim's arm as well. "Yep, he has the same tattoo. Do you know what it represents?"

"Not yet, but I'll check as soon as I get back to the office."

"Please. It might be important and give us a lead on this case."

She nodded. "Uh-huh." She didn't think that it was as important as he did, but she would check Google Images when she got back to the office. She had forgotten to do so after the second murder.

"This guy's been dead for less than three hours because rigor hasn't set in yet."

"Hang on to something," a deputy sheriff told them as he started the engine of the bass boat. "We're going back to the boat dock."

"Okay," O'Mahern acknowledged.

When they got back to the dock, crime scene techs as well as the coroner were waiting for them. The detectives got out of the boat and let them do their work.

O'Mahern's cell phone went off, and he answered it. "O'Mahern."

"Jackson, I'm forming a task force with you in charge, so I need you to get back here. The meeting is set for 10:00 a.m."

"Yes, sir. We're on our way." O'Mahern turned to Palmer. "That was the sheriff, and he's forming a task force with me in charge. He's also called in the FBI and the state police."

"Great," she said.

"I'm not as overthrilled by that as you might be. I'd rather continue the investigation on my own than with a task force."

"Yeah, but we aren't getting anywhere with the case fast. Maybe they can help us do that."

"I sure hope so."

On the way back to the office, Palmer remembered that the psychic had seen a man being killed by an arrow. "That psychic saw this murder accurately."

"Yeah, that's scary. Unfortunately, it didn't help us prevent it."

"Maybe she will see more and give us a call."

"We can only hope she doesn't see any more, but if she does, I hope it leads us to the murderer next time."

Chapter 30

Dallas, Texas, November 22, 1963

A ir Force One touched down on Love Field at 11:40 a.m. on the sunny fall day. President John F. Kennedy waved to the crowd as he departed the blue-and-white plane decorated with the presidential seal, *United States of America*, and the American flag on the side. He was greeted by Texas Governor John B. Connally Jr. and his wife, Idanell, as well as many other local dignitaries. Then he got into the rear of the open presidential limousine along with his wife, Jacqueline. In front of them sat the dark-suited governor and his wife, who went by Nellie and wore a black coat and small red hat to help keep her warm. The svelte president was dressed in a dark gray suit while the beautiful Jackie wore a pink overcoat and matching pillbox hat, a hat that gained popularity because of her wearing it.

Secret Service Agent William R. Greer drove the presidential limousine, and Agent Roy H. Kellerman sat in the passenger seat. Behind the black limo was a group of eight Secret Service agents riding in a convertible. Responsible for the president's protection, the highly trained agents scanned the crowds, roofs, windows, overpasses, and streets for any trouble as the motorcade proceeded. Alongside and in front of the motorcade were Dallas motorcycle policemen. Other agents and police also lined the streets, so protection came from everywhere.

At first, the motorcade passed through some residential neighborhoods. President Kennedy told Greer, "Stop here. I want to shake hands with these people."

The procession came to an abrupt stop, and the president shook hands with some enthusiastic Texans. A couple of blocks later, the president stopped the procession again to greet people. The police and Secret Service didn't like the president stopping unexpectedly, but there was nothing they could do to be more prepared.

When the motorcade arrived in downtown Dallas, the streets were lined on both sides with local residents; people were thrilled to get a glimpse of the nation's leader. The president told the Secret Service agents who were standing on a special platform on the back of the limo to get off as they were blocking his view. They did as he requested, but one agent was perplexed by the request and put his hands out to the side as if he couldn't understand what was going on.

At 12:30 p.m., the slow-moving motorcade snaked past the Texas School Book Depository. The president waved to the crowd. A Secret Service agent in the car behind the president radioed the Trade Mart, where the president was to speak. "The president will be there in about five minutes," he said.

Suddenly, a shot rang out, but it missed its target. Then two seconds later, another shot. President Kennedy felt a sharp pain in his neck and moved his hands to the area. A rifle bullet cut through him like a jet through a cloud, exited his body close to the knot in his dark blue tie, continued on to hit the governor in the back, passed through Connally's right nipple through his right wrist, and finally came to rest in his thigh.

And another shot was fired. This one struck Kennedy on the top of the head, causing a massive head wound. He lurched forward in his seat. His mind went blank.

Agent Kellerman heard the shots and turned to see the president and governor fall forward in their seats. "Let's get out of here, we're hit!" He then radioed the lead car, "Get us to the hospital immediately."

Another agent from the following car jumped on the back of the limo to shield the president; Jacqueline Kennedy reached back to help him up. People along the street panicked and began running away from the scene.

Meanwhile, Dallas motorcycle patrolman Marrion L. Baker, who had been in the motorcade, heard the shots. He knew it was the sound of a high-powered rifle. He looked up and saw pigeons scattering from their perches atop the Book Depository building. He raced to the building, dismounted, and parked his Harley-Davidson motorcycle. The black uniformed policeman removed his white helmet and set it on the bike. He made his way through the crowd and entered the building.

"Can I help you?" asked Roy Truly.

"I heard some gunshots, and I think they came from this building."

"I'm the building superintendent. I'll help you look through the building."

"Great. I think the shots came from one of the upper floors."

He pointed toward the stairs. "This way."

They ran up the stairs to the second floor. Baker saw a man walking away from him in the lunchroom. "You, come here!" Baker barked at him.

The slim man dressed in a plain brown shirt stopped and turned around. He started walking slowly toward the officer. Truly had continued toward the third floor but stopped when he heard Baker yell, so he came back to the officer.

"You know this man?" Baker asked as the man got closer.

"Yeah, he's the new guy here," Truly said when he recognized the dark-haired Lee Harvey Oswald.

"Never mind, go on your way," the officer instructed Oswald.

"Okay, sir," Oswald said. Then he turned around and walked away with the Coke he had just purchased in the lunchroom.

Baker and Truly went up to the third floor to continue their search.

As they searched the building, the presidential limousine arrived at Parkland Memorial Hospital. A team of physicians were waiting. They examined President Kennedy immediately and noticed that he was still breathing and detected a slight heartbeat, but there was no pulse. The doctors performed a tracheotomy on Kennedy to improve his breathing. At 1:00 p.m., the president's heart stopped. He was declared dead.

Fifteen minutes later, Patrolman J. D. Tippit was on patrol downtown when he came upon a man who fit the description—slender white man of medium height with black hair and no facial hair—of a suspect wanted in connection with the assassination. He pulled his black-and-white patrol car over to the curb.

"Hey, you," Tippit said to the man. "Come over here."

Oswald walked over to the passenger-side window of the police car. "What do you want, Officer?"

"Where were you forty-five minutes ago?"

"Working."

"Where?"

"The Book Depository."

"Okay. You're coming with me."

Tippit got out of the car and went around the front to handcuff Oswald and take him into custody. Oswald saw him get the handcuffs out of his pocket, so he pulled a revolver from his pocket and started shooting. Four bullets hit their mark; Tippit fell to the ground and died instantly.

Domingo Benavides heard the shots from his pickup truck and saw Tippit lying next to his police car. He also spotted Oswald, who was walking hurriedly from the scene. Benavides stopped his dark brown Chevrolet pickup truck and rushed to the downed officer. Blood was pouring from Tippit's wounds. The auto repairman saw he could do nothing for the officer, so he went into a nearby store to call police.

Oswald emptied the spent cartridges from his revolver as he walked away. He turned the corner from the shooting and saw a taxi driver crouched behind his cab. "Poor dumb cop," Oswald told the scared driver.

When Oswald arrived at Jefferson Boulevard with his gun still in his hand, a man asked him, "What's going on?" Oswald ignored him and kept walking. He passed a gas station and ditched his light tan jacket in the parking lot as he wanted to change his identity. Then he shoved the gun in his left pants pocket and slowed down his walk so as not to gain suspicion.

A police car came down Jefferson, so Oswald ducked into the front entrance of a shoe store to get out of sight. The police car passed in a hurry. The shoe store owner, Johnny Calvin Brewer, saw Oswald and became suspicious of his activity. So when Oswald continued on his way, Brewer followed him. Oswald came upon the Texas Theater and ducked in the side door of the theater to get off the street. Brewer told the cashier, "A suspicious man just entered the side door of your theater. I think police are after him. You better call them."

"I will," she said and called the operator. "Operator, get me the police!"

A few seconds passed.

"Police department."

"I think you're after a man who just ducked into the Texas Theater illegally."

"We'll get patrol cars over there right away."

Within minutes, several Dallas police cars arrived at the theater. The house lights were turned up. Police approached Oswald, who started to reach for his gun. The officers jumped him and hit him in the face several times, one blow landing on his forehead and the other landing on his nose. They got the slender Oswald under their control, cuffed him, and took him downtown for questioning.

Police checked his background and felt they had the right man. When Oswald was in the marine corps, he was court-martialed for shooting himself in the elbow with an unauthorized handgun. Then he was court-martialed for fighting with his sergeant. He was court-martialed for a third time when he fired his gun without reason into the jungle while on guard duty. After he left the marines, he defected to Russia in 1959 and renounced his American citizenship. He reconsidered his decision two years later as he found Russia rather boring in comparison to the United States. He married a Russian woman, Marina Prusakova, and was able to get her documents to go to the United States with him. When he returned to the United States, he was arrested in New Orleans earlier in the year for disorderly conduct after getting into a scuffle while passing out leaflets in support of Cuba, the leaflets titled *Fair Play for Cuba.*

Police also found the rifle that Oswald had used, a C2766 Mannlicher-Carcano rifle, and matched his fingerprints to it. The rifle had a telescopic lens, making it easy for Oswald to kill the president from the sixth floor of the Book Depository. The rifle fired a 6.5-millimeter bullet that traveled at 1,904 feet per second, which is why it went right through President Kennedy and the governor.

Two days later, Oswald was to be transferred to the county jail in an armored car. The press had gathered for the occasion. Television cameras rolled as Oswald, who was dressed in a jacket, emerged from the basement flanked by detectives who held him by the arms. Suddenly, Jack Ruby stepped in front of him, pulled out a Colt .38 revolver, and fired one shot into Oswald's abdomen. Oswald winced and groaned in pain. Then he fell to the ground. Pandemonium broke out!

"He's been shot," a television reporter said. "Lee Oswald has been shot."

Minutes later, he was taken to Parkland Hospital where he died an hour and a half later.

For the seventh consecutive time, Tecumseh's curse had claimed a president who was elected in a year ending with zero. The thirty-fifth president of the United States had been elected to the office of the presidency on November 8, 1960.

Chapter 31

Present Day

All the detectives and some deputy sheriffs gathered in the conference room at 10:00 a.m. as ordered by Sheriff Joshua Andrews. Nobody took a seat. They started examining the portable whiteboard that had been wheeled into the room—the murder board containing pictures and information from the three murders. They spoke in hushed tones to one another about the case and what the meeting was all about, sounding like a bunch of bees buzzing in the room. Rumors had already flown around the department before the meeting was called. Many had already speculated that a task force was being formed as a result of the murders. The dozen police officers quieted down immediately when the sheriff and Jackson O'Mahern entered the room.

"I've called you all together to tell you that you're all now working on this serial killer case. We need to get this thing solved right away before everyone starts panicking. I'm authorizing overtime for everyone on this task force for the rest of this week. Cancel all your appointments for the week to come. O'Mahern is the lead detective on this task force, so you will take orders from him. Jackson, it's all yours."

"Thank you, Sheriff. We've had three murders now in four days. They all have a similar MO . . ." O'Mahern moved over to the board and went over all three murders in detail. That took about ten minutes as he detailed the crime scenes, murder weapons, and leads.

"The state police and FBI are being called into this case, as well as the local police departments," O'Mahern continued. "So we will have lots of manpower, Forensics, and whatnot. I'd like to introduce Clay Downing. He's a consultant for the FBI and specializes in profiling."

"Thanks, Jackson," said Downing. "After analyzing the three murders, here's who I think you are dealing with. The pattern of this killer fits more with a psychopath than a serial killer because of several things." Downing held up his arm and extended the index finger on his right hand. "One, because a serial killer usually takes some time off between murders." Then he held up two fingers. "Two, because serial killers rarely change weapons. This person used three different weapons, but they were all weapons used by Indians centuries ago. You're dealing with a murderer, and it doesn't matter whether he or she is psychopathic or serial. I think the killer is likely a male, but since all males were killed, a female could be the culprit, but I doubt it. And you can't rule out a couple, although those are rare. I'd say the age of the murderer is somewhere between twenty-five and forty-five. Because of the weapons used, you should be looking at someone who owns those things, like a reenactor or collector, unless he's just trying to throw you off. Like I said the murders are too close together to fit the usual serial killer. The killer may have suffered a psychotic break recently or timed the murders to coincide with some kind of event. I might be able to narrow the field after you do some research and find more connections between these victims. You—"

"Excuse me, Clay. We have made one other connection between the three victims. They all have the same tattoo, a hawk." O'Mahern turned and looked at Palmer. "Were you able to find out more about those tattoos?"

"Yes," Palmer replied. "They are all much the same and similar to the one used as a logo by the Order of Hawks. There's a club here in Lafayette."

"Then we need to investigate that club to see if it provides us with a lead in this case," O'Mahern said. "We also need to check into where they got those tattoos as well, and perhaps that will give us another connection. That's all we could find in common so far with the victims, Clay."

"Good, we have something to go on," continued the profiler. "Check out all the tattoo parlors in the area. Perhaps they all went to the same one. Who knows? He decided to kill them all. Who knows? Anything's possible. You should also canvass all the victims' families and friends to find any other connections. And see if they had a common thread such as a shared enemy. I can't believe these murders are random. Any questions?"

"What do you think the motive could be for these killings?" a deputy sheriff asked.

"Considering you have three murders in such a short span, I'd say someone might be doing it for the thrill of it, or they're seeking attention."

"Is the MO for these murders like any other current serial killers around the nation?" a detective asked.

"No, not really. Killings like this seem confined to your area. Anyone else?"

"Could this be the work of a professional killer?"

"No, I don't see anything that leads me to believe a pro is at work here—just some maniac is what I think. Any other questions?"

The room fell silent.

"Thanks for your help, Clay," Jackson said. "Now let's hear from Forensics, Melody Quinten."

"Thanks, Jackson," the redheaded long-haired Melody said. She was a short middle-aged woman who was not overly attractive. She held up a picture of the arrow and showed it around the room as she spoke. "We've taken a quick look at the arrow that killed the latest victim. It was made from Port Orford cedar with trimmed turkey feathers. A two-inch steel point did the damage to the victim. The point was attached to the arrow using sinew—definitely a homemade job. It replicates arrows that were first used in the late seventeenth century. We are going over it to see if we can get any DNA off of it. We have copies of this picture for all of you in case you come across any other arrows during your investigation. That's all I have for now."

"Thanks, Melody. We have a list of suspects, and I'll be giving each of your teams some to contact. Like the man said, contact their family and friends. We need to find more connections. I will have one of you check financials and someone else check phone records to see if there's any connection there. The FBI is looking at their computers and checking their e-mail, Facebook page, and stuff like that. Also, talk to your CIs and see if there's any word out on the street about these murders. If you get any good solid leads, let me know right away so I can coordinate what action to take. We will reconvene at seven p.m. tonight to go over what we have found out today. The sheriff has granted us overtime. We need to solve this right away before we have any more victims. Okay, see me individually for assignments. And don't say anything to the press. We have a press conference set for noon, so it will be covered live by the local television station. Are there any other questions?"

"Thank you, Jackson," Sheriff Andrews said. "Now get out there and get me some results, people." Andrews had already planned to run again for sheriff next year, so he thought it was important to get these murders solved right away for his own political agenda. The county commissioners wanted them solved quickly as well.

For the next half hour, Detective Sergeant O'Mahern went over assignments with the other detectives while Palmer went through lists of suspects to give them. They would look at all reenactors in the area and start interviewing Native Americans who lived in the area as well. By the time they were finished, it was lunchtime and nearly time for the press conference. Media from all over the state had gathered on Lafayette, thirsty for the latest news on the murders.

Chapter 32

Washington DC, March 30, 1981

After a speaking engagement at the Washington Hilton, President Ronald Reagan walked out of the hotel at 2:30 p.m. surrounded by his entourage of Secret Service agents and Washington DC police officers, who were dressed in their rain gear for the cold rainy March day. Small groups of people, some carrying umbrellas to protect them from the light showers, had gathered near the hotel to catch a glimpse of the president. Reagan, wearing a dark blue suit with a white shirt and plain dark-blue tie, saw the people waving at him from across the street, so he waved in return.

"President Reagan!" one onlooker yelled as the president waved.

The remark brought a smile to the president's face. He turned and waved in another direction. "Hi, how are you doing?" the president responded.

Bam! A shot rang out.

The first shot from a gun put the Secret Service agents into action immediately. Senior Agent Jerry Parr was behind the president when he heard the pop. The president thought it was a firecracker. Instinctively, Parr knew it was a gunshot and that it was aimed at his commander in chief. Parr grabbed President Reagan by the waist and pushed him into the presidential limousine. As he did, a bullet ricocheted off the presidential limousine and entered the president's left side. The agent pounced on top of him to protect him. The president grimaced in extreme pain.

Bam!

Another bullet hit Press Secretary James Brady in the head, and he fell to the pavement.

Bam!

DC policeman Thomas Delahanty was struck by a bullet.

Bam!

Agent Timothy McCarthy was also struck by a bullet.

Bam! Bam! The other two bullets missed.

"Jerry, get off!" Reagan shouted. "I think you've broken a rib." He didn't realize he had been shot.

The agent immediately eased off the president.

Then the president coughed up some frothy blood. "Jerry, I think the broken rib has pierced my lung." He took a handkerchief from his pocket and wiped his mouth.

"The president's been hit!" Parr shouted at the driver. "Get us to George Washington Hospital!" The limo sped off with a police escort.

The scene of the shooting was chaotic. Some officers ducked or put up their hands in response to the gunshots while others looked around for the shooter. A police officer in a slicker as yellow as a ripe banana and two officers in black raincoats saw the shooter and took him to the ground, much like defensive linemen tackling a running back.

Other Secret Service agents ran to the pileup as well. One African American agent pulled his revolver from under his dark blue coat, ready to use it if necessary. "Get back!" he yelled.

"Get an ambulance!" an agent ordered.

"All right, stand back!" an agent demanded.

"Get that patrol car up here now, Officer!" a Secret Service agent in a gray suit wielding a small machine gun yelled. "Get it up here."

"Call for an ambulance quick," said another agent, who was attending to the wounded agent.

"We got to get us a unit!" another black agent requested. "A police unit!"

The agents and officers yelled many demands, lending to the confusion.

"Got a handkerchief?" an agent asked a police officer. The officer handed him one so he could stop the bleeding of a downed officer.

"Get that ambulance up here, please," requested another Secret Service agent.

"Get out of the way," a Washington DC police officer demanded of an ABC television cameraman.

A patrol car pulled up, and the agents manhandled the suspected shooter over to it, but they couldn't get the back door open. So they took him to another patrol car as an ambulance pulled up to the scene. The three injured men lay on the wet pavement with agents and officers trying to do what they could until the paramedics arrived to help.

A few minutes later, the presidential limousine arrived at the George Washington University Hospital; an emergency team had been alerted and was waiting for their arrival. The president got out of the limo on his own feet and headed into the hospital with Parr right by his side. As he came into the hospital emergency room, Reagan suddenly grew weak. "I'm having trouble breathing," he told a nurse. Then his knees got rubbery, and he began to fall. Parr and the nurse caught him before he went down. He was placed on a stretcher, and the team took him to the operating room for immediate treatment. "I forgot to duck," the president joked as they hurried him to the operating room, Secret Service men flanking their every move.

The team began cutting his brand-new suit away from his body to get him ready for surgery. Reagan said a silent prayer to God as they prepped him. He had lost a lot of blood—about half of his blood supply—and his blood pressure was very low, so he was going into a state of shock. Before they put him out for the surgery, he quipped, "I hope you're all Republicans." The president never stopped with the jokes even as his life hung in the balance.

Some doctors in the team that had assembled thought he might not live at this point. It took surgeons two x-rays and almost an hour before they found the bullet. It had passed within an inch of the president's heart. The bullet had damaged his lung, so surgeons sewed up his tattered lung, recovered the bullet, and were done in two hours.

Ironically, nine days before the assassination attempt, Reagan had visited old Ford's Theatre in Washington DC with his wife, Nancy, for a fundraiser. He looked up at the president's box where President Abe Lincoln was shot and thought that with all the protection he had from the Secret Service, even he was not safe enough against someone with determination to kill him. He was right.

Meanwhile, police were booking John W. Hinckley Jr., a twenty-five-year-old drifter from Evergreen, Colorado, with attempted murder on the president and a dozen other charges. He had nearly killed four people with his German .22 revolver, a Saturday night special, and six Devastator explosive rounds. Hinckley pleaded not guilty by reason of insanity.

Hinckley had developed an obsession with Jodie Foster, who played a prostitute in the movie *Taxi Driver*, which he saw fifteen times during the summer it came out in 1976. In the movie, actor Robert De Niro played Travis Bickle, who plots to assassinate the president. So Hinckley planned to win her over by assassinating the president. He first trailed President Jimmy Carter from state to state until he was arrested in Nashville, Tennessee, on a weapons charge.

When Reagan became the new president, he went after him. The day before he attempted the assassination of Reagan, he wrote a letter to Foster describing his sinister plan. "I'm going to kill the president tomorrow," he wrote.

During surgery, a press conference was held at the White House. The media wanted all the answers they could get about the president and his condition.

Secretary of State Alexander Haig Jr., dressed in a pinstriped suit, told the press, "Constitutionally, gentlemen, you have the president, the vice president, and the secretary of state in that order, and should the president decide he wants to transfer the helm to the vice president, he will do so. He has not done that. As of now, I am in control here, in the White House, pending return of the vice president and in close touch with him. If something came up, I would check with him, of course."

Vice President George H. W. Bush was in Dallas, Texas, at the time of the shooting and returned to Washington as soon as he got word of the attempted assassination.

When Reagan awoke, he scribbled his first words on a pad of paper: "All in all, I'd rather be in Philadelphia." Those words came from humorist W. C. Fields.

President Reagan remained in the hospital for twelve days. As he left the hospital on April 11, a reporter yelled a question his way, "What are you going to do when you get home?"

"Sit down," the president remarked. Reagan had a sense of humor, and the American public liked that.

More than a year later, Hinckley was found not guilty by reason of insanity and put away into St. Elizabeth's Hospital, a mental institution. Investigators found out that during his college days, he became depressed and twice played Russian roulette. He even took a photo of himself holding a gun to his dark-haired head. Hinckley wore his hair short with some bangs in front; he was actually a handsome young man.

Hinckley once told a reporter, "Guns are neat little things, aren't they? They can kill extraordinary people with very little effort."

President Reagan forgave Hinckley in his prayers for what he did.

Reagan went on to serve as president until January 20, 1989, and didn't die in office. He lived until June 5, 2004. Apparently, Tecumseh's curse was finally broken. Or was it?

Chapter 33

Present Day

After O'Mahern and Palmer finished assigning suspects to the other detectives, they went to the coroner's office to look in on the latest victim, Monty Wentworth. Dr. John Jurgenson was typing up a report on his computer.

"Have you confirmed the identity of this latest victim yet?" O'Mahern asked.

"Yeah," Jurgenson, who was dressed in his whites, said as he came to his feet. "His wife was in here about thirty minutes ago."

"How did she react?"

Jurgenson got up from his chair. "Oh, she cried quite a bit. You can probably rule her out unless she shoots an arrow like a champion bow hunter. I don't think she was capable. She's a woman of about five feet in stature and probably weighs a hundred pounds soaking wet."

"Anything else I should know about the death?"

"Not really. He definitely died from the arrow. It hit him in the back and slid through his kidney. It nearly went through him. He probably never saw it coming."

"Could you determine how close the shooter was?"

"Oh, that's very hard to say, but probably within fifty feet."

"How long ago did he die?"

"I'd say it wasn't long after dawn that he got it. Have you found where he was when he was shot?"

"Nah. We'll probably never have that answer. We only know where he launched from near Battle Ground. His pickup truck was found a little while ago."

"If you could narrow down the time," Palmer said, "we'd be able to figure out approximately where he was when he was killed. Because then we could take the speed of the river and subtract it from the time the body was found."

"You're right, but figuring out the exact time of death hours after you find a body makes it difficult to figure out. The cold temperature makes a difference too. I'll do some more figuring and see if I can come up with a more definitive TOD. I'll give you a call. Okay?"

"Sure, Doc," Palmer said.

"We need to get out there and do some police work," O'Mahern said. He could see that the coroner and Palmer were getting into it again and didn't want that. "Let's go, Palmer."

"Thanks, Doc. See ya," Palmer said.

"Bye." Jurgenson turned and went into the room where Wentworth's body was stored to see if he could narrow the time down. He didn't think he could, but he would try to satisfy the detectives.

The detectives made their way to Palmer's car, and O'Mahern got an idea. "Let's go by the weapons expert again—"

"Jim Buchanan."

"Yeah, that's him. I want to check out his alibi, and maybe he can help us out with these other weapons that have been used in the murders."

"That's a good idea," Palmer agreed. "I have his number in my phone. I'll call him to make sure he's there."

"Good, we don't have any time to waste on this case. The sheriff wants it solved like yesterday."

She pulled her cell phone out from her pocket. "Or at least before there are any other murders."

"That's for sure."

Palmer called him before starting the car and confirmed that Jim Buchanan was indeed at home. Then she maneuvered quickly around some cars in downtown Lafayette on her way there, driving much faster than the speed limit as the driving conditions were good—the streets were dry and the sun was shining. The murders had taken on more of a sense of urgency now that a serial killer or some homicidal maniac was on the loose. Where would he strike next? That was the question that was going unanswered.

O'Mahern wasn't troubled by Palmer's driving. He too wanted to get there as soon as possible to get some questions answered. He didn't think of Buchanan as a viable suspect, but he didn't want to rule him out just the same. One thing he learned over the years was that anyone was capable of murder.

They arrived at Buchanan's home, and he answered the door promptly since he knew they were on the way there. He was dressed casually in a long-sleeved blue-and-white striped shirt and denim jeans. After greetings were exchanged, the three went to the weapons display room.

"Our coroner has ruled that a tomahawk could have been used for the second murder," O'Mahern said. "You have some of those, don't you?"

"A couple. They're over there."

He pointed to a case in the center of the room. The case was much like those used in jewelry stores to show off their goods; it had two shelves and was full of Indian weapons, including tomahawks, war clubs, knives, arrowheads, spearheads, arrows, and a bow. One of the arrows looked just like the one used in the third murder.

"Here is my collection of Native American weaponry. As you can see, I don't have a lot of them, but more of a sampling of them. However, they are originals and some are quite expensive."

"Do you mind if we take a closer look at them?"

"Sure. I'll have to get the key to unlock the cabinet."

Buchanan left the room to get the key.

"At least he keeps them under lock and key," Palmer said.

"Yeah, but all someone would have to do to get them is to break the glass."

Palmer nodded. "True."

Buchanan returned and unlocked the case. He removed the two tomahawks that he had. He handed one to Palmer and one to O'Mahern.

"That one was used by the Shawnee," he said about the one he gave to Palmer.

"How do you know that?" she asked.

"The Shawnee liked to have a spike on the opposite side from the blade."

"So Tecumseh might have had one like this?"

"I'm sure he did. He was the chief of the Shawnee and one of the most famous Indians who ever lived."

"How about this one?" O'Mahern asked and pointed at another in the case.

"That kind of tomahawk is more of a generic one. It was used by many different tribes."

"Would you mind if we had them analyzed?" O'Mahern asked. He could give them to Forensics to see if they had any trace of blood, and he could give it to the coroner to match to the wound.

Buchanan put his hands on his hips and said, "Are you considering me a suspect, Detective?" He was now getting annoyed that even he would be considered as a suspect, and it showed on his face with a scowl.

"I consider everyone as suspects. Where were you this morning about dawn?"

"There was another murder this morning?"

"Yeah. We think it occurred sometime after dawn. A man was killed with an arrow."

"Oh boy. You mean we have a serial killer here?"

"Yes. Now where were you this morning?"

"I was in bed until about dawn. Then I went to my favorite place for coffee, Starbucks. I had breakfast with my friend Don Kirkland. You can call him if you wish."

"We will."

"If your alibi doesn't pan out, we'll come back for these later with a search warrant."

"Be my guest. They've been in that case for years. I've never used them for anything." Buchanan said, and his baritone voice increased in volume.

Palmer jumped in. "Okay, okay. The latest weapon used this morning in a murder was a bow and arrow, much like the arrow you have in your display case. Do you know of anyone who makes their own arrows?"

"I don't know of any of the Indian reenactors who make their own arrows. Some vendors sell homemade arrows at the Feast of the Hunters' Moon."

"Do you have a list of those vendors?" Palmer asked.

"Sure, I can give you a list of them and their contact numbers from the festival last month."

"That might be helpful," O'Mahern said.

"Let me go make a copy of the list."

"Thanks, Jim," Palmer said.

As Buchanan went to his office, O'Mahern asked Palmer, "How do you think this list of vendors will help us out?"

"I don't know exactly, but it might give us a lead on someone. We could at least investigate those who make those types of arrows to see if it might be one of them. If they make the arrows and sell them, they probably sell all those other weapons that were used. That would give them the means to commit the murders."

"I guess. We'll give it to someone else to research. I'm not in the mood to do a needle-in-the-haystack search for leads."

"That's your decision."

"I'll give it to someone at this evening's briefing unless someone comes to me earlier needing some more work."

Buchanan returned with a copy of the list, which contained more than a hundred vendors. He handed the list to Palmer. "You can rule out the food vendors on this list. I've put a star next to a couple I know who sell those types of arrows. Not many vendors sell them. I just don't know all of the ones who do. I also wrote the number of my friend who can confirm my whereabouts this morning."

"That will be helpful," Palmer said. "Thanks so much for your help."

"Anything I can do."

Buchanan let them out. On the way to the car, Palmer called the number he had given for his friend. The friend confirmed that he had breakfast with Buchanan. His alibi was solid. Palmer never thought of Buchanan as a suspect; O'Mahern did.

O'Mahern got a call on his cell phone. When he looked at the number that was calling him, it rang a bell. It was the psychic.

Chapter 34

Washington DC, February 7, 2001

Robert Pickett finally woke up around 9:00 a.m. at the old cut-rate hotel in downtown Washington DC, a five-story hotel that had been around for more than a hundred years. He turned on the television to watch the news and weather while he slowly woke up; the television was a large old analog set that sat on a cheap old tan dresser made of pressed wood. The off-white walls brightened up the place even though the drapes were still closed. A couple of pictures of Washington DC monuments adorned the walls. One was of the White House, his destination later in the day.

After watching the news for a few minutes, he went into the bathroom to take a shower and get ready for the day. He flipped on the light, and the yellow-painted walls shone like the sun. Pickett wiped the sleep matter from his brown eyes and threw some water on his dry, wrinkled white face to help him wake up. Then he brushed his yellowing teeth with whitening toothpaste, stained from thirty years of smoking. He thought the toothpaste would help make his smile brighter and help him get a better job. Pickett then looked in the mirror at his scraggly beard and hair. He was running low on money and could no longer afford a haircut, so he cut his hair using a dog trimmer. He pulled it out of his bag, plugged it in, and started trimming himself. He wanted to look good when he spoke to the president later about his lawsuit against the Internal Revenue Service. Pickett had worked for a dozen years for the IRS but left under pressure from his boss. Afterward, he decided he had a case against his boss, the IRS, and his union, the National Treasury Employees Union; so he filed lawsuits against all of them. The federal court in Indiana had recently given him a month to show why his remaining lawsuit should not be dismissed. After the first two lawsuits were dismissed, he threatened to commit suicide, and his mother had him committed for psychiatric help. That was a year ago.

After dressing in a cheap black suit, Pickett ate a breakfast bar he had brought along on his trip from Evansville, Indiana. Then he loaded the Smith & Wesson .38-caliber revolver he had purchased the year before, a used black police revolver that was in good condition. He bought it after being accepted on an instant background check in a gun store in his hometown. He only intended to use it if necessary to gain access to the president.

A bright sunny day with temperatures in the thirties greeted him as he left the motel and got into his dark blue 1990 Buick Skylark. He started the car and let it warm up for a minute before proceeding. The ex-IRS worker lit up a generic cigarette while it warmed up as he could no longer afford the Marlboros that he had smoked when he worked. Like him, the car was getting old and needed to warm up to run properly. He felt he was younger than the car in comparative ages, kind of like a dog in which a year for a dog is like seven for a human. Since his car had more than one hundred thousand miles, he thought of it as being equal to one hundred in human years. He would turn forty-eight this year.

Pickett drove to the White House and parked along Nineteenth Street two blocks away. He ignored the parking meter, figuring that if he got a ticket, he wouldn't pay it anyway. He only passed a few people on his way to the White House, none of which made any greeting to him, and he ignored them as well. Pickett was deep in thought on what he would tell the president.

When he arrived at the entrance to the White House, he went up to the entrance. "I'd like to see the president," he asked.

"Do you have an appointment?"

"No."

"Then that's not possible, sir. You will need to call his office to request an audience with the president."

"Oh," Picket responded. He turned around and walked away. He decided to walk around the black picket fence that surrounded the building before trying to enter another entrance to the White House.

At about 11:30 a.m., Pickett was getting cold and took up a position at the southwest corner. He was getting frustrated that he just couldn't go into the White House and talk to the president. He pulled out his pistol, aimed, and fired three shots in the direction of the Executive Mansion; but the bullets harmlessly went into some trees that blocked his view of the building.

Secret Service agents heard the shots and quickly rushed to the area. They saw Pickett trying to hide in some bushes in the Ellipse.

"Sir, come out of the bushes," an agent yelled. "We want to talk to you."

Pickett waved his gun in the air and replied, "I'm not giving up."

"Sir, we just want to talk."

"Oh, no you don't."

"What's the problem, sir?"

There was silence. The agents communicated with superiors and tried to figure out what to do next.

Meanwhile, Washington Police showed up with more units. A police helicopter hovered high above the scene; television crews began showing up. Crowds began forming. The agents decided to try a more direct approach with Pickett.

"Sir, please toss the gun out."

"No, I need it. I need it to kill myself." Pickett waved the .38 revolver around and then held the gun to his mouth.

"Okay, sir. Calm down."

He nodded. "Okay, okay."

"Drop the gun!" an agent commanded.

Pickett then put the gun to his temple. His hand shook.

"We need to take him down," one agent whispered to the other.

"I agree. Let's move in on him."

The agents moved forward. Pickett lowered the gun and pointed it in their direction. The agents stopped.

"Drop the gun!"

Pickett failed to do as directed. He aimed the gun at them; the gun shook in his hand.

One of the agents targeted Pickett's leg. He fired and hit Pickett in the knee. Pickett went down and dropped his gun as he did. They rushed him and took him into custody.

Pickett was taken to the hospital and treated for his wound. He had to undergo vascular surgery and a psychiatric evaluation.

President George W. Bush was at the White House residence at that time but was not in any real danger, although it was determined that a bullet from the gun could have reached the White House if Pickett had aimed it properly.

A court later sentenced Pickett to three years imprisonment on July 2001 in connection with the incident.

George W. Bush, who was elected in 2000 as the nation's forty-third president, had dodged Tecumseh's curse.

Chapter 35

Present Day

"Detective O'Mahern," he answered his cell phone although he knew it was the psychic.

"I've had another vision," Sandra Barksley said.

"Not another murder?"

"No, I saw a man that's tied up in a chair and a man with a gun and badge."

"A police officer?"

"No, he was a detective like you, I assume, because he wasn't wearing any police uniform. The badge was on his belt, just like yours."

"Do you think you could identify the officer or the guy tied up from photos?" O'Mahern asked.

"Maybe. I don't know. My visions are not that vivid. The detective was closer, but he had on a hat."

"What kind of hat?"

"It was a ball cap with a *P* on it?"

"Like Purdue?"

"Yeah."

"I'd like you to come down to the station to look at photos of some police officers."

"Sure, I could do that. I just don't know if I could identify the officer."

"That's okay. Like they say, nothing ventured, nothing gained."

"Okay, I'll be there soon."

After he hung up, he turned to Palmer. "That was our local psychic. She's had another vision. This time, she sees a man tied up along with a man with a badge."

"A police officer?"

"Detective, like us."

"Did she know who it was?"

"No. She's coming to the office to check out photos."

"Just because she saw a police officer doesn't mean he was killing the man. Maybe he was saving him."

"Right, unless she saw him actually torturing the guy."

Barksley soon arrived at the station to look at photos. After looking at all the police officers in the county, she came up with nothing. Then they showed her state police officers—still nothing. Then they showed her all the suspects in the case and pictures of some reenactors they had received from the historical society, but she didn't recognize any one of them from her visions.

"That's all the photos I wanted to show you," O'Mahern said.

"I'm sorry I didn't recognize anyone."

"That's okay. Call me if you get a clearer picture of this guy."

"I will," Barksley said and left.

After she left, O'Mahern turned to Palmer and asked, "That was a waste of time. Who have you got for us to interview?"

Palmer looked at the short list of suspects and replied, "I picked out a guy by the name of Hunter Jennings. He's an Indian reenactor and is part Indian."

"That must be the Hunter part."

"You're probably right. He lives in Battle Ground."

"That makes him a likely possibility since all the murders occurred there. Any priors?"

"Not much. The latest is a public intox charge last year in Lafayette."

"That's what he gets if he comes here and drinks too much. Are there any bars in Battle Ground?"

"No, but there's a restaurant that serves alcohol."

"That explains why he comes to Lafayette to drink. Is he married?"

"No. He's divorced."

"Let's go. I'll drive." He wanted to drive his own car just so he could smoke that day in it.

"Okay."

Knowing now where to go, O'Mahern pulled out of the parking lot and drove toward the bridge in West Lafayette to take Indiana 43 toward the town. O'Mahern used his cigarette lighter to light up a smoke; then he opened his window to let the smoke out.

"Must you?" Palmer said.

"Yeah. This case is driving me to smoke more."

"Uh-huh."

"What's this guy's age?"

"Fifty-seven."

"Any registered weapons?"

"Several. He has some hunting rifles and a handgun registered."

"Anything else I should know?"

"Not really. Have you heard from any of the other detectives?"

O'Mahern responded, "Nobody has come up with anything earth-shattering enough to call me today. And the sheriff wants this case solved as quickly as possible. He's already tired of the media coverage. He doesn't mind the locals, but those from Indy and Chicago are a real pain in the ass. They're like stalkers or worse—bloodsuckers."

"Yeah, they can be a pain," Palmer said. "I had one reporter all over me when I returned from lunch. She knew I was from Battle Ground. I told her that I couldn't talk to the press, and she didn't like that much."

"They've been bugging me too. They know I'm the lead detective in the case, so they want to hear it from the horse's mouth instead of our media spokesman or the sheriff. I'm glad I don't have to talk to the media. They sometimes get it wrong."

"Tell me about it."

A little farther down the road, they came upon the Trail of Death sign. "You know they're going to have to redo that Trail of Death since someone has started a new death trail right here in Battle Ground," commented O'Mahern.

"Yeah, at the rate this is going."

"Have you ever traveled along that trail?"

"No, but I've seen different parts of it along the Wabash. I think I'll put that on my to-do list."

"Oh, you have a bucket list?" queried O'Mahern.

"Sort of. I'd like to do some traveling. I'd like to see the Rockies, so I guess I could take that route to get to Kansas, then go beyond to Colorado. What's on your bucket list?"

"Catching this psycho is top on the list right now. After that, I wanna go to a Purdue bowl game if they make it this year. At the rate they're going, they should make it to a bowl. Not the Rose Bowl though. They aren't good enough for that."

"There's always the Old Oaken Bucket game with Indiana."

"Yeah, your school. We should win that one hands down."

"Wanna bet on that?"

"Twenty bucks, and I'll give you six points."

"You're on."

He turned his attention back to driving as they approached Battle Ground. "Where do we turn up here?"

"Go right at the next light," commented Palmer. "His house isn't far after that."

They arrived at an old farmhouse just out of town, a house painted white with green trim, which had little curb appeal as overgrown evergreens adorned either side of the front door and infringed on the entrance. Palmer went ahead and knocked on the door.

A man about six foot tall wearing a Purdue T-shirt and black sweats answered the door. He hadn't shaved in a couple of days, so it made his face darker than it already was. His long black hair was pulled back in a little ponytail at the back of his head.

"Hunter Jennings?" asked Palmer.

"Yeah, how can I help you?"

"Police." Palmer pulled up her dark blue sweater to show her badge. After introductions, he invited them in. The living room was messy with an Xbox sprawled on the floor, plates stacked up on the scratched oak cocktail table, and some clothes in disarray on the couch.

"Sorry, but the place is a mess," Jennings said, throwing the clothes into a laundry basket. "I'll move these clothes to the laundry room where they belong. Today is wash day."

As Jennings left the living room to take the laundry basket full of clothes away, the detectives started looking around curiously. O'Mahern examined the stack of magazines on the cocktail table: *National Geographic*, *Sports Illustrated*, and others. Palmer looked at the books Jennings had in an oak bookcase, most dealt with history, but one got her attention: *The Encyclopedia of Serial Killers*.

Jennings returned to the living room. "Have a seat, Detectives. What's this all about?"

O'Mahern sat on the worn blue-and-red-print couch while Palmer plopped down in a matching chair. Jennings sat in an old wooden rocking chair.

"We're investigating some crime," O'Mahern said. "So where were you this morning about daybreak?"

"So there was another murder this morning?"

"Yeah, just answer my questions."

Jennings nodded. "Okay. I woke up about that time. Then I fixed some breakfast and started doing my wash. I have the day off."

"Where do you work?"

"I'm an auctioneer and work mainly weekends for a number of different auction companies. I buy and sell things at auctions as well."

"Where were you Sunday night about dusk?"

"Here. I had an afternoon gig in Lafayette and came home about five p.m."

"How about Saturday night at dusk?"

Jennings looked out the front window and thought for a second. "I worked in the morning and afternoon. I got home about five that day too."

O'Mahern became silent as he thought about his answers, so Palmer asked, "So I understand you're an Indian reenactor at the Feast of the Hunters' Moon."

"That's right. Done that for ten years now ever since I got a divorce. Best move I ever made."

"Do you own a musket?" Palmer continued.

"Sure do. In fact, I have an original that I bought for a thou some years ago."

"Can we see it?"

"Sure, the gun cabinet is in my spare bedroom."

"We'll go with you," O'Mahern said.

They followed him to the small bedroom, which had no bed at all, but was being used as a storage room for his collection; it contained stacks of magazines, boxes of clothes, and a plethora of junk. Also in the room were a treadmill and a small flat-screen television for viewing while he worked out. He unlocked the gun cabinet containing the musket, several hunting rifles, a bow, and some arrows that appeared to match the arrow that killed the latest victim. As the door opened, a tomahawk fell out of it onto the floor.

"Let me see that tomahawk."

O'Mahern thought he had the murderer since Jennings had no alibi for the murders and had all the possible murder weapons. He examined the tomahawk and saw what he thought was some blood on the blade. "Mr. Jennings, I need you to come to our office to answer some questions. I'm taking this tomahawk in for our Forensics people to check it out."

"Why's that?"

"It looks like it has dried blood on it."

"It's not blood. It's fake blood."

"They will confirm that then."

"You can take me in, but I'm not answering any more of your questions without an attorney. I know my rights." His angular face turned red to reveal his anger.

O'Mahern looked at Palmer and rolled his eyes. He certainly didn't want Jennings to lawyer up at this point. That would make his job that much more difficult, but if the tomahawk turned up as the murder weapon, then he'd have the guy anyway. Palmer read him his Miranda rights.

"You can contact your lawyer once we get downtown," O'Mahern said.

Jennings kept quiet during the ride to downtown Lafayette; the detectives only talked about the weather and a snowstorm that would hit in a few days. Once they arrived at the sheriff's office, they put Jennings in an interview room after he called his attorney.

"I think he's hiding something," O'Mahern said, scratching his scalp.

"I agree, but we aren't going to get it from him."

"Maybe not. Get a search warrant for his house so we can go through it more carefully and see if we can find more incriminating evidence than the tomahawk."

"Will do."

Jennings's attorney showed up at police headquarters about thirty minutes after being called. Lester Mullins was known to represent criminals in the past and was not well liked by the department because of that. He was shown to the interview room by Palmer. The three were soon joined by O'Mahern.

"So what are you charging my client with?" Mullins said as he adjusted his light blue tie. The blue tie matched his eyes, and he had a full head of blond hair. He was a diminutive man of Norwegian descent.

"Murder times three if our search warrant turns up the necessary evidence to charge him, and I think it will."

"You should charge him or release him."

"As you know, we can hold him for twenty-four hours, so he's spending the night here," O'Mahern said. "I'd like to ask him some more questions."

"We've already decided not to answer any more of your questions."

"Okay, we're putting him in a holding cell, and you can go back to your office. We will contact you tomorrow about charging him, or we'll release him."

"Don't say anything to them," Mullins warned his client.

"Right," Jennings concurred.

O'Mahern was now certain that he had the killer because of his reluctance to answer any of his questions, lack of alibi, and possible murder weapons. Palmer wasn't so certain.

Chapter 36

Longboat Key, September 11, 2001

O n Tuesday morning about 6:00 a.m., President George W. Bush awoke in his VIP suite at the Colony Beach and Tennis Resort on Longboat Key, Florida, a key near Sarasota in western Florida. He looked out his window at the beach facing the Gulf of Mexico; the western sky was being transformed from black to blue by the rising sun. The dark blue in the sky was much like the dominant color in his room as the bedspread was blue with shells on it and the painting above the bed was of the ocean—even the carpet was dark blue. Bush was going to take his morning jog along the beautiful beach before breakfast. A jog along the beach would be easier for the Secret Service to provide him with more privacy and security than a jog along the road.

As the president got dressed in his sweats and sneakers, a white panel van showed up at the entrance of the hotel. Two men of Middle East descent got out of the van and entered the lobby, one dressed in the traditional clothes of a Middle Eastern man with a white dress called a thoub and a head cover called a shumagg, the other man clothed like a Floridian with tan shorts and a short-sleeved white dress shirt. He also carried a television camera on one shoulder.

When they entered the hotel lobby, they were greeted by three Secret Service agents, who became very suspicious of them right away because of their nationality. Two of the agents reached inside their sport jackets and put their hands on their pistols in case they were needed immediately.

"Can we help you?" asked one of the agents.

"We are here to see the president," the man in the Arab clothing said. "He was going to give us a poolside interview this morning."

"I'm sorry, but you need an appointment, and the president has no appointments until later this morning. What is your name?"

"Joshua Avakian."

The agent looked down at a list of names. "I don't see your name on this list at all. You will have to leave."

"Tell the president that I would like to get an interview with him sometime."

"Who are you with?"

"I'm a reporter for the Arab Television Service. Here is my card."

"I will let the president know."

The two men turned around and left.

A couple of hours later, two jets slammed into the Twin Towers in New York City. Another jet crashed into the Pentagon, and another crashed in a field in Pennsylvania. The nation was under attack by terrorists from the Middle East. The Secret Service thought that terrorists were testing the security of the president when they showed up that morning in light of the day's events. They considered it a viable assassination attempt.

President Bush, who was elected in 2000, had dodged Tecumseh's curse again, but America had suffered a huge loss. Nearly three thousand Americans lost their lives that day. The United States considered itself at war with terrorists.

Chapter 37

"Since the state police headquarters is so close to our latest suspect's house, I called them to go collect that musket and any other evidence at his house. While they're doing that, we will go visit that Order of Hawks' place. Where is it?" said O'Mahern.

"On South Sixteenth Street," Palmer responded.

"Let's go. You drive."

"Okay."

It was almost 6:00 p.m., so they didn't have much time to check out the lead since the task force was meeting in about an hour. Palmer took only about ten minutes to get to the building, a gray metal building located in a residential area not far from the county fairgrounds. There were several cars parked outside, so a number of members were there. O'Mahern hoped the president was there, but he'd talk with anyone who knew the victims.

They walked in the lobby and straight to the bar, where everyone was located. They were all drinking, and some were eating dinner.

Palmer asked the bartender, "Is your president here tonight?"

"Yeah, he sure is," she responded and pointed to him. "That's him at the end of the bar."

The president was a big guy, probably all of three hundred pounds and over six feet in height, dressed in a Purdue sweatshirt that stretched tightly over his belly and some of his black jeans. He was drinking a large beer on tap.

O'Mahern led the way over to him and flashed his badge as he came up to him. "Detective O'Mahern, and this is Palmer. We have some questions for you, Mr. President. What's your name?"

"Doug Verse. What's this about?"

"We're investigating the recent murders in Battle Ground, and it just happens that all three victims had the same tattoo, a hawk that looks just like the hawk in your logo. We were wondering if they were members of your club: George Baen, Patrick Daviess, and Monty Wentworth."

"Monty's dead too?"

"Yes, he was killed this morning," O'Mahern said.

"God, I hadn't heard about that one. We went to Patrick Daviess's showing earlier today and plan to go to George's tomorrow. They were all members here, but not very active. They might come once a month or so."

"Did they hang out together?" O'Mahern asked.

Verse responded, "They knew each other, but they didn't come here together unless it was for a special event."

"Have they been members long?"

"I don't know that without looking at our records."

"Please get their records so we can look at them as well."

"I usually don't share those records."

"This is a murder investigation. Don't make me go get a subpoena, or otherwise we'll be taking a very close look at this place for other things, and you'll be shut down considering those illegal gaming machines you have in the back room," threatened O'Mahern. He didn't know the machines were there; he was just bluffing.

"I'll go get those records for you right now." Verse shrugged, swiveled around on his barstool, and went to the office.

"And get us a list of your members as well."

"Right."

"What do you think?" O'Mahern asked Palmer, who had been quiet during the interview.

"I don't think there's anything unless they have some secret society that we don't know about."

"I'll ask him."

Verse returned with many papers. "Here's a copy of each of their records for your files and a membership list."

"Thanks. Were they part of any secret group that you might have?"

"You're confusing us with the Masons," replied Verse. "We don't have anything like them. We're a fraternal organization that supports freedom, God and country, and other patriotic things like that."

"Okay. Just wanted to know."

"You're welcome, Detective."

"Here's my card in case you hear something."

"I'll keep my ears open."

"Thanks," Palmer said.

On the way back to the station, O'Mahern looked at the three records and didn't see anything that jumped out at him. "The connection is there, but I don't see how it helps this investigation," he said.

"Not unless they all pissed off the same guy at the club and he's out for revenge."

"Unlikely. I think this is a dead end. We'll have someone go through this membership list to see if it turns up any suspects worth interviewing."

"Do you see Hunter Jennings on the membership list?"

"No."

"Did you have someone check out the tattoo parlors?"

"Yeah. Maybe they'll have a report for us at the meeting."

At 7:00 p.m., all the detectives and sheriff's deputies assigned to the case met in the conference room for an update on the multiple murder case. Much of the chatter before O'Mahern showed up was about the suspect he had brought in earlier in the afternoon. They thought the case might have been solved, and he was going to make an announcement to that effect.

"I wish I had some good news about this case," O'Mahern started. "We had a guy that was right for these murders in Battle Ground, but it turns out the tomahawk we recovered wasn't the murder weapon after all. The red stuff I saw on it turned out to be fake blood. The guy lawyered up on us, and we let him go a little while ago. So we are back to square one on this case. Have any of you got any leads?"

"I haven't got any good leads, but how did the media find out so much information about this case?" asked a deputy sheriff.

"What information did they reveal?" asked O'Mahern.

"On the six o'clock news, the local channel called the killer the Savage Slasher because he had killed with a musket, a tomahawk, and an arrow. I thought that information wasn't given to them."

"I can understand the arrow because many people saw that in the last victim, but we didn't tell the media about the musket or the tomahawk, so we must have a leak somewhere. Did any of you talk to the media?"

There was silence in the room.

"Oh well, shit happens. I'm not really worried about that. I'm worried more about catching this guy before he kills again. Anyone got any real good suspects at this point?"

Everyone was looking around, seeing if someone was going to raise their hand or speak up. Nobody did.

"Well then. We really are back to square one. Hopefully, we won't have any more murders. Does anyone need some additional work for this case?" Two detectives held their hands up. "See me after the meeting. Any questions?"

"Have we connected the victims yet?" one of the detectives asked.

"Just the tattoos. Did that turn up anything, Bo?"

"Dead end. Turns out there were three different tattoo parlors who did the work."

"No other commonalities other than the tattoos and they are part of the Order of Hawks. I'm going to go through your reports and see if I can link them together. I think that will be the key in solving these murders. We will meet again tomorrow morning at ten a.m. The FBI is sending in a team from Washington, so they will brief us then. Now go home and get some sleep."

After the meeting, Palmer left while her partner met with two detectives and gave them some more possible suspects to interview on Wednesday. O'Mahern then went back to his desk to try and put the pieces together. He was downhearted and really wanted to get a break in the case. The national media had already descended on the northwestern Indiana city like flies on cow piles and were constantly pressing for interviews and any information they could squeeze out of the police, relatives, or others.

He started looking through all the information the detectives had gathered from their interviews to see if there was any more connections to the three men who had been murdered. O'Mahern had another report from Forensics from earlier in the day about some footprints that turned up by the creek. The techs thought the footprints were made by moccasins. He saw that Palmer had sent them back out to the monument and wondered what prompted her to do that. She certainly hadn't talked to him about it. He was thinking about doing an all-nighter, but he was tired. He figured he'd work as late as his body could take, which wasn't much longer.

Sheriff Andrews closed the door to his office as he left to go home for the night. He stopped by O'Mahern's desk on his way out. "How's it going with the case?"

"Nowhere yet."

"Did that psychic give you anything?"

"Yeah, but what she gave us hasn't helped us. She thinks a police officer may be involved in it because she saw a detective in her vision. We had her look through all the photos we had of police officers we have on file, but she didn't recognize any of them."

"That's too bad."

"I'm afraid if we don't find someone soon, somebody else is going to die."

"I know. Hopefully, this team from the FBI will turn up something," the sheriff said as he left.

"Yeah."

Chapter 38

Tbilisi, Georgia, May 10, 2005

Tuesday turned out to be a warm day in the former Soviet republic of Georgia. Vladimir Arutyunian had come to Freedom Square to hear President George W. Bush and Georgian President Mikheil Saakashvili speak. As he stood in the crowd, he got too warm and started sweating, his black leather jacket and black shirt absorbing the sun like a sponge soaking up water, his full head of lush black hair toasting his head. He wore dark sunglasses to shade his eyes from the bright sunlight. In his hand, he snuggly held a hand grenade wrapped in a tartan handkerchief to conceal it as he waited for the right time to throw it.

President Bush took the podium, his dark blue suit and lighter blue tie contrasting with the red-and-white decorations behind him, giving the scene a USA patriotic look as the people behind Bush were dressed in all-white clothing. Shortly after he began speaking, Arutyunian pulled the pin from the deadly device and threw it toward the Georgian leader, who was sitting about fifty feet from Bush.

The hand grenade landed with a thump in the stands near President Saakashvili and his wife, First Lady of Georgia Sandra Roelofs, and First Lady of the United States Laura Bush. The startled trio sprang up from their seats and rushed off the stage. Fortunately, the device did not explode.

Security officials ran to the grenade and safely took it away. The handkerchief was so tightly wrapped around the device that it failed to go off.

In the confusion, Arutyunian swiftly made his way out of the crowd and escaped.

After the incident, Georgian officials asked the Americans for help in identifying the man who threw the grenade, so the FBI was called upon to assist with the investigation. When FBI agents studied photos of the crowd, they saw an American professor with a long camera lens high up in the stands who might have taken photos that could help in the investigation. They contacted the educator, and sure enough, he had a photo of an unidentified man in the crowd holding the tartan-wrapped grenade. They turned the photo over to Georgian officials for identification. Georgian Interior Minister Vano Merabishvili issued the photo to the press on July 18, 2005, for information leading to the arrest of the man in the photo for a reward equivalent to $80,000.

Two days later, a man called the police hotline: "I know who that man is. He is Vladimir Arutyunian. He lives with his mother in Vashlijvari."

With that tip, Zurab Kvlividze, the head of the interior ministry's counterintelligence team, took a team of agents to Vashlijvari. The team arrived that evening and surrounded the old two-story house. Officer Kvlividze knocked on the front door and said, "Police, open up!"

Nobody answered.

"Break it down," Kvlividze ordered.

They busted in the door, and Arutyunian started shooting at them with a Russian submachine gun. He hit Kvlividze in the chest and wounded a couple of other agents in a hail of bullets. Arutyunian bowled over an officer as he attempted to escape out the back door, running toward the woods.

Agents continued firing at him and finally hit him in the leg, but he ducked into the woods just the same and soon disappeared. Kvlividze died in the skirmish.

The Georgian Special Forces were called to comb the woods. They soon found Arutyunian and took him into custody.

Two months later, a United States federal grand jury indicted Arutyunian for the attempted murder of President Bush.

In January 2006, a Georgian court tried him. At one appearance in court, he entered the courtroom with his mouth sewn shut; he had somehow got a hold of a needle and thread in jail. The court found Arutyunian guilty of the attempted assassinations of Bush and the Georgian president and the murder of Officer Kvlividze. They sentenced Arutyunian to life in prison without parole.

President Bush, who was first elected in 2000, finished his second term of office on January 20, 2009; he could not run for a third term because it is no longer allowed. FDR was the last president to serve more than two terms. He had avoided Tecumseh's curse three times during his presidency. The curse seemed to be over—or was it?

Chapter 39

Present Day

On the way home, Palmer decided she needed to do more research on the Battle of Tippecanoe, and the best place for that was at the Tippecanoe Public Library. She remembered there was a room there containing Indiana books and nearly every book ever written about the local area, including Battle Ground. She looked at the clock in her car as she started it and figured she better hustle to get there before they closed in twenty minutes. On the way to the library, she noticed the first signs of Christmas, a grand old home in downtown Lafayette decorated with hundreds of Christmas lights and a couple of lighted deer in the front yard. She hadn't bought any Christmas presents yet; it was the least of her worries right now.

When she arrived at the library, a large modern building in downtown Lafayette, she headed straight to the Swezey Room of Indiana History in the rear of the library. An announcement was made: "The library will close in ten minutes. Please bring your materials for checkout to the main counter now. Thank you."

She rushed to the room at the rear of the library, a room that contained six tables with two chairs at each table and surrounded on three sides by books rising about ten feet. She started at one end and began looking for a shelf containing local books. After several minutes, she found it. The book was titled *The Battle of Tippecanoe*, published in 1900. She looked at the table of contents and decided it contained all the information she needed about the battle. Just then another announcement was made: "The library is now closed. Please proceed to the checkout."

As she left the room, a young woman at the desk just outside the doorway to the room got up from her seat and said to her, "I'm sorry, but that's a reference book and needs to stay in that room."

Palmer pulled her brown jacket away to show her badge. "I need this book to do some research tonight. I'll bring it back in the morning," she explained.

"Well, I'll have to get the head librarian to approve that request."

Palmer reached into her pocket and handed her a business card. "Here's my card. Just give it to her and tell her I need it for research for this serial killer case I'm working on."

"Oh, I'll give it to her. Just wait here a sec."

The woman departed through a door marked Staff Only and into the catacombs of the library, away from the bookshelves.

When she disappeared from sight, Palmer didn't wait around for an answer and quickly left. As she went through the first set of front doors, the alarm went off.

Two girls at the front desk looked in her direction. Palmer flashed her badge at them and proceeded out the final set of doors to her car that was sitting just outside the door. She'd become a thief in the night while adding some excitement into the normally dull and quiet library.

The girls looked at each other in a puzzled way, not knowing what to do. Generally, they'd call the police and report the theft, but she was the police. The head librarian showed up at the front desk and explained to them what had happened. Then she decided to call the sheriff's department to lodge a complaint about the officer.

Meanwhile in Battle Ground, Bill Harrison was about to go to bed when his doorbell rang. He opened the front door of his one-story ranch home and was surprised to see a gun pointed at him.

"What's the gun for?" he asked as he raised his hands in the air.

"To make you do what I tell you to do," the copper-faced man in the black coat said.

"What do you want?"

"Just shut up and do what I tell you to do."

"Ah, whatever you say." Harrison thought he recognized the man, but he wasn't sure. He figured this must be a home invasion. "What do you want?"

"Oh, I want to kill you, but I don't want to make it too quickly."

"Why are you doing this to me?"

"Let's just say it's revenge."

"Revenge for what?" Harrison was really confused now.

"For being a relative of President William Henry Harrison."

"What on earth are you talking about?"

"Oh, he was responsible for killing hundreds of my brothers."

"That was a long time ago."

"Yeah, it was. But my people have long memories."

"What can I do to rectify what he did?'

"Die. I'm tired of your questions."

With that, the visitor put a pair of handcuffs on him and tied a cloth tightly around his mouth so he couldn't say another word. It would also silence the screams.

When Palmer arrived at home, she grabbed a vitaminwater out of the refrigerator and sat in her most comfortable chair for reading, a light tan chair and a half with several pillows on either side. The chair was in her living room, containing a matching couch and an end table between the couch and chair. They pointed toward a thirty-two-inch flat-screen television that sat upon a glass table. The room also had a large white bookcase sitting against one wall that contained books and some knickknacks.

She took a sip of water and started reading the book slowly and carefully as if she was going to be tested on the material. She arrived at a page containing the names of the officers who served on the American force at the battle. She looked down the list and found the same last names of three men who were slain by the serial killer: Daviess, Baen, and Wentworth. Suddenly, she realized the connection between the three victims: they were all related to someone from the Battle of Tippecanoe. She opened up her laptop, a Dell computer, and started doing some research online. In her search, she came across Tecumseh's curse in About.com: "American History." The article talked about the first president who died from the curse: William Henry Harrison. That's when it suddenly dawned on her who the next victim could be. She closed her laptop and called her partner with the news, although it was now past midnight.

O'Mahern was fast asleep in his bed when the cell phone woke him up after about ten seconds of playing his favorite island song, which reminded him of the Bahamas. "O'Mahern."

"Were you asleep?"

"Yeah, I usually sleep at night."

"Sorry. I think I've figured out the killer's next target."

"And who might that be?"

"I think it's going to be Bill Harrison, the president of the historical society."

"Why's that?"

"I've been doing research on the battle, and the murderer has been killing people with the same name as those Americans who fought in the battle. They must have been descendants of those men."

"Interesting."

"Plus, there's Tecumseh's curse."

"Curse?"

"Yeah. Supposedly, the Shawnee Prophet or Tecumseh put a curse on William Henry Harrison and the presidency of the United States after being defeated at the Battle of Tippecanoe. When Harrison became president, he died exactly one month after being inaugurated into office. Bill Harrison was elected to his office exactly a month ago today."

"That all sounds a little far-fetched, but not as bizarre as a ghost doing the murders. You better call him to see if he's all right."

"Will do."

"Then call me back and let me know what you find out."

She looked up Harrison's number in the Lafayette phone book and called his home. The phone rang three times, then a recorder came on. She hung up without leaving a message. She called O'Mahern back.

"He's not answering, so I'm going over there now."

"Now? Why don't you wait until morning."

"No, I need to go now. Today is exactly a month after the day he took office, just like the president. He could already be dead."

"I didn't think the day started until after my first cup of coffee."

"Very funny. You can stop and get one on the way down there."

"I will. Where does he live?"

"Battle Ground."

"Of course, why did I ask. What's the address?"

"He lives on 225 just after you turn off of 43."

"Okay. But my TomTom likes an address."

"It's the first house on the right after you turn."

"Very well. I know I can find it then. See you there in a little."

She decided to call the town marshal and asked him to go there because he would be there in minutes while it would take her about fifteen minutes to get there. All she got was a recording. She had his cell phone on her phone, so she called it—again a recording.

Palmer called the Tippecanoe County Sheriff's dispatcher. "Do you have any units near Battle Ground?"

"No, but we could ask the state police, which has an office nearby."

"That's right. Yeah. Have the state police send a unit to the first house on the right side of 225 after you turn off of 43. Bill Harrison lives there. Tell them he may be the next target of the serial killer, and we need to take him into protective custody immediately. I'll be there as fast as my car will get me there in the meantime."

"Will do. I'll also dispatch a backup unit from our department."

"Great idea."

Palmer literally ran out the door of her house, flipping the front door closed as she flew out. She ran to her car and leaped in it. She hit the throttle as if it was some kind of drag race, the tires yelling on the pavement. She had second thoughts on the maneuver after she squealed the tires that late at night, but she didn't care. Time was of the essence. Palmer was tired, but finding out who might be the next victim gave her an adrenaline rush. She sped down Interstate 65 in her Chevrolet Capri as if it was some kind of Grand Prix circuit. The expressway was nearly deserted at this hour, except for some eighteen wheelers headed to Chicago or Indianapolis in the opposite direction. As she drove, she hoped she wasn't too late. The surreptitious murderer had struck at either sunset or sunrise. The local newspaper had dubbed him the Battle Ground Murderer since all the murders had occurred in or near the small town. She arrived at Bill Harrison's house in about fifteen minutes. An empty state police unit sat in front of the house.

She got out of her car and approached the house quickly. Then she heard several gun blasts and saw light flashes coming from inside the house. *Oh my god, I'm too late,* she thought. Instead of barging through the front door like the cavalry, she nervously withdrew her pistol and went over to the front window to see if she could see what was going on since the drapes were open slightly. What she saw was Marshal Redbird sitting on the floor next to the wall. Blood was streaming from his shoulder. She also saw Bill Harrison tied up to a dining room chair. She entered the front door with her gun lowered and pointed at the ground. As she entered, she saw the state policeman lying facedown, motionless on the floor. Blood was oozing out of a head wound and forming a pool on the floor.

"What happened?" she asked.

"The killer ran that way," Redbird said as he rose to his feet. He pointed to the back door, which was wide open.

Harrison mumbled something through the towel around his mouth, but it wasn't understandable.

Palmer ran to the back door and outside. She looked around and saw nothing but darkness. No movement.

She came back into the house, and the marshal had risen to his feet. Palmer pulled out her phone and hit a speed dial to dispatch.

The marshal pointed his gun at her. "Drop the phone and your weapon, Detective," he ordered.

"What are you doing?"

"Kick your weapon over here."

Palmer folded up her phone and put it in her pocket. Then she dropped her gun on the floor and booted it over to him. She remembered that the psychic had said the policeman in her vision had a hat with *P* on it, like the one the marshal was wearing.

"Don't tell me. You're the serial killer?" she asked in a surprised tone.

"Yeah, that's right. And you're my next victim."

Just then O'Mahern came charging through the front door. The marshal turned his gun on him and fired several times.

One round hit O'Mahern on the right hand. It made his shot go off to the right and made his gun go flying. The other bullet hit him on the right chest and made him fall backward to the floor from the force of the shot.

Palmer, who was standing barely five feet away from the marshal, gave a swift karate kick to the marshal's gun hand. His gun went flying through the air. She followed up with another kick to his groin. Redbird bent over from the pain. She then hit him in the back of the neck with a karate chop. He dropped to the ground. Palmer figured that she had done him in, so she took the handcuffs from her belt to put them on him. As she reached down to grab his arm, he rolled over and swiped her leg with a bowie knife. Blood spurted from the cut on the back of her leg just below the knee. She fell in extreme pain.

The marshal rose up and was about to drive the big blade into her torso when a bullet struck him on the same shoulder. He fell backward to the floor. Palmer looked over at her partner and just smiled. O'Mahern had managed to get off a shot with his derringer from his prone position on the floor. Palmer roughly cuffed Redbird, who moaned. O'Mahern called for an ambulance.

"Now you're under arrest," she said.

Later that morning at St. Elizabeth's Hospital East in Lafayette, Sheriff Joshua Andrews entered the room of his two injured detectives. A bouquet of fresh-cut flowers on the table between them brightened up the stark-white hospital room. O'Mahern was reading the newspaper, which had just been delivered to his room. Palmer was reading a detective novel.

"How are you guys doing?" the sheriff asked.

"Not bad, Sheriff," said O'Mahern.

"Just fine," Palmer added. "How is that state cop doing?"

"He'll survive. Although the bullet went through his head, it didn't hit any vital areas, and he's showing signs of recovering."

"That's good."

"So how did you figure out Harrison was the next victim?" the sheriff asked while looking at O'Mahern.

"She did, not me."

Palmer explained how she borrowed a book from the library and researched it, which led her to Harrison.

"You need to return that book ASAP. They called and complained about that. Considering that it led to you figuring out where he was going to hit next and solved the case, I'll overlook it this time. I don't like my officers breaking the law to solve crimes even if it was a minor infraction."

"Yes, sir. It will never happen again."

"Okay. Well, I thought about how you two did together. Maybe I'll keep you together as partners."

O'Mahern and Palmer looked at each other and thought that's not what they really wanted. O'Mahern then remembered the movie *The Odd Couple*. Palmer sighed.

Chapter 40

Present Day

On Friday morning, Sheriff Joshua Andrews opened the door to his office and called out, "O'Mahern, Palmer, my office."

Whenever he did that, it usually meant someone was in trouble, so the two detectives looked quizzically at each other. Both wondered what the chief wanted. Palmer straightened her purple satin blouse, which was crumpled up from sitting at her desk.

As they entered his office, the sheriff moved around his large oak desk and sat on his oversized leather chair; he motioned for O'Mahern and Palmer to take a seat.

"I wanted to pass on to you that Marshal Redbird came to a plea agreement with the prosecutor last night, and he'll be serving the rest of his life behind bars," the sheriff told them.

"Well, that's good, but he deserves the death sentence," O'Mahern commented.

"Yeah," Palmer agreed.

"Well, it saves the county a whole bunch of money and trouble convicting him of the three murders, attempted murder, criminal confinement, and other crimes," the sheriff explained.

"That's good," O'Mahern said.

"It turns out that he was related to a Potawatami Indian by the name of Chief Cardinal, who was shipped to Kansas during the Trail of Death march there in 1838."

"That's interesting," Palmer said.

"Oh, I get it. A cardinal is a redbird, hence the name," Palmer deduced.

"You're right. I've decided to reorganize the department and create a homicide division. You two will be it. Jackson, I'm promoting you to lieutenant. You'll get a pay raise too. Julie, you're his assistant, and you'll get a small raise as well. I'm doing this for several reasons. The raises are a small way of rewarding you for your work in the serial killer case. You'll be getting an award for that later today from the county commissioners, so you'll have to go back home to get a sport coat and tie on, Jackson. You're attire is just fine, Julie."

"Could I possibly get my hair done for it?" Julie asked as she flipped her locks.

"Sure. The ceremony is at one p.m., so you can do that during your lunch hour."

"Thanks, sir."

"Can I get my hair done as well?" said O'Mahern.

The sheriff ignored his quip and went on. "I'll be assigning you two other detectives to work in this division starting next week as well. When you don't have a current murder case, you'll be digging into cold cases. In fact, your first case will be a cold one in which some DNA evidence has linked us to a suspect, but you need to dig further to build a case against this guy. Here's the folder. You'll work at your existing work stations until the office is rearranged over the weekend with your own section at one end of the room. Any questions?"

"What do you want us to do with the cases we're working on now?" O'Mahern said.

"Just give me the folders, and I'll take care of them. Right now, you have only one case. This cold one."

"Sounds good to me," Palmer said in relief. She had been given a drug-dealing case to work on before the murders that she wasn't having much luck solving. Murder was a lot more interesting to her. She felt working with O'Mahern again was okay as long as he quit trying to hit on her all the time. She really didn't want to get involved with someone in the department, especially her boss.

O'Mahern and Palmer shook the sheriff's hand and thanked him for the new assignment. As they returned to their desks, O'Mahern commented, "And I thought we were going to get our asses chewed."

"Yeah, it was good news instead. What do you want me to do first in this new case?"

Edwards Brothers Malloy
Thorofare, NJ USA
September 29, 2016